RYAN RULE: BONUS CONTENT EDITION

NEW YORK RUTHLESS: BOOK 1

SADIE KINCAID

RED HOUSE PRESS

As always, for my incredible boys.
And, for every single reader who has made my dreams come true!
Love Sadie x

CHAPTER 1

JESSIE

*M*y lips curl into a smile as Nikolai runs the pad of his thumb down my cheekbone and along my jawline until it's resting on my lower lip. He pulls southwards, opening my mouth slightly. The smell of him, of whisky and cigars, assaults my senses, making my eyes water. Leaning forward, he towers over me. "You did good," he smiles.

"Thank you," I whisper with a flutter of my lashes.

"*Moya Kroshka,* I will give you your reward later." *My little one.* His pet name for me.

I smile at him because I can't trust myself to speak. Grabbing hold of my wrist, he bends his head lower, pressing a soft kiss against my temple. He's so close that I can see the vein pulsing in his neck. I imagine slicing a cold steel blade across it and how I would stand over him and smile as he clutched at his throat, desperately trying to stop his life from slipping away from him.

I hate Nikolai Semenov with every fiber of my being.

Suddenly, the sound of an explosion rocks the whole room, making my ears ring in my head. It's quickly followed by rapid gunfire and it makes us both look up to the door. My heart races in my chest and my pulse thrums with energy as I try to wrench myself from Nikolai's grip.

"Ivan!" he snarls to his bodyguard who nods solemnly as he draws his own weapon.

I can only stand and stare at them in shock until the adrenaline kicks in and I manage to wrench my wrist from Nikolai's hand. The action unfolds as though I'm watching a movie and I'm not really a part of it. Before Ivan can even reach for the door handle, it blows off its hinges with a deafening boom. *Shit, Jessie. This is no movie!*

Instinctively, I cover my ears and dive beneath the desk. The room fills with flying splinters of wood, and smoke that catches the back of my throat. I cough into my hand as Nikolai barks orders in Russian, and then my heart almost stops when I look up from my hiding place. They walk into the room like the four horsemen of the apocalypse. Each of them fills the doorframe as they pass through it. Two of them hold semi-automatic weapons aloft as they scan the room for any signs of life.

Everything that follows happens so fast, but despite that, I see it as if in slow motion. Nikolai takes the first bullet. It flies straight through his neck and he drops to the floor, coughing and spluttering as the blood gushes out of the wound. Ivan takes the next two in his chest and stomach and he slides down the wall he was standing beside, leaving a trail of blood on the expensive damask wallpaper.

I crouch further behind the desk, covering my mouth to stop me from coughing, and praying that whoever those men are, they don't see me through the dust and smoke-filled air.

The one who is so obviously in charge walks straight toward my hiding place. All that's visible are two black shoes and black suit pants. He crouches down until he's looking directly at me with the greenest eyes I have ever seen. "You missed one, brother," he says in a voice that makes me think of rich velvet. I detect the hint of an Irish accent and realize that Nikolai has far more enemies than I had been aware of.

One of the men who's holding a semi-automatic approaches and aims the gun at me. I can't see the face of the gunman, only the muzzle of his weapon.

"Please. I'm not one of them," I protest.

The one crouching in front of me cocks an eyebrow. "You weren't working for the Semenovs?"

I swallow hard. I'm here in Nikolai Semenov's inner sanctum, dressed in jeans and a hooded sweatshirt, so I am clearly not one of his many whores. Not to mention, I'm sitting under a desk that has half a dozen computers on it.

"I was working for him, yes," I say, running my tongue over my lip. "But not exactly by choice. I have no allegiance to the Semenovs. I swear."

"You understand that we can't just let you walk out of here? You've just seen us kill your boss and his bodyguard," he says with a nod to his brother, who moves his gun closer to me.

"Wait," I shriek. "I can help you."

He narrows those incredible green eyes at me. "And how exactly do you think *you* can help *us?*" he asks with a smirk.

"I'm a hacker. That's what I did for Nikolai," I say as I edge forward and climb out from under the desk. I will not cower or hide away any longer. That's never been my style. I'm damn sure I'm as strong as any man in this room.

He stands too and steps back, allowing me some space. I pull my shoulders back, craning my neck so I can look him in the eye. "And I'm the best."

He laughs out loud as his brother beside us repositions his gun. "You think?"

"I know," I snap back at him. "Let me prove it."

"How?" He runs a hand across his jaw and then nods to his brother, who lowers his weapon.

"Whatever you need. I can hack into any security system

3

anywhere. Banks. Casinos. I can access personal records. There is nothing I can't find out as long as I have enough time. Take me with you and if I don't prove my worth in two weeks, then you can do whatever you want with me."

"Why do you assume that taking you with us is a better outcome than ending your suffering right now?" He narrows his eyes at me again.

I tilt my chin and glare at him. "I'll take my chances."

"So? Two weeks? You just allow me and my brothers to keep you hostage for two weeks?"

"I'm not exactly a hostage if I'm not being held against my will, am I?"

He frowns at me. "Don't you have any family who might be looking for you, Little Hacker?"

"No. I have no-one."

He looks behind him at the men I now know to be his brothers. they're the biggest men I've ever seen in my life and they're clearly identical twins. The sight of them makes my heart hammer in my chest as they bring so many buried memories rushing to the surface of my brain. I take a deep breath. *They are not them, Jessie!*

"She wouldn't be the worst house guest we've ever had," one of them says with a shrug and the other nods his agreement.

"She might come in useful, Shane," the one beside me with the gun adds.

Shane scowls and turns to the one who just spoke his name. "Or she might turn into a massive pain in our asses, Conor. And we could save ourselves a lot of trouble by ending this right now."

I look at the man he called Conor, who sucks in a breath before he responds. "It's your call. But it can't hurt to see what she's made of. If Nikolai had her working for him, she must be good."

I watch Shane's jaw working as he considers what to do with

me. My life is literally in his hands and I wonder what else I can do to convince him to spare me. I heard the Irish accent when each of them spoke and go with my last resort. "I also make an amazing soda bread," I offer. I worked in an Irish pub for six months when I was nineteen and home-made soda bread was one of our most popular sellers.

The hint of a smile plays on Conor's lips while Shane shakes his head in apparent annoyance. "Fine. Bring her," he snaps to Conor before turning around and walking out of the door.

CHAPTER 2

JESSIE

I sit in the back of the SUV, sandwiched between the twins, who I now know to be Liam and Mikey. The two of them are so huge, their thighs are pressed tightly against mine as the three of us share the back seat. They're identical twins, but I can already tell them apart by virtue of the small scar below Liam's left ear and the fact that he's about an inch taller than his brother. I have an eye for detail and I'm a quick study. They're skills that have helped me to survive for so long on my own.

Apart from telling them my name, I've said nothing else since we left Nikolai's house. I have listened though, to every single thing that they've said. It doesn't take me long to realize I'm in a car with the Ryan brothers—the heads of the New York branch of the Irish Mafia. These guys are ruthless, and they own half of New York, but I've never come across them personally before. I suppose the Russians and the Irish don't gel that well?

Shane is the oldest of the four, and everything about him, from the way that he talks to how he holds himself, tells me he's their leader. Conor drives the car. He's Shane's second—the closer. Smooth talking and charismatic. The twins appear to be quite a few years younger and, from what I can gather, are largely the muscle.

"You okay there, Jessie?" Liam turns and says in his soft Irish lilt. He has a twinkle in his dark brown eyes and what seems to be a genuine smile on his face. "We're almost home."

"I'm good. Thanks," I say with a nod. In fact, I'm not sure how I feel. I'm incredibly relieved to still be alive. I'm happy that Nikolai Semenov and his most loyal soldiers are all dead. But I was so close to finding *him*. And now it feels like I'm taking ten steps backwards.

"You'll like our place," Mikey says on the other side of me. I turn my head to him and offer him a faint smile.

The brothers begin to talk amongst themselves again. They're discussing their nightclub and how they plan on dealing with the trouble they've been having there for the past few nights. I half listen, keeping an ear out for any snippets of information that might be useful to me, but my mind wanders. What the hell is my next move? It took me almost two years to get close enough to Nikolai that I was allowed into his inner circle —even if it was the seventh circle of hell.

I look at the two oldest Ryan siblings sitting in front of me. Like their brothers either side of me, they wear the finest Italian leather shoes and impeccably tailored suits. They're all tall, dark, and stacked, as well as very easy on the eye. Besides any of that, though, I get a good feeling about them and I've learned to trust my gut. It rarely lets me down.

They are notorious. They do bad things, but that doesn't always mean that they're bad men. I imagine there are lots of people who would disagree, but I suppose I have a different morality barometer than most people. The things I've seen and lived through have taught me that sometimes good people do terrible things to get by in this world.

I lean back in the leather seat and close my eyes. The warmth of Liam and Mikey on either side of me is strangely comforting. Their conversation washes over me, and I absorb it all. Perhaps a few weeks or months working for the Ryan brothers, because I *will* prove my worth to them, will be a good thing. I can lay low and regroup. Gather more intel while I decide what to do next.

Because I am so close. I know he's out there somewhere.

Waiting.

I can almost feel him.

CHAPTER 3

JESSIE

The Ryan brothers' apartment is freaking huge. It must cover the entire top floor of the building. I look around me, with my mouth hanging open as I follow Liam and Mikey along the hallway. Their older brothers went into the nightclub that makes up the ground floor and basement of this building. Or part of it, at least. From what I could see when we drove in, half of it is used as a parking lot for the building. It's packed with top end, high spec cars, and I wonder if they all belong to the brothers or whether someone else lives in this block.

"You want something to eat? Or maybe a drink?" Liam asks as I walk behind him, my sneakers making a satisfying soft squeaking sound on the solid wooden floor.

"A cold drink would be good," I say as I hoist my backpack further onto my shoulder.

"This way." He cocks his head, and we turn left and into the biggest kitchen I have ever seen in my life.

"What do you fancy?" Mikey asks as he opens the massive refrigerator and sticks his head inside. "Soda? Juice? Water?" He pulls his head back out and looks at me with a grin on his face and, for a moment, I almost forget that I am basically their prisoner. I could be here on a date the way they're both so at ease and casual about the whole thing. My mind wanders for a few seconds. A date with one of these hot brothers? Or both of them?

"What's it to be?" Mikey asks again.

"Uh?" I blink at him. "Oh, water. Please."

He hands me a bottle before tossing one to Liam and grabs himself a can of soda. I take a long drink and the cool liquid feels like heaven against my raw throat. When I look up, they're both sitting at the kitchen island watching me. I shift uncomfortably under their gaze. I know that I asked to come here, and I know they seem like good guys, but I can't help wonder what the hell I've let myself in for here. I mean, what the hell do I do now?

Sensing my unease, Liam smiles at me. "We won't bite, Jessie."

"Not unless you want us to." Mikey flashes an eyebrow at me and laughs and the sound makes me shiver in a not unpleasant way.

"I was just wondering what happens now?" I say with a shrug, trying to appear tough and confident while my heart hammers against my ribcage.

"It's up to you. We have plenty to do here. A games room, gym, a huge TV in the den. We also have a library and a rooftop pool," Mikey says before taking a long swig of his soda.

I don't answer as I stand there staring at them. What the hell is this place?

"Or we could just show you where you'll be staying?" Liam offers.

"Yeah, that would be great," I reply, wondering if maybe they'll chain me up in a room with no windows.

"You're in the room next to ours," Mikey says as he jumps off the stool.

"You guys share a room?"

"Shared a womb, we can share a room," Liam laughs.

"Oh?" I blink at them. I don't know why that surprises me.

"Hey. We share a room, not a bed," Mikey adds.

"Well, unless we have good reason to," Liam says and they both laugh out loud.

"I don't understand," I say, aware that I'm frowning at them now.

Liam rounds the island and bends his head close to my ear. "Sometimes, we share *everything*, Jessie," he says with a low growl that turns my insides to jelly.

"Come on," Mikey adds as he saunters past us and out of the kitchen with his can of soda in his hand.

* * *

I THANK the twins for showing me how to use the electric window blinds and the TV and close the door behind them before taking another look around. If this is the guest bedroom, then I can't even imagine what the brothers' rooms must be like. A king-size bed dominates the space in the center and vast floor to ceiling windows make the room bright and airy. There's a huge TV on the wall and a small bookcase complete with full shelves of books. I kick off my sneakers and realize the floor is warm to the touch. Damn, they must have underfloor heating. This place is fancy!

Throwing my backpack onto the bed, I can't help but smile. I could get used to living in a place like this. Shaking my head, I catch myself before I get too comfortable with that thought. There is no getting used to a place like this for me. No getting used to anywhere. It's been that way for as long as I can remember, and I can't imagine a time when it will ever be any different.

Sitting on the bed, I open my backpack, take out my laptop and open it up. Relief washes over me as it fires to life when I turn it on and the document I was working on is still there on the screen. It's a list of the bank details of some of Nikolai's contacts. Both his enemies and the people he considered his friends. He was an incredibly suspicious man, and it didn't take me long to convince him that one of the best ways to monitor his associates was to monitor their money. Everything always leads back to the money in the end.

It gave me the perfect cover to delve into the financial history of almost every member of the Russian mob. Almost. I still haven't found what I was looking for, and I still have some work left to do. Nikolai was reluctant to give me the details of some of the top names, but he was getting close. I whispered in his ear every chance I got, reminding him how his enemies were trying to topple him, feeding his paranoia and suspicion like a loving owner feeds a pet. But I was so focused on the rest of the Russian mob, that I didn't even see the Irish one coming. And now I'm at a dead end. I'll have to start back at the beginning of this list and follow each individual money trail until it leads me to the top. It will be a much longer process, but time is something I have plenty of.

A soft knock at the door makes me jump. "Come in," I say, expecting one of the brothers. But it's not one of them who pops their head inside the room. It's a woman who looks to be in her late thirties, with dark curly hair.

"Jessie?" she asks.

"Yes," I reply, closing my laptop over and nervously rubbing my hands on my jeans.

She steps inside the room carrying a medical bag. "I'm Dr. Adams," she says with a smile. "But you can call me Lisa."

"Oh? Hey, Lisa." I blink at her.

"Conor called me and asked me to check you over. Make sure you're okay while you're staying here?"

"Okay," I say with a frown. This is either the highest level of consideration in hostage taking, or there is a hidden agenda here.

Lisa walks toward the bed and places her medical bag down beside me.

"How are you feeling?" she asks.

"Is that a trick question?" I reply. Does she know why I'm here, or that the Ryan brothers almost killed me earlier?

She tilts her head slightly and smiles at me. "No. I believe there was some sort of explosion? I know the Ryan brothers well, Miss Heaton."

I roll my eyes, wondering just how well, and she chuckles softly. "I was also told you asked to come here?" She takes a blood pressure cuff from her bag and indicates that I should hold out my arm.

"I suppose so," I say as I pull off my hooded sweatshirt until I'm sitting in only my tank top. I don't add that I didn't feel I had much choice at the time.

"Shane and his brothers will look after you. I know what they are, but they're good men," she says as she places her stethoscope in her ears. "They just want to make sure you are fit and well and don't need any medical treatment, especially after what happened today."

"Huh!" I snort.

"Well, if you have some sort of internal bleeding and die in bed tonight, it would be a bit of an inconvenience for them to find somewhere to bury your body, wouldn't it?" She flashes an eyebrow at me and I burst out laughing. Dr. Lisa has a dark sense of humor and I decide immediately that I like her.

"So, you know the brothers well, then?" I grin at her.

"I'm their physician," she replies with a knowing smile. "Nothing more."

Dr. Lisa gives me a thorough medical and confirms I don't have any internal bleeding and am unlikely to die in my sleep tonight. I figure she's about done when she pulls a huge needle from her bag.

"What the hell is that for?" I ask. "I hate needles."

"I need to take some blood and run some tests."

"What kind of tests?"

"To make sure you don't have illnesses that the brothers need to be aware of."

"Such as?"

"Blood-borne diseases you could infect them with should you ever cut yourself, for instance. STIs. And also, I'll do a pregnancy test too."

"Jesus!" I hiss as I hold out my arm. "What are they planning on doing with me?" I attempt a joke, but my insides are churning.

"It's just a precaution, I assure you," she replies.

I smile at her and nod. *Never let anyone see how afraid you are, Jessie.* A lesson from my father. A sudden surge of grief almost overwhelms me as thoughts of him and my mom and my little brothers force themselves into my consciousness. I haven't thought about them for a long time, but seeing Liam and Mikey today flicked some kind of switch and now I can't stop thinking about them. I do whatever I can to keep my memories of them at bay because it hurts too much not to. But, as painful as it is to think about the night they were taken from me—slaughtered in front of my eyes—it destroys me when I remember the happy times. When I recall how much I loved them. How much they loved me. When I remember what a team the five of us were.

I blink away a tear and focus on the sharp scratch of the needle piercing my skin. Pain grounds me. No matter what might happen here at the hands of the Ryan brothers, I know without a doubt that I have endured worse. I was sixteen years old when I learned that monsters were real, and unlike the princesses, maidens or the damsels in distress in the fairytales my mother read to me, there was no-one left to rescue me.

CHAPTER 4

CONOR

$\mathcal{I}$ sense Shane's irritation with me as we walk through the corridors of our nightclub. I know he expected me to back him up earlier when the twins had suggested bringing a hostage home was a good idea. My younger brothers are like excitable toddlers. To them, Jessie is a shiny new toy for them to play with. It's not often we have visitors or guests to our home, and the idea of having a new person actually living with us is tantamount to a kid getting a puppy for Christmas. At least for Liam and Mikey.

I had some altogether different motives for agreeing to her request, though. I've been unfortunate enough to have more dealings with Nikolai Semenov and his family than my brothers. Notoriously vicious, paranoid and straight up crazy, anyone not related to him by blood, who could gain his trust and also have the backbone to work with him, obviously has something special about them.

I hadn't even noticed her when we'd first walked into the room. The smoke from the twins blowing the door off had blurred my vision. Shane had gone straight to her, though. When I'd heard a woman's voice, I'd assumed it was one of

Nikolai's whores. I didn't particularly enjoy the thought of putting a bullet in her head, but she had seen us and we couldn't afford any comeback. I'd been ready to kill her at Shane's word. Then she crawled out from under that desk, dressed like a teenage boy, but unable to hide those incredible curves, and with long flaming red hair tied up in a ponytail. She squared up to Shane, all five foot four inches of her, and challenged him. Nobody spoke to Shane like that. Never. And especially not with a semi-automatic in their face.

I don't believe in love at first sight or any of that shit, but this woman made my heart pound and my dick hard. She is a tiny fucking powerhouse and all I could think about was how she has bigger balls than most of the men I'd ever met. If she wants to work for us, then we should fucking let her.

Shane glances at his watch and frowns. "We need to make this quick. I don't like having some stranger in our house and not being there."

"Relax. The twins will keep an eye on her. I'm pretty sure she's not exactly jumping for joy at the prospect of us kidnapping her."

"We didn't fucking kidnap her. She asked to come with us," he snaps.

"Yeah. Because it was either that or die. What choice did she have, really?"

"Semantics," he says with a dismissive wave of his hand. "We have no idea who she is or why she was working for Nikolai, or if we can trust her at all."

"Well, like she said, if you're not happy in two weeks, you can go back to your original plan," I say with a shrug. I already know that Jessie Heaton is going to impress us. You don't get to work that closely with one of the top Russian faces if you're not shit hot at what you do.

"If she hasn't murdered us all in our beds before then," he snarls.

16

"What? She's about one hundred and twenty pounds wet through. You're really worried she can take you?" I laugh and he scowls at me.

"Just call Henry and get him here now. I want this dealing with, so I can keep an eye on our little hacker upstairs."

I take my cell from my pocket and call our head bouncer to find out where he's at and leave Shane pacing the corridors in annoyance.

* * *

AN HOUR LATER, Shane and I walk into the penthouse apartment on the top floor of the building we own. We've just finished our meeting with our head bouncer, Henry, and his team, putting plans in place to deal with the recent trouble that's been happening in our clubs.

Shane is still pissed. "Make sure the hacker is settled and she isn't causing any trouble," he snaps before stalking off to his office.

I shake my head and bite back a smile before heading down the hallway to the kitchen, where I find my two younger brothers.

"Where is our house guest?" I ask.

"She's in her room. Lisa got here about ten minutes ago to check her over."

I nod. "You asked her to do the full range of tests, yeah?"

"Yes," Liam says with a grin and Mikey chuckles.

"What's so funny?" I snap. Between Shane's moodiness and the twins goofing around like teenagers whenever they get the chance, I sometimes feel like I'm the only sane one living in this place.

"Just you asking for the whole nine yards, that's all. You planning on having some alone time with her, Bro?" Liam says, his grin widening further.

"Grow the fuck up," I snarl as I stalk toward the refrigerator and take out a beer. The twin's juvenile behavior doesn't usually bother me at all. At twenty-six, they're eight years younger than me and they're both pretty funny most of the time. But today they've touched on a nerve. Because I have been thinking about Jessie Heaton, and what she would look like naked and tied to my bed since the moment I laid eyes on her. It's taken me by complete surprise, because I haven't looked at a woman like that for a long time.

"Hey, I'm not judging you, Con," Liam goes on. "She is a fiery little pocket rocket and I totally see the attraction. I wouldn't mind a piece of that ass for myself."

"Hmm," Mikey nods his agreement.

"Fuck you," I say as I turn to face them. "Both of you."

Mikey laughs out loud. "We're just fucking with you, Conor."

"Yeah," Liam agrees. "To be honest, it's nice to see you taking an interest in her. It's been a long time."

"I have no fucking interest in our new hostage," I snarl at them before taking a swig of my beer.

"Good to know," Liam says as he stares at me. "Leaves the pathway open for me and Mikey then." He grins at me.

"Stop fucking with him." Mikey nudges Liam on the arm. "He can't help it if he's got a hard on for her."

I down the last of my beer and slam the bottle onto the counter. "You two are a pair of assholes!" I snap and then I stalk out of the kitchen and along the hallway. I almost bump into Dr. Lisa when I do.

"Hey, Conor." She takes a step back and sucks in a breath. A few years after my brothers and I came to New York, and she was fresh out of med school, she saved Mikey's life. A fight broke out in our club one night and someone stabbed him in the gut. He lay bleeding out on the dance floor and Lisa knew exactly what to do. She's been our personal physician ever since. She asks no questions. She is loyal, and she is fucking good at her job. Whenever we need her to, she patches us up and makes sure we're always at the top of our game. I don't know what we'd do without her.

"How is she?" I nod toward the door she has just come out of.

"Surprisingly well for a woman who has just been kidnapped," she says with a flash of her eyebrows.

"I guess she's pretty tough. We found her working for Nikolai Semenov."

"Shit! She must be then. Is that where you all went today?" she asks, her eyes full of concern.

"Yes."

She reaches out and places a hand on my arm. "I know it must have taken a lot for you to go there. Are you okay?"

I swallow hard. I don't want to have this conversation, and especially not with her. She's desperate to fix me. If I gave her even the slightest suggestion that I'd consider speaking to one, she'd have a shrink in here within five minutes. She doesn't understand that what Nikola Semenov did to me can't be fixed —not like that anyway.

"When will you have her results back?" I ask, ignoring her question.

She stares at me, her eyes searching my face as though she might find the answer to her question written there. Eventually she shakes her head and sighs. "I'll have them in a few days. I'll send them over to you as soon as I do. I can tell you now that she's not pregnant though."

"Oh? How?"

"She has a contraceptive implant in her arm. And she's on her period. Do you have any provisions here for her?"

"No." I shake my head.

"I could have some sent over. But, she'll need clothes too." She shoots me a look of disapproval and I can tell she'd like to yell at me for being so dumb.

19

"Thanks for the offer. But, I'll sort some stuff out for her. And, she was kind of a surprise. We had no idea she'd be there, and we certainly didn't plan on kidnapping her and bringing her back here."

"So, why did you? Kidnapping isn't exactly your style, Conor. Not women, at least."

"She asked to come with us. And I don't know." I shake my head. "But there was something about her. The way she stood up to Shane. You should have seen her."

Lisa smiles at me and I realize it's because I'm smiling too. "She seems like a woman who can handle herself. But, just be careful. You have no idea who she really is."

"You sound like Shane."

She shrugs. "Well, maybe that's because we both care about you, and those knuckle-head little brothers of yours."

"Well, I think I'm pretty capable of handling a five-and-a-half-foot computer geek," I arch one eyebrow at her.

She laughs out loud. "Oh, Conor. I'm pretty sure she could turn you and your brothers inside out if she wanted to, sweetheart. So don't say I didn't warn you."

Then she pushes up onto her tiptoes and gives me a soft kiss on the cheek. "Take care of yourself, handsome. I'll be in touch as soon as I have those results."

I watch her walk to the elevator and lift my hand to my cheek to wipe away the lipstick stain she will have left there. She's wrong. I can handle Jessie Heaton. But just how much I'd like to handle her might become a problem.

CHAPTER 5

JESSIE

I sit on the enormous bed in the guest room and stare at the blank screen of the TV with no idea what the hell I'm doing. Why on earth did I ask to come here? I should have pleaded with them to let me go instead.

My stomach growls, and I look down in annoyance. Food would be great right now, but I don't know if I'm allowed to leave this room. I have awful cramps too. The first two days of my period are always the worst. Of all the days for it to arrive! I have two tampons in my backpack, but nothing beyond that.

Soft knocking at the door interrupts my train of thought. "Come in," I shout and a second later Conor walks through the door, holding a brown paper bag in one hand and what looks like a clothing store bag in the other.

He walks in and despite the vast space, he somehow manages to dominate the entire room. Still dressed in his suit pants and a crisp white shirt, he has his sleeves rolled up and there's a tattoo of some kind of bird peeking out from beneath the material. My heart flutters in my chest and I'm not entirely sure it's purely through fear. In fact, I doubt it has anything to do with fear at all.

21

"I thought you might need some things," he says as he places the bags on the bed beside me.

Sitting up, I swing my legs over the edge as I take the brown paper bag and peer inside. It contains five boxes of tampons in various sizes as well two different types of pads, a box of Advil and a huge bar of Hershey's. The flush creeps unexpectedly across my cheeks as the realization that he knows I'm on my period hits me.

He clears his throat. "Lisa said you needed that stuff and I didn't know which type, so..."

"You got this stuff yourself?" I blink at him.

"Yeah." He shrugs. "It seemed the quickest and easiest option."

"Thank you," I say with a sudden rush of gratitude to him.

Get a grip, Jessie! He only bought you some freaking tampons and a bar of candy!

"It's not a problem. There's some basics in there too." He nods to the large clothing store bag. "I know the owner of the store and she picked those out for you."

I drop the brown bag and open the large pink and white one. It contains panties, at least two bras, socks, jeans and t-shirts. I pull out a pair of jeans and look at the label.

"How did you know my size?"

He shrugs. "Sizing people up is kind of my thing."

I nod and wonder how he has honed those particular skills. "Thanks," I whisper.

"We can get you some decent stuff in the next couple of weeks, but that should see you through until then."

I smile at him and my stomach growls loudly.

"You want to come join us for dinner?" he asks as he indicates the open door with his head.

I chew on my lip as I consider his question. Do I just go sit and eat dinner with the men who have essentially kidnapped me?

"We won't bite, Jessie. I promise. And Mikey has cooked."

"Mikey cooks?" I arch an eyebrow at him.

"Yep. He's good too. He trained to be a chef for two years," he says as he holds out a hand to me. "Come. Eat."

The gnawing hunger pains in my stomach decide for me. I reach out and take his hand and the spark from the touch of his fingertips on my palm almost makes me pull back. I look up at him, wondering if he felt that too. But, if he did, he hides it well.

I allow him to clasp my hand in his and then I follow him out of the room and toward the kitchen, where the smell of Mikey's cooking makes my mouth water.

* * *

FIFTEEN MINUTES LATER, I'm sitting at the table with the four Ryan brothers eating a delicious chicken parmesan. They laugh and joke and talk about things that I imagine brothers must talk about. The new film one of them wants to watch on Netflix later, the amazing pizza place that just opened up in Brooklyn, the new waitress in their club who has been flirting with both Liam and Mikey separately, while thinking they're the same person. They include me in their conversation too, as though I'm an old family friend or a welcome guest. And I realize after a few mouthfuls of Mikey's excellent food, that I'm smiling as I listen to them chat.

Shane is quieter than the other three and I suspect he listens more than he speaks, but every so often I catch him staring at me and I know he's sizing me up. He is the protector, and I am an intruder into their world.

I look down at my food every time I catch his eyes on me. If he knew who I really was, I doubt he would have invited me into his home so willingly.

CHAPTER 6

CONOR

*I*t's been three days since Jessie came home with us and she's been the perfect houseguest so far. She walked into the kitchen about two minutes ago and doesn't seem to have noticed that I'm here. I take the opportunity to watch her. The tight jeans and tank top I had my contact at the boutique in Manhattan pick out for her fit her perfectly. She stands on her tiptoes to reach the cereal from the top shelf of the cabinet and the tank rides up, revealing her full round ass and a glimpse of the tanned skin on her back. I got her size spot on, but then I've hardly stopped looking at her curvy little body since we left Nikolai's house.

"Damn!" she curses as her fingers barely brush the edge of the box.

I watch her as she jumps, but she doesn't quite have the co-ordination right to grab the cereal at the same time. "You need some help there, Angel?" I ask, suppressing a smile.

Turning sharply, she stares at me. "I didn't see you there," she stammers, and then she glances at her watch. "What are you doing skulking around in the kitchen at this hour of the morning?"

Pushing my chair back, I stand up and walk over to her. "I could ask you the same thing?"

She blows a stray strand of hair from her face and shakes her head slightly. "I couldn't sleep, and I was hungry. You?" She crosses her arms over her chest and I can't help but laugh. I have almost a foot and one hundred pounds on her, but she glares at me with such defiance in her eyes that it makes me want to put her over my knee and spank her ass. My cock twitches at the idea.

Reaching above her, I take the box of cereal from the shelf before handing it to her.

"Thank you," she whispers, as though she's momentarily forgotten that she's supposed to be annoyed at me. It's obvious that she was raised to have good manners.

"You're welcome. And I've just finished work," I finally answer her question. "Our club is open until six am."

"Wow! And you work there every night?" she asks as she shoves her hand into the box and pulls out a fistful of Lucky Charms.

"No. Just a few nights a week. Would you like a bowl?" I arch one eyebrow at her.

"No, thanks." She grins before tossing some dry cereal into her mouth and walking over to the table with the box.

I watch the way she moves. She calls herself a computer geek, and she dresses like a teenage boy, as though she wants to give off an energy that she's clumsy or awkward. But she's not at all. She is graceful and sexy. Every sway of her hips only accentuates her delicious curves. I wonder for a fraction of a second if I'm welcome to sit with her. But, fuck it! This is my house and I'll sit where I want.

"Why can't you sleep?" I ask as I sit on the chair opposite her.

She swallows the mouthful of dry cereal. "My mind is in overdrive. I need something to distract me."

Her words bypass my brain and go straight to my dick. *No, Conor, that is not the kind of distraction she is talking about!*

I close my eyes and draw in a breath before I answer her. "Read. Watch TV?" I suggest.

"I'm too hyper to read right now. And there's only so much TV a gal can watch, you know?" She flashes one eyebrow at me.

"You've been here for three days. You're really bored already?"

"Out of my mind! I promise you I'm really good at what I do. Give me a chance to prove it to you. Give me something. Please?"

The way she says the word please makes my cock start to fire on all cylinders. Jesus! I've only been talking to her and watching her eat some fucking cereal. How the hell am I going to live with this woman and keep my hands off her?

Avoidance. That's how.

"Please, Conor?" she says again, this time with a flutter of her eyelashes and all the blood rushes straight to my groin.

"Keep batting those eyelashes at me like that, Angel, and I can promise you I'll distract you so hard you won't even know what day it is," I growl at her, the words coming out before I've even considered the implications of what I'm saying.

It doesn't seem to scare her off though. She narrows her eyes at me and leans forward. "I bet you would, big guy. But, all I'm looking for is some work to keep me busy. Promise."

I stare at her, licking my lips as I fall into those bright blue eyes. "You any good with hacking into security systems?"

"Yes. It's my specialty." She grins.

"Good. There's a club downtown. I need the footage of a fight that broke out in there two nights ago. Can you get that?"

"If it exists, I'll get it for you. What's the name of the club?"

"Angelino's."

"Consider it done," she says with a satisfied smile as she sits back in her chair and stuffs her hand back into the box of Lucky Charms.

"You should really use a spoon and a bowl. Mikey won't be happy if he catches you manhandling his Lucky Charms like that."

Her blue eyes twinkle as she bursts out laughing, and I realize the massive double meaning inherent in that statement.

"On second thoughts, maybe he would?" I laugh too. "Now, I am going to find me some sleep. You think you can get me that footage before I go back to work tonight?"

She stands up, wiping the cereal dust from her hand on her jeans and walks around the table until she's standing so close to me, I can smell that she's used the vanilla body wash I bought her. "I could probably get it before you even fall asleep," she purrs, and my cock throbs in appreciation.

I bend my head low, so my lips are close to her ear. "Well, by all means, Angel, if you do, feel free to come in and tell me all about it. I don't need much sleep anyway."

Her breath catches in her throat and the sound only makes me harder. But she doesn't step away from me. "I'll get onto it as soon as I can," she says softly, and it's only then that she steps back and looks up at me, chewing on her bottom lip. I can't tell if she's trying to look like a sex kitten desperate to be fucked, or if that's just her default setting.

I am so damn tired, I can hardly think straight. But Shane would lose his shit if I start fucking our hostage and even my frazzled brain realizes that.

"I'd appreciate that, Jessie," I say as I straighten up and walk out of the kitchen.

CHAPTER 7

JESSIE

*W*alking along the hallway toward the gym, I can't stop my thighs from trembling with each step. Shane told me this is where I'd find Conor and the thought of seeing him working out makes that warm, wet heat build in my core. As if he isn't hot enough in regular clothes. He left me a quivering hot mess after our encounter in the kitchen earlier this morning when he was openly flirting with me.

I'd been so freaking horny that I'd gone straight back to my room and had to relieve myself before I spontaneously combusted. Imagining it was his fingers on me rather than my own had seemed like a good idea at the time, but now, I'm not so sure. Certainly, it's not going to help me feel any less flustered around him. If it's not bad enough that he is possibly the hottest looking man I have ever come across in my life, with his chiseled jaw, dark beard and his deep brown eyes, he's also funny and charming too. The perfect Jessie trifecta!

I push open the door to the gym and step inside. The room is silent except for the sound of his heavy breathing. He's wearing just his shorts and sneakers while he does pull-ups about twelve feet away from me. He's wearing his ear buds and obviously hasn't heard me come in.

I stand here and watch him. His muscular back and shoulders flex each time he moves and his powerful forearms bulge with the effort. A sudden image of him holding himself over me flashes before my eyes. I wonder how good those muscles would feel beneath my fingertips. He has ink all over his back and shoulders and I tilt my head to try to make out some of the images as he moves. I can see some Celtic symbols, an angel and a phoenix.

I'm almost in a trance watching him when he drops to his feet and pulls out his ear buds.

Clearing my throat, I let him know I'm in the room and hope that he doesn't realize I've been ogling him for the past five minutes. He spins around and grins at me. "You got something for me?" he nods toward my laptop in my hands.

"Yeah," I say, trying to sound really cool and calm while my heart races like a Bugatti and my pussy begins to throb with need. "That footage is here when you want to see it. Shane said you were heading straight out after your workout, and you said you wanted it today, so?" I shrug awkwardly.

He nods before picking up a nearby towel and wiping the sweat from his face. Then he begins to rub the towel over his shoulders, chest, and abs. I know I should look away, but I can't. Never before have I felt so jealous of a square of Egyptian cotton as I do right now.

"Great. Let's see it then." He beckons me toward him and I walk over, opening the laptop and pressing a button to bring the footage onto the screen. I pass it to him, but he continues drying himself off. So instead, I stand there awkwardly holding it for him as he leans close to me and watches the action unfold, and I'm forced to smell his fresh sweat mixed with his expensive cologne. And damn, if it doesn't make me feel like jumping his bones right now.

The footage was easy to find, and it means nothing to me. It's just a bunch of guys having a fight, but it obviously means something to Conor. His eyes narrow and his jaw clenches while he watches. "Fuckers. I knew it!"

"Is everything okay?"

"Yeah. Just some people back in the city who aren't supposed to be, that's all. Nothing me and the twins can't take care of later."

"Oh. I see," I say as I shift my weight from one foot to the other. He smells so freaking good! How can someone smell so damn good when they've just worked out? Dear God, my ovaries are about to explode.

"You did good, Jessie," he says with a smile before he leans down to pick up a bottle of water from the floor.

Pride swells in my chest. I am good at what I do, and maybe now that he knows it too, I might get my hands dirty around here. I wasn't lying earlier this morning when I told him I was bored. Looking for the man who killed my family has brought me to a complete dead end. The only files that might have held some information were destroyed by the Ryan brothers when they torched Nikolai's house after we left. Not that I held out much hope of finding anything. The man who killed my parents and my brothers seems to have disappeared.

Although, I know he hasn't. He didn't just disappear that day. But I haven't seen him for almost eight years and there is no trace of him anywhere. I know he's alive, though. Even if I wish I didn't.

"You okay?" Conor asks, snapping me from my thoughts. "You look like you're in another world?"

"What? Sorry!" I shake my head. "I was thinking about something, that's all. Is there anything else I can do for you?"

"I'm sure Shane will find you plenty to keep you busy once I tell him how easily you got this."

"Good. Thanks," I say absent-mindedly.

He reaches out and cups my chin with his hand and I almost jump back with a jolt at the feeling of his warm skin on mine. I can't remember the last time anyone touched me with such concern or tenderness. It makes the tears prick at my eyes.

"You sure you're okay? Did you see something on here that bothers you?" He nods toward my laptop.

I snap it closed and shake my head. "No. Nothing. And I'm fine. Seriously."

He drops his hand, but he continues to stare at me. "Okay," he finally says. "I need to grab a shower before I head to work."

"Of course," I nod a little too quickly, as though to convince him I'm not currently picturing him naked in said shower and imagining the water running over all the hard contours of his body.

"Thanks again, Jessie," he says softly before he throws his towel over his shoulder and walks out of the gym.

CHAPTER 8

SHANE

I watch Conor walking out of my office and sit on the edge of my desk. He's just finished telling me how quickly Jessie got the footage that he requested from Angelino's club. I know how good their security systems are, and the fact that she got what he needed so quickly impresses me, as much as I hate to admit it. Maybe I'll have some use for her after all? I still don't trust her, though. And I don't like the effect she's having on my younger brothers. They're like dogs on heat around her, and sooner or later one of them is going to fuck her. I can smell it in the air.

Closing my office door, I take my cell out of my pocket and walk back to my desk. The soft leather creaks as I sit and lean back in my chair while I scroll through my contacts for the number I need. As soon as I find the name I'm looking for, I press dial and listen to the ring tone.

Jax answers on the fourth ring. "Hey, amigo. Long time no speak."

Jackson Decker is the human equivalent of a highly trained sniffer dog. There is no information, no skeletons in any closets, that this man cannot find. When me and my brothers first moved to New York, we did some work for Jax's boss, Alejandro Montoya, and we impressed him so much that he recommended us for more jobs. Before we knew it, we were the go to men for arms in the New York area, and because of our roots and our father's name, we made a successful challenge for the top. Alejandro and Jax are two of the few men I consider to be friends.

"Hey, Jax. It's been far too long, buddy. I have a trip to L.A. coming up soon. We should catch up."

"I'm still recovering from the last time I met up with you and your brothers, Shane," he laughs, and I can't help but smile at the memory of the weekend in Vegas he's referring to.

"I promise no whiskey this time. Okay?"

Jax laughs again. "Deal."

"I was wondering if you had time to help out a friend?"

"For you, of course. What do you need?"

"You sure Alejandro won't mind me distracting you?"

"Hey, you know me. I never sleep anyway. Besides, he's a lot more chilled these days now that he's a family man."

"Of course. How old are his boys now?"

"Almost nine months. A right handful. But fucking adorable," Jax chuckles. "So, what is it you need me to do?"

"I want you to look into someone for me. I'll send you her picture and the information I have, which isn't a lot, but I think she's lying to me about who she is, and I want to know why."

"Okay. Send it on over. When do you need it by?"

"As soon as possible, buddy. She's living in my house right now."

"Oh? You finally looking to settle down, amigo?"

"Not a chance. I don't even know how to describe what she's doing here. A willing hostage, maybe?" I shake my head at the words as they come out of my mouth.

Jax laughs down the phone. "Sounds complicated. But I'll get on it."

"Thanks. I owe you one."

"A bottle of that fine Irish whiskey when you visit will do just fine. I'll let you know when I have anything."

I thank him again and end the call just as there's a knock at my door. I assume it's the hacker as my brothers don't knock.

I sit up in my chair and straighten my jacket. "Come in."

She opens the door and sticks her head inside. "You wanted to see me?"

"Yeah, I do." I nod, and she walks into the room. She's dressed in her own jeans, paired with one of Conor's t-shirts, which dwarfs her petite frame. But even the oversized top does little to disguise her incredible curves.

My cock twitches, and I curse under my breath. What the fuck? It's not like I've never seen a beautiful woman before, but something about her and the way she looks at me makes me want to bend her over my desk and fuck her until she screams my name.

She hovers uncertainly by my desk and a part of me contemplates leaving her standing there and watching her fidget under my gaze. But I'm not sure that would help my cock behave itself and so I indicate the chair for her to sit down. She takes the seat and crosses her legs, tossing her long red hair over her shoulder and training those bright blue eyes on mine.

CHAPTER 9

JESSIE

*S*hane sits behind his desk, wearing one of his impeccably tailored suits that fits the contours of his body so perfectly, it could have almost been painted on him. His hands are steepled under his chin as he stares at me, his eyes running over my face and body as he appraises me. I lick my lips as I sit opposite him, waiting for him to tell me why he has summoned me to his office this afternoon.

"Conor tells me you hacked into the security feed of that hotel within a few hours?" he eventually asks.

"It wasn't a complicated system," I say with a shrug, immediately shifting to my default mode of playing down my talents. Now that I have his attention, I've shown him all I need to for now. Stay humble. Don't let people know just how good you are until you absolutely have to. Then they will always underestimate you. Another lesson my father taught me that I will never forget.

Shane narrows those incredible green eyes at me and I shift uncomfortably under the heat of his gaze. "How exactly does a girl from …?" he flashes an eyebrow at me and waits for me to fill the blank.

"Minnesota," I remind him of what I told him and his brothers a few days earlier. I've told so many lies that I used to worry that one day I'd forget the truth myself.

"How did a girl from Minnesota end up working for Nikolai Semenov?"

My heart starts to hammer in my chest, but I perfected the art of lying under pressure a long time ago. Now, it comes as easily as breathing. I look at him calmly. Time to bring my A game! "I hacked into a college system for the daughter of one of his men. I impressed him with my skills and he offered me some work. I guess he just kept being impressed because within six months, I was living in his house and I was his go to tech person."

"You lived with him?"

"Yep."

He frowns at me. "How did that happen?"

"He was a very paranoid and suspicious man. Before long, he was in need of my services on a daily basis. It made sense for him that I would move in."

"And did it make sense for you?"

"Well, Nikola Semenov was a hard man to say no to," I say with a shrug. "I didn't have much choice."

"So, you were his personal hacker? That was all?"

I shift in my seat again. "No," I reply as I look down at the floor.

"He fucked you too?" he says, and I flinch at the ease at which he asks me that question.

"Sometimes," I admit. This is the truth, at least.

"And you were okay with that?" He tilts his head to one side as he stares at me.

"Again. He is a hard man to refuse. So, I didn't," I say with a shrug as I glare back at him. I won't allow him to use my body and my choices to intimidate me.

His green eyes roam over my body, reminding me of a panther sizing up its prey. But something about the way he looks at me has the heat searing between my thighs. The truth is, Nikolai Semenov made my skin crawl, and I hated every moment of his hands or his lips on my skin. But I needed him, and I'm not against using any means at my disposal to get what I want—or to simply survive. The prospect of Shane Ryan, or any of his hot brothers demanding anything from my body, however, makes me shiver in an altogether different way.

He clears his throat. "Rest assured, there is no expectation that you provide those services around here," he finally says.

I nod at him and experience an unexpected twinge of disappointment. That would certainly make my time here more interesting.

"That's not to say my brothers won't try," he adds with the flicker of a grin. "But you're under no obligation to agree. They were raised right. So, don't feel bad about turning them down. They can have their pick of any woman from our club downstairs."

I nod again, and it takes all of my effort not to scowl at him. He's just made me feel completely worthless, and incredibly small, and I expect he knows it. I wonder if that was his intention. From the little I've managed to find out about the Ryan brothers, they're all business and little pleasure. I know that can't be completely true. Men like these have to blow off steam sometimes, but whatever they do, they're discreet about it. No relationships to speak of. No scorned exes waiting to dish the dirt. No jilted one-night stands who are desperate for revenge.

The Ryan brothers have many business enemies for obvious reasons, but very few people who seem to hold a grudge for any personal ones. At least, none that I could find. I've hardly been able to dig up anything at all on their personal lives, other than the fact that they moved to New York about ten years ago, quickly rising through the ranks until they became the undisputed heads of the Irish Mafia. Their reign has been challenged many times, but never successfully. Perhaps Shane Ryan is worried that if I get too close to his brothers, I might get too close to him.

I sit up straighter in my chair. "That's good to know. Thank you," I say with a forced smile.

He rubs a hand over his jaw and his tongue darts out to lick his lower lip. An image of him using that tongue somewhere else on my body forces itself into my mind and I squeeze my thighs together to stem the rush of heat there. *Behave yourself, Jessie!*

Shane picks up a brown folder from his desk and hands it to me. "I want you to get access to this man's life. Bank accounts. Medical records. College. High School. Employment. I want to know everything about him."

Taking the folder from his hand, I resist the urge to peer inside. "Who is he?"

"Someone I am very interested in," he replies coolly. "Do you have what you need?"

"I have my laptop, so I can get what you need. But I could do it faster with access to a desktop too," I reply as my eyes flicker to the computer on his desk.

"I'll arrange for a desktop to be delivered for you tomorrow. You can set it up in the library."

"Okay. When do you need this information by?"

The noise of his cell phone ringing interrupts our conversation, and he pulls it from his pocket, frowning as he glances at the screen. "As soon as possible," he snaps. "I need to take this."

I realize I am being dismissed and stand up with the folder in my hand. "There's no rush for the desktop. I'll have the information to you by tomorrow," I say before turning and walking out of his office with a deliberate sway of my hips. This is my chance to show Shane Ryan exactly what I'm made of and prove to him I can be an indispensable asset to him and his brothers. It offers me the perfect cover while I continue my true goal in life, to find the man responsible for murdering my entire family.

CHAPTER 10

JESSIE

I finish writing the last page of notes and snap my laptop closed. Stretching my arms above my head, I stifle a yawn and check the time on my watch. It's a little after 3 a.m. I've been in the library looking into Shane's mystery man for the past six hours. Although he made it clear there was no urgency to his request, I want to get it to him as quickly as possible. I sense that he has the last word on whether I get to stick around here, and I want to prove my usefulness. Strangely, I want to impress him too. I'm not usually driven by my ego, but something about Shane Ryan and his brothers makes me want to show off my talents.

Closing my notebook too, I pick up my laptop and head out of the library toward my temporary bedroom. As I pass Shane's office, I notice the light is still on. I pop my head through the door. He's sitting at his desk and the soft glow of the computer screen illuminates his handsome face.

I clear my throat to announce my presence, and his head snaps up. He frowns. "Hacker?"

"Hey. You never told me that guy was in Ireland," I say with a tilt of my head.

"Take a few more days if you need to," he says with a shrug.

"Oh, I have your information. I was just surprised to find he doesn't live in the States. I was surprised by a lot of things actually." I arch one eyebrow at him.

"You have the information already?" He leans back and rubs a hand across his jaw.

"Yep, it didn't take me long."

If he's impressed, he gives no indication of that fact. "What did you find out?"

I stride into the room and sit down opposite him. "Why are you so interested in a schoolteacher from Cork, anyway?"

"Why I need the information is of no consequence to you, Hacker. The sooner you learn that, the better. Now, what do you have for me?" he growls.

I place my notepad on his desk. "He's a schoolteacher. Two sisters. His mom is still alive, but his dad died three years ago. He lives alone. He's never been married but he does have a girlfriend. They have no children. He studied at the University of Liverpool and teaches at the local high school in Cork. He has no criminal record. He broke his collarbone playing rugby when he was seventeen and he has two fillings. Every other piece of mundane information about him is in the notepad. Is there something I'm missing here?"

He scowls at me. "You tell me, Hacker. Isn't that the whole fucking point?"

I stare at him as I go over the information I discovered today in my head. Unless Noel Callaghan is really a deep cover MI5 agent with no past, then I got everything there is to know. But even if he were, I'd have found something. "No. That's everything," I say, sitting up straighter in my chair. "He's as clean as they come."

Shane nods and picks up the notebook. "I'll take a look at this anyway."

"Right. I'm off to bed then." I stand up and yawn. "Goodnight."

"Night," he says absent-mindedly as he goes back to his computer screen.

I shake my head and walk out of his office. A thank you would have been nice.

Since I'm so annoyed by Shane, I don't even notice Conor standing in the dark hallway until he speaks. "Working late?"

When I look up, he's leaning against the kitchen doorframe, his legs crossed at the ankles and his arms folded over his chest.

"You could say that," I reply as I walk toward him. "You?"

"You could say that," he grins as he mimics my response. He doesn't move out of the doorway as I reach it and I stand and look up at him. His eyes are so dark and intense. I feel the tightening in my abdomen as I stare into them. He is so freaking handsome.

He narrows his eyes at me. "What were you and Shane up to at this time of night?"

"He asked me to look into someone for him. I just finished up. Now, I'm off to bed."

Something flickers in his eyes and then he bends his head low. He smells of whisky and expensive cologne. He lifts his hand to my hair, taking some and curling it around two of his fingers. "You could come back down to the club with me?"

"I have nothing to wear. Besides, isn't it almost closing time?"

"No." He smiles. "A few hours to go yet."

"Well, you'd better get down there and see to your customers. Or maybe there's a special someone down there waiting for you?"

He laughs softly. "A special someone?"

"Hmm. Shane tells me you and your brothers can have your pick of women at the club."

"Is that so?"

"Can't you?"

"What do you think, Jessie?" he says, his voice low and husky as he inches closer to me until his warm breath skates over my cheek. "Can I have *any* woman I want?"

I swallow as his dark eyes burn into mine and the heat sears between my thighs. "I'm sure you can," I breathe.

"But what if the one I want is off limits?"

My pulse thrums against my skin as he edges closer. "Then you'll have to find another one. I'm sure there are plenty of women who would be happy to share your bed, Conor."

"You might be right about that, Angel," he growls. "Most of the women at the club would die to come up here."

"So, why don't you bring them up here, then?" I raise my eyebrow at him.

He shakes his head. "I don't really do that kind of thing."

"Why not?" I purr, feeling a strange sense of satisfaction and happiness that he doesn't bring randoms home from the club every night.

He presses his lips lightly against my cheek. "It's complicated."

"Isn't everything?" I groan as he drops one of his hands to my hip. His fingers press into my flesh and I lean into him. My breathing grows faster as my heart pounds in my ears. He moves his head slightly, lightly dusting his lips across my skin and my insides turn to molten lava.

"Jessie," he growls.

"Conor!" Shane's voice slices through the air. "Chester is looking for you."

The moment broken, Conor straightens up and I take a step back. "I'm on my way back downstairs now," he says and then, without even a glance in my direction, he walks down the hallway toward the elevator.

Shane disappears back into his office and I lean against the wall, letting out a long slow breath as I try to calm my racing heart and the throbbing between my thighs. Living with the Ryan brothers is going to be more of a challenge than I expected.

CHAPTER 11

SHANE

*E*ighteen days. That's how long it's been since Jessie came into our lives. Somehow, she has slipped into our world and our daily routine seamlessly and effortlessly, as though she's always been here. It's a skill to both blend into the background while also making yourself indispensable.

My brothers are calmer and more content with her around. Mikey and Liam's usually boundless energy and their constant trawling for trouble whenever and wherever they can find it, is lessened, dampened by their late-night talks with her, and her laughter. She loves to listen to their stories and they love to embellish them for her entertainment. I see the biggest change in Conor. That haunted look in his eyes disappears when she's near him. I've been worried about him since his ordeal last year. I was even coming around to Lisa's idea about getting him some sort of therapy. Who knew all he needed was a curvy red-head with a smart mouth?

My brothers watch her. No matter what she's doing, they're looking at her. And I watch them watching. There's a sexual energy that's growing with each passing day, and something soon is going to have to give. It seems to vibrate through any room that she's in. I wish my brothers would go out and get laid just to defuse the tension. Maybe then I could stop watching her as well.

I watch for other reasons too. I'm waiting for her to put a foot out of line. Although she hasn't yet. Her two-week trial period passed without acknowledgement from any of us. I suspect that neither her nor my brothers wanted to bring my attention to the fact, and they've done their best to avoid any mention of how long our intruder will be staying with us.

The truth is, Jessie has proven herself repeatedly. She's skilled and efficient, leaving me with no doubt that she is one of the best at what she does. Since that first assignment I gave her when I asked her to look into my cousin's fiancé back in Ireland, she's asked no questions about anything else I've given her to do.

If I were to bring her in to my office and review her two-week trial, I'd have nothing but good things to say about her. I'd have to tell her that she's made our lives easier, and has proven herself an asset to our business. I would tell her that she seems to be the perfect addition to our team. She brings something to our close-knit unit that I didn't even know was missing. She appears to be the perfect fit.

Except that she's not. Because Jessie is a liar.

Jax has been looking into her for two weeks, and all he's discovered so far is that she's a ghost. She's definitely not Jessie Heaton from Minnesota, although she covered those tracks well. The fact that Jax is still following the trail of dead ends and false leads tells me we're dealing with someone who has worked damn hard to cover up who she really is. I have no idea who I've allowed into our home. I don't know who she's really working for, or who or what she's running from.

And that makes her the most dangerous person I know.

CHAPTER 12

JESSIE

$\mathcal{I}$ sit at the kitchen table opposite Liam— me working on my laptop and him scrolling through his phone— and it's nice not being alone in a room. He and I seem to spend a lot of time together and we've developed an uncomplicated relationship where we can sit in comfortable silence. I've probably spent more time with the twins than anyone else since I got here, and they're both such enjoyable company that I often forget I'm practically a prisoner here. If I asked to go somewhere, I doubt the brothers would stop me, but they'd damn sure escort me there. Entry to this apartment and the garage downstairs is via an electronic fingerprint system. I could hack it and override it if I really wanted out, and I guess they know that. But the truth is, I'm happy here.

When I've finished what I'm working on, I close my laptop with a snap, making Liam look up from his phone.

"You fancy some lunch?" I ask him.

He tilts his head and looks at me. "What you making?"

"Me? Nothing. I was thinking we could ask Mikey to rustle us up a grilled cheese."

Liam grins at me and nods. "He does make the best grilled cheese."

"Let's ambush him when he comes in after his workout, then?" I flash my eyebrows at him.

"Deal," Liam agrees as he puts his phone down on the table.

"So, what did you do while Mikey was training to be a chef then?"

He sucks in a breath and runs his hands through his hair. "I've only ever worked for Shane," he says with a shrug. "But Mikey always wanted to be a chef."

"Why didn't it work out? He's a great cook."

Liam nods. "Yeah. But it's kind of hard to be anything other than what we are when you're a Ryan."

I nod at him because I know all about not being able to escape the shackles of a name. I'd like to know more, but I don't want to push him. Liam is the quietest of the twins and although he and I get on great, I figure it takes a lot for him to open up to people and he'll talk to me when he's ready.

"Shane did his best to help us live a different life, don't get me wrong," Liam goes on, feeling the need to defend his older brother. "He never wanted to leave Ireland, but he came here for us. Mostly for me and Mikey."

"Oh?"

He shakes his head. "Some shit went down. We were sixteen. He brought us here. Mikey trained to be a chef. But me, well..." He looks down at his hands and starts picking at his fingernails.

"You what?"

"Shane is the boss. Conor is the negotiator. Mikey is the funny one who cooks great food and can also make a bomb out of the ingredients of most people's pantries. And me, well, I guess I'm just the fuck-up."

I blink at him. Wow! "Well, that's not how I see it," I say as I pick up a grape from the fruit bowl on the table and pop it into my mouth.

He arches an eyebrow at me. "And how do you see it, Jessie?"

"You're the buffer."

"The what now?" he says with a frown.

"The buffer. The person who stops Conor and Shane from killing each other, or Mikey from blowing too much shit up. You're the one who keeps them all that little bit calmer."

Liam narrows his eyes at me. "You think?"

"That's what I see anyway." I shrug just as Mikey bounces into the kitchen.

"We got this place to ourselves tonight, kids. The folks are going out." He grins at us as he rubs his hands together. *The folks* are how he sometimes affectionately refers to Shane and Conor.

"Where are they going?" Liam asks.

"The O'Malley's wedding. They forgot all about it," Mikey replies. "And they're staying over at the hotel too."

"Who are the O'Malley's?" I ask.

"Old family friends." Liam pulls a face. "Boring fuckers, the lot of them."

"Why aren't you two going then?" I take another grape and watch as Mikey pulls off his sweaty gym shorts until he's standing there in just his skintight boxer briefs, and I try not to choke on the grape I've just eaten. I've seen them both bare-chested plenty of times. They constantly walk around shirtless and my ovaries are just about getting used to it, because they are both huge and ripped. But, damn, if there isn't the outline of the hugest cock beneath the gray cotton of Mikey's underwear.

Dear God, these boys are fine!

"You checking out my tattoo, Jessie?" Mikey asks with a chuckle, referring to the tattoo of a phoenix that he has on the very top of his right thigh.

"Yeah," I reply as calmly as I can. "That's some nice ink."

He nods to himself as he walks toward the utility room and disappears inside. I swallow hard. If he comes out of there naked, I might just pass out. But my modesty is spared when he walks out a few seconds later with a white towel wrapped around his waist.

"So, why aren't you two going then?" I ask again.

Liam and Mikey share a look, and Mikey shakes his head and winces.

"We've been banned from any weddings because at the last one, Mikey here got caught fucking the bride in the restroom. At the reception." Liam laughs.

My hand flies to my mouth. "Mikey?" I stifle a laugh. "Really?"

He nods as he walks over to the table and sits down. "Yeah, but…"

"But what?" I gasp. "That's awful!"

"So, why are you smiling then, Red?" He flashes an eyebrow at me.

"Because it's just so… so bad."

He shrugs. "What can I say? She only married him for his money. And I was young, dumb and full of–"

I hold my hand up to stop him talking. "Yeah, I don't need to hear the end of that sentence, thanks. But, wow! No wonder you're banned from weddings."

He nods proudly.

"But why aren't you allowed to go?" I turn to Liam.

"Oh, me? Well, when the groom found Mikey balls deep in his new virginal wife, he tried to cut off his head with a butter knife. So, I might have knocked him unconscious and then used his brand-new Maserati as our getaway car."

I hold my hand over my mouth as I burst out laughing. "You boys are so bad," I say with a shake of my head when I'm able to talk.

"You have no idea, Red." Mikey arches an eyebrow at me. "So, what are we doing tonight? All night rager?" he suggests.

Liam sighs and rolls his eyes.

"How about a movie marathon?" I offer, and both of their eyes light up.

"You're not going to make us watch any more where the dog dies, though, are you?" Liam says. "That fucking cut me up that."

"No more dogs dying." I smile as I recall them both sniffling, watching *Marley and Me* with me a few nights earlier. "How about *Fast and Furious*? We could stay up all night and watch all eight?"

"Or, we could watch two, and then crack open the tequila and play some poker instead?" Liam suggests.

"Strip poker?" Mikey grins.

"What? You two hardly wear any clothes as it is. The game would be over in like, five minutes." I pop an eyebrow at him.

"Makes it easier for you to win then, doesn't it, Red?" he fires back.

"You don't exactly wander around here fully clothed yourself." Liam laughs, and I shoot him a look of mock indignation. "You keep stealing my shirts and wearing them."

"I know." I bite my lower lip. "But they're so comfortable. Plus, they're so big on me, they're just like a dress."

Mikey leans onto the table and props himself up on one elbow. "Yeah, but do you wear anything underneath it, Red?" He winks at me.

"Well, I guess you'll have to beat me at poker to find out," I say with a grin.

"Fuck!" he chuckles. "You're going to get us in a whole load of trouble, Red."

I open my mouth to respond, but just then Shane and Conor walk into the room and the conversation changes to the O'Malley's wedding.

CHAPTER 13

MIKEY

"Are you sure you're okay if we stay out all night? You won't do anything stupid?" Shane asks as he fastens his watch.

I look over at my twin and roll my eyes, and he stifles a laugh. Shane is in a foul mood and if we piss him off too much, then he might just stay home and put a stop to our planned night of fun with our new house-mate.

"We'll be fine. I'm pretty sure me and Liam are capable of looking after a one-hundred-pound computer nerd for the evening."

"She's not a nerd," Liam snaps in her defense, and I shake my head at him. My twin brother has it bad for Jessie. Not that I blame him. I mean, she is pretty cute, has an ass that I could happily eat my dinner off, and she's funny too. Hence, our planned night of popcorn and movies, followed by tequila and poker. If we're really lucky, we might just get to play strip poker.

"He's just kidding," Conor says as he walks into the kitchen. "Aren't you?" He narrows his eyes at me.

I nod in response to his question. "Shane thinks we can't be trusted to keep an eye on our hostage for the night." I arch an eyebrow at Conor and he does his best to hide his smile while shaking his head in exasperation.

"They'll be fine. Now let's go so we can get this over with. I hate spending time with the O'Malley's. I can't believe you've agreed we'd stay at their hotel," Conor snaps.

"Oh, quit your whining," Shane barks. "Let's go. You can drive."

"Have fun." I smile before shoveling a spoonful of Lucky Charms into my mouth.

"Just behave yourselves," Shane warns.

"Don't do anything I wouldn't do," Conor adds with a smirk.

"Well, that's a pretty vast range of shit we can do then," Liam says as he takes a can of soda from the refrigerator.

"We'll be back first thing," Shane says before they walk out of the kitchen.

"Don't rush!" I shout after them.

"You think Jessie has finished her bath?" Liam asks me as soon as our brothers have disappeared from sight.

"Why don't you go find out?" I flash my eyebrows at him.

"Don't be such a perv." He punches me on the arm. "I mean like go knock on her door or something, numb-nuts."

He takes a drink of his soda and stares at me for a few seconds. "I'll go check."

"I'll get the popcorn ready."

* * *

HALF AN HOUR LATER, Jessie sits between Liam and me on the sofa while we watch *Fast and Furious*. She sits cross-legged, holding the bowl of popcorn on her lap as the three of us eat.

Once the bowl is empty, I take it from her and put it on the floor, but she doesn't shift her position. She's wearing one of Liam's old baseball shirts and she was right earlier, it is as long as a dress on her small frame, but only a very short one. I try to focus on the movie, but my eyes are constantly drawn to that space between her thighs. I imagine what it would be like to put my hand there. What she would feel like? Smell like? Would she taste as good as I think she would? My cock grows harder with each passing minute and the more I try to stop thinking about all the filthy things I'd like to be doing to her, the more difficult it becomes.

I don't know if Jessie is aware of the growing sexual tension on the sofa, but Liam is looking at that space where the popcorn bowl was a few minutes earlier too, and I know that it's no longer popcorn he's thinking about eating. Maybe she does know, because she wiggles her ass slightly and that damn t-shirt rides up even higher.

When I realize I'm staring, I close my eyes and suck in a breath. But fuck if I don't feel her warm, soft fingers resting on my leg. The heat of her skin on mine makes my cock stand to attention. I open my eyes and place my hand over hers. She turns hers palm side up, threading her fingers through mine. Then she gives me a quick smile before she pulls our joined hands into her lap, until they're right where that bowl just was. The heat from the space between her thighs is so fucking obvious now that my hand is there, and it's driving me crazy.

Liam slides an arm around her shoulders and then we all just sit there like that for a few minutes watching the movie—or at least I'm trying to. I am so fucking aware of the fact that my knuckle is about one inch from her pussy. If I straightened out my little finger, I could touch her through her panties.

My cock is getting so hard it's becoming painful and I use my free hand to discreetly shift it into a more comfortable position. When I glance sideways at her to see if she's noticed, she has her head turned toward Liam. I stare at them as he reaches out his free hand and cups her cheek. Then he's leaning into her, pressing his lips over hers. She kisses him back and his hand drops to her leg. My eyes are drawn to his fingers as he gently squeezes the inside of her thigh while the two of them continue to tongue each other. I suck in a breath as my dick feels like it is about to explode.

She squeezes my hand tightly and I don't know if it's the effect of Liam kissing her, or she does it on purpose, but she groans and drags our joined hands closer to her body, until my knuckles are pressed against her panties.

Fuck! They're already damp. My cock twitches because all I can think about is how wet she must be beneath them. I graze the back of my fingers over her pussy though the fabric, and she groans into Liam's mouth as she untangles her fingers from mine.

Double fuck! I figure this is my cue that I'm not a spectator here. Turning my body to hers, I reach up and pull her hair back from her face, planting a kiss on her neck and making her moan softly. I keep kissing her there, sucking and nibbling at the tender skin as I pull up her t-shirt with my free hand. My fingertips brush over her stomach, down to the band of her panties. Her breathing grows faster as I continue kissing her neck, while my fingers dip beneath the waistband of her underwear, sliding lower until I reach her slick folds.

I brush two fingers between them. "Fuck! You're so wet, Red," I breathe against her skin.

Her clit is already swollen, and I rub it softly as the groan of pleasure rumbles through her throat. She presses herself against my palm and I increase my pressure while I keep sucking on her neck. Listening to my brother swallowing her whimpers and moans as he kisses her, while I play with her pussy, makes me want to make her moan even more. I slide two fingers lower and my cock throbs as I realize just how much she's fucking dripping for me.

For both of us.

Edging myself closer to her, I push two fingers inside her

and she gasps out loud as she wrenches her lips from Liam's. Her slick heat drips all over my fingers as I push deeper inside. She squeezes me tight, pulling me deeper into her, and I know there is no way I'm leaving this room without feeling this pussy on my cock.

CHAPTER 14

LIAM

I look down at my brother's hand in Jessie's panties as he finger-fucks her and it might just be the hottest thing I've ever seen in my life. The stain of her arousal is visible on the scrap of black fabric as the room fills with the wet sound of him pumping his fingers in and out of her dripping pussy. My cock feels like an iron bar and I palm it through my shorts to get some relief.

She's still looking at me, her eyes dark with lust as she bites on her lip and tries to stop herself from moaning.

"I can smell how wet you are, baby," I chuckle as I slide my hand up the inside of her thigh. "You like Mikey touching you like that?"

"Yes," she breathes.

"She's fucking soaking, Liam. If she smells this good, can you imagine how good she tastes?" Mikey groans as he thrusts his fingers in and out of her.

"Fuck!" I grunt as I imagine just that. I look into her eyes. "I want to taste you, baby."

She nods and my cock throbs in anticipation.

Mikey looks at me and winks, and I reach down and grab her hips, swinging her around until she's lying on the sofa. Mikey turns too, so that her back is pressed against his chest while he still has his fingers inside her, working her for me.

She holds onto his forearm with both hands. "Mikey," she moans, and my cock twitches at the sound. I'm going to make sure she's moaning my name pretty soon.

Taking hold of her panties, I peel them slowly down her legs as Mikey keeps playing with her. The top of her thighs and his hand are slick with her arousal and I lick my lips at the realization that I'm about to taste her. I have wanted her from the minute I laid eyes on her.

Placing my hands on the inside of her thighs, I smile as they tremble beneath my touch. Mikey slides his fingers out of her and a rush of her cum trickles out of her opening, making her moan loudly.

"Fuck, Jessie. You are soaking wet, baby. You really like Mikey's fingers, huh?"

She can't answer me, because Mikey tilts her head up and kisses her as I push her thighs wide apart. I should probably take my time and savor this, but I can't wait a minute longer. Dipping my head, I push the flat of my tongue against her hot entrance and her hips jolt upwards. I suck her delicious juices and she bucks against my tongue so much that I have to wrap my forearms around the back of her thighs to hold her in place.

She groans loudly, but when I glance up, Mikey has his hand on the back of her neck, crushing her face to his as he devours her mouth and swallows her sounds of pleasure.

I dip my head low again and lick the length of her folds before I swirl my tongue over her clit, and then I stay there, sucking and nibbling the swollen bud of flesh until Mikey can't swallow her screams any longer. I slide a finger inside her as she comes for me and coats me with the sweet release of her juices.

Her thighs tremble violently, and I look up at her. She's so fucking beautiful when she comes. Her blue eyes burn dark with lust and her cheeks are flushed bright pink.

"Liam," she moans as her eyelids flutter.

Mikey chuckles softly. "We've hardly even started yet, Red."

CHAPTER 15

JESSIE

*M*y head spins and the blood thunders in my ears as I lie with my back pressed against Mikey's bare chest and his arms wrapped around me. Liam lies with his face still only inches from my pussy after he's just given me the most incredible orgasm of my life. Although, I suppose he can't take all the credit—Mikey did get things started pretty nicely. I was already on the edge by the time Liam got his magical tongue anywhere near me.

I had no idea the twins saw me that way. I've spent so much more time with them than with Conor or Shane since I've been here. They're fun and easy to be around, and they're both pretty hot. But I always thought they saw me as a buddy, or an annoying kid sister they like to make fun of.

Until tonight when I was sandwiched between them on the sofa. I've seen them shirtless before. I knew they were ripped, but being wedged between those muscular biceps and forearms made me feel all kinds of things that I'd never felt about them before. Whether it was the weeks of flirting with Conor that had me all on edge and horny, I don't know, but all I could think about was sex.

"You ever been with two guys before, Jessie?" Liam growls, reminding me that I am still sandwiched between two super hot dudes and I am dripping onto their sofa.

"No," I say as a thrill of pleasure shoots through me. I mean, who hasn't fantasized about being with two guys, right? Especially when they're as gorgeous and attentive as these two.

"You want to?" Mikey asks as he brushes my hair back from my face.

"Yes."

"Good, because you've got me as hard as iron here, baby," Liam growls as he kisses the inside of my thigh.

Mikey presses his lips against my ear. "You ever been fucked in the ass?"

"Yes," I breathe as I look down at Liam between my thighs just in time to see him flashing a wicked grin at his twin brother.

I'm about to ask what that was about when Mikey reaches down and lifts my t-shirt up. "Let's get you naked, Red," he says softly, and the tone of his voice makes my insides melt like butter.

I raise my arms in compliance and he peels the oversized shirt over my head and throws it onto the floor. I snake my arms back and around Mikey's neck as his hands slide over my breasts, down over my stomach and between my thighs as he rubs my clit with the fingers of one hand, while he pushes one of my thighs flat to the sofa with the other. Liam leans over me and trails kisses in the opposite direction, working his way up until he reaches my breasts and he sucks one of my nipples into his hot mouth while he rolls the other one between his finger and thumb.

The pressure of Mikey's fingers and Liam's mouth has me panting with need. I try to grind against them both, but they hold me still between their hard bodies. All I can do is look on helplessly as they tease me, bringing me close to the edge over and over again.

"Look at me, Jessie," Mikey growls.

I tilt my head to him as he leans down and kisses me while he keeps rubbing my clit and pressing my thigh to the sofa, so I am open wide. There is so much flesh pressed together that it's becoming hard to tell where one of them ends and one begins. I'm vaguely aware of Liam's hand moving from my breast. It skates over my stomach and then brushes over his brother's hand before he pushes two thick fingers inside me, and suddenly the two of them are bringing me to another intense, earth-shattering orgasm.

I buck and shudder between them as their mouths and their hands coax the last tremors of my climax from my body.

"I think she's ready, Mikey," Liam breathes against my skin.

"I think you're right," Mikey agrees, and I lie between them feeling completely boneless, wanting to ask what the hell they mean whilst barely being able to form a coherent word.

Liam pushes himself up onto his knees and holds out his hand. "You okay, Jessie?" he asks.

I nod as I allow him to pull me into a sitting position. Behind me, I'm aware of Mikey sliding off his shorts and then he lays back down on the sofa and places his hands on my waist. "Turn around, Red," he says, and I oblige, catching my first glimpse of his cock as it stands thick and tall and glistening with pre-cum.

Without thinking, I bend down and take it in one hand, licking his arousal from the tip and he groans out loud. "Don't, Red," he groans. "I'm already on the edge, and I don't want to come in your mouth. Not yet, anyway." He arches one eyebrow at me.

I lift my head up and look at his handsome face. "Do you have a condom?"

"We do. But I promise you I'm clean. We both are. We get

tested every six months and our last one was four weeks ago. There's been no-one since."

"Don't you ever wear condoms?"

"Always," he breathes as he brushes my hair back from my face.

"So why not now?"

"Because the doc told us you're clean and you're on birth control. And I really want to feel that pussy on my cock, Red." I feel a sudden rush of wet heat at the thought and I move to straddle him. "So, please, slide yourself onto it before I come just from looking at you," he adds.

I take his hard length in my hand and then guide it into my wet entrance. I slide down, my walls squeezing him as I take him all the way. He's big, but I'm so wet from the orgasms that there's only a slight burn as he stretches me wide open. I roll my hips and smile as his eyes roll back in his head.

"Damn, you feel good on my cock, Red," he grinds out the words as he places his hands on my hips. "But you need to keep still until Liam gets back."

I only just realize that Liam is no longer here.

"Where ..." I start to ask but Mikey sits up and sucks one of my nipples into his mouth and I get completely distracted.

"God, you have a hot mouth," I groan as I try to buck my hips against him.

He bites my nipple just a little too hard and I yelp in half pleasure, half pain.

"Be still," he growls.

The sound of footsteps behind me alert me to the fact that Liam is back. The snap of a cap opening makes me realize exactly what's about to happen next, and my legs start to shake at the prospect.

Mikey lays back down, pulling me with him so I am flat against his chest. He keeps one arm wrapped around me, while his free hands fists in my hair and he pulls my mouth to his, slipping his tongue inside and kissing me deeply. The sofa dips behind me and Liam's warm hands are rubbing gently over my skin.

"This will be cold, baby," he says as he squeezes lube over the seam of my ass. "But necessary," he chuckles as he slips one finger over my dark entrance before pushing the tip inside. I gasp at the intrusion, pulling my lips away from Mikey.

He strokes the back of my neck. "Relax, Red. We can stop whenever you want to. Okay?"

"Okay," I breathe.

Liam keeps edging his finger inside me until he's all the way to his knuckle and then he gently pumps it in and out as I get used to the feeling of being full of him.

"Jessie, try to stop squeezing me so much, baby," Mikey groans.

"Okay," I pant but how the hell am I supposed to stop? Having these two sexy guys fucking me at the same time is mind blowing.

Liam withdraws his finger and I let out a breath. I suck in another one as he presses the tip of his cock there instead. "Help me out, Bro," he growls to Mikey who wraps both arms around me.

"I'm going to hold you still, Red. Once he's inside, you can move all you want, okay?"

"Okay."

"I'll go slow. I won't hurt you," Liam says softly from behind me and my body relaxes. Because I know that's true. I am completely safe here.

Liam pushes deeper inside and the burning stretch is pleasurable too.

"Fuck!" Liam grunts. "She's too fucking tight."

Mikey releases me from his grip and cups my face in his

hands. He kisses me again, his tongue swirling against mine, and my body melts into his as Liam is able to push further inside me.

"Damn, Jessie, your ass is so fucking hot," he grinds out as he starts to move his hips.

"You should feel her pussy," Mikey chuckles as he lets me up for air. "Now, do you want to move or you want us to?"

"You," I breathe.

He looks past me and winks at his brother and then they start to move in a perfect fucking rhythm that makes my body thrum with an energy like I have never felt before in my life. Liam peppers my back with kisses while Mikey nibbles my neck and all I can do is moan their names as they work my body like they've known it forever.

I'm so close to the edge for so long that I feel like I might fall into oblivion.

"You feel so fucking good, Red," Mikey breathes in my ear.

"You're fucking perfect, baby," Liam growls as he thrusts his hips harder.

I plant my forearms on the sofa beside Mikey's head and push myself up slightly, and then something catches my eye from the corner of the room. I turn my head and gasp as I realize Shane and Conor are standing there, staring at the three of us.

"Oh, God," I whisper. "They're back early."

"I'm not stopping, Red," Mikey groans, as he tightens his grip on my hips and pumps into me. I'm still looking at Conor and Shane and the heat flushes my cheeks as they watch us, but all my body can focus on is Liam's lips on my neck, Mikey's hands on my hips and the exquisite feeling of being filled by the two of them at the same time. Shane shakes his head and storms down the hallway away from us. But Conor takes a seat and continues watching us, and that makes it even hotter.

Mikey turns my face back to his. "I want you to look at me while you come, Jessie," he pants as he pulls my hips downwards at the same time he thrust upwards. "Fuck!" he roars as he spills his seed inside me.

The look on his face, Liam's soft kisses on my neck, his cock twitching in my ass, and knowing that Conor is watching all of it, makes my body sizzle with energy. The vibrations ripple out from my core to every nerve ending I have.

"Damn, Jessie," Liam groans as he loses himself too, just as I do.

My head is spinning. I pant for breath as I lay back down on Mikey's hard chest. Liam lies on top of me and plants a kiss between my shoulder blades. "You're incredible, Jessie," he whispers.

"Hmm," Mikey agrees as he brushes my hair from my damp forehead. "You are."

I smile as I lay my cheek against his chest. Liam slowly slides out of me, but he holds himself up on his powerful forearms and rests his body against mine. The three of us are slick with perspiration and cum, but I realize I don't care. I'm not ashamed to admit that I've used my body as a weapon in the past. But, as a sixteen-year-old girl at the mercy of a monster, it was the only weapon I had. The men in the circles I've always run in, powerful men with too much money and not enough conscience, are used to taking what they want anyway. I always figured it couldn't hurt to get out in front and give them what they want on my own terms. And if that means I get to use it to my advantage sometimes, then so be it. But I cannot remember a single time in my life when I have ever felt this desired, this wanted, or this cared for. Yes, Liam and Mikey and I just did something that I'd never in a million years thought I'd be down with, but I felt completely cherished by them the whole time.

I blink away a tear as it pricks at my eyes and it rolls down my cheek onto Mikey's chest.

He places his index finger under my chin and tilts my head up. "Hey, are you okay, Red?"

"Yes." I smile at him. "More than okay." I lay my head back on his chest and snuggle against him and his twin. I had almost forgotten what being cared about feels like. It's only now that I realize Conor has disappeared.

CHAPTER 16

CONOR

I knock on the door to my younger brothers' room and wait for them to answer. Why the fuck am I fidgeting like a nervous teenage boy?

"Yeah?" one of them shouts.

Opening the door, I stick my head inside. They're in their own beds, with no sign of our house guest in there. "Where's Jessie?"

"She's taking a shower," Liam says with a yawn.

I look toward their bathroom and frown. There's no water running.

"In her own room, bro," Mikey adds. "She said something about going shopping?"

That she has remembered our shopping trip makes me smile and I silently curse myself. She spent last night being railed by my two younger brothers and that tells me all I need to know about me and her.

Despite that, I can't stop thinking about her. I can't get the image of her incredible body shuddering as she came loudly for my brothers out of my goddamn head. When I went to bed last night, I jerked off twice to it, but it did nothing to relieve the tension. I close the door and leave the twins to go back to sleep before walking along the hallway to Jessie's room.

I knock. And wait.

"Come in," she shouts, and I open the door wide as she's putting her hair up into a ponytail. She's wearing those skin-tight jeans and a tank top, and I start to have second thoughts about today. How will I spend the whole fucking day with her? Because I can't stop replaying last night's highlight reel in my head. When I look at her now, all I can see is her being fucked by my brothers, and instead of making me back off, it only makes me want her more. What the hell is wrong with me?

"Hey," she says breathlessly as I walk into the room. "I'm almost ready. We're still going shopping, right?" She gives me a huge, genuine smile and I can't help but wonder if it's for me, or it's because she's still on a high from her exploits last night. But how the fuck do I say no to her?

"Yeah. Course we are. Meet me in the basement in ten."

"Great," she says with another megawatt smile.

I walk out of her door and close it behind me, resting my forehead against the cool wood and letting out a long sigh.

JESSIE IS quiet during the car ride. She seems nervous. I suppose I can't blame her when she is fully aware that I sat and watched her being fucked by my brothers last night.

We arrive at the boutique forty-five minutes later. The owner, Callie Thomas, is an old friend of mine, and she's closed the store for the afternoon for me. This isn't the first time I've brought a woman clothes shopping here, and I always make sure Callie is well compensated for her trouble. This is the first time I've ever brought a woman I'm not fucking, though. I shake my head in exasperation at that realization as we reach the door where Callie is waiting.

"Conor," Callie says with a smile, wrapping her arms around me and enveloping me in a cloud of sweet perfume. "It's so good to see you, darling." She pulls away and looks at Jessie, who is hovering nervously behind me.

"This is Jessie." I place my hand on the small of Jessie's back and guide her toward the entrance. "She's staying with us for a while and she needs a whole new wardrobe."

Callie nods. "You have a beautiful figure. I'll enjoy dressing you today," she says as she openly looks Jessie up and down. "I have some beautiful pieces for you to try."

Jessie seems even more nervous now as I gently push her through the doorway and into the shop. Callie shows us to the fitting room and I sit in one of the huge, plush velvet chairs. At least I'll get to enjoy today's show if I'm lucky.

"What's your style, Jessie?" Callie asks as she whips out her measuring tape and starts measuring her waist and hips.

"Um. Casual, I suppose. I like jeans. T-shirts. A few hooded sweatshirts would be good. I don't need a lot."

Callie looks at me and frowns, and I can't help but laugh. The women I've brought here in the past rarely have such simple tastes.

"Bring some dresses too," I say.

"Yes. Dresses!" Callie claps her hands together.

"I don't really wear dresses," Jessie protests.

"But you might need one if you ever want to come to the club? Or go out somewhere? Just try some?" I suggest, hoping that I might be the one to take her to such places.

"Okay. Dresses," Jessie agrees.

"And some underwear too, Callie," I add, and I watch in perverted satisfaction as the flush creeps over Jessie's cheeks.

"Of course." Callie winks at me, and then she disappears out of the dressing room.

Jessie turns to me with a slight frown on her beautiful face. "What kind of place is this?"

"It's a boutique. Callie owns it and she's an old friend."

She nods. "So, you do this a lot? Bring women here and watch them try on clothes? Is that, like, your thing?"

"I used to do it. Not so much anymore. I don't have to watch if you don't want me to. There's a curtain over there." I nod toward the corner of the large room. "But I have already seen you completely naked. So?" I shrug.

She blushes deeper. "About that..." she says, just as Callie walks back into the room.

"I pulled some of these for you earlier. Conor told me your size, and these are a few pieces I thought you might like." She says that last part to me rather than Jessie. She knows my tastes well.

Jessie takes the clothes from her, and Callie leaves again. She holds up the first item of clothing. It's a short black mini dress with leather and mesh panels.

"You think this is me?" She arches one eyebrow.

"You won't know until you try it on." I sit back in my chair, hoping that she's going to try it on right here in front of me, while also wondering how the hell I'll hide my raging boner when she does.

"Here goes," she says with a grin as she peels her tank-top over her head.

My mouth goes dry as I watch her undressing, stripping down to her tiny black cotton panties and her bra. I can't take my eyes off her and I know that she knows I'm staring at her. When she finally has the dress on, she gives me a twirl.

"What do you think?" she asks with a smile.

"It looks fucking incredible," I answer honestly, and completely unguarded.

She blushes again, but she's smiling widely. "I haven't worn anything like this for a very long time," she says, almost to herself.

"What do you think?" I ask her.

"I like it. It makes me feel…"

"What?"

She bites her bottom lip as she looks at me, her cheeks flushed pink. "Sexy? Is that big-headed to say that?"

"No," I laugh. "Especially not when it's one hundred percent true. You look hot, Angel."

She sucks in a breath and I'm sure I feel something pass between us. My cock is growing harder with each passing second, and I'm not sure I'm going to make it through this afternoon without burying myself in her.

The moment is interrupted by Callie coming back into the room, armed with lots more clothes, and piling them onto the empty chair. She stays with us, helping Jessie try on various outfits. I continue watching Jessie. She gets more relaxed with Callie and me as the day goes on. She complains good-naturedly every time Callie insists she tries on something that's not her usual style, but she does it anyway, and she likes almost everything that Callie has chosen. The woman has good taste.

After two hours, Jessie has tried on almost all the clothes and I have a raging hard on from watching her shimmy her incredible body in and out of them all afternoon. Callie looks at the small pile remaining, which comprises only underwear. She picks up a matching red lace bra and panties and holds them out. Jessie chews her lip and looks at me, and I almost pass out with the rush of blood to my cock.

"Leave us," I growl to Callie and she nods before slipping silently out of the door.

"You want me to try these on too?" Jessie asks, her voice sounding like the purring of a kitten.

I could ask her what she wants. I should ask her. But I am too far gone. I need to see her naked. "Yes."

"Okay," she breathes as she reaches behind her and unclips her bra. Her heavy breasts spring free. Her nipples are already hard, and they seem to pebble further under my gaze. She hooks her fingers under the waistband of her panties and then slides them slowly down her legs before kicking them off her feet. My eyes roam over her entire body greedily, in case I never get this opportunity again. She takes the red lace set and puts it on just as slowly, and I don't think I have ever been this turned on by a woman putting her clothes *on*.

"Well?" she stammers as she holds her arms out wide.

"You look fucking beautiful. I would say that you know that, but I'm not sure you do?" I arch one eyebrow at her and she bites her lip nervously.

My dick is going to bust out of my zipper any second, and I groan in frustration. Sitting forward, I put my head in my hands. "Fuck!"

"What is it?"

I sit back up and run my hand over my face. "You'd better get dressed, Jessie. Or…" I swallow. I can't even finish the sentence.

"Or what?" she asks, and I swear she must know exactly what she's doing to me. How could she not?

Standing up, I walk over to her until we're standing just inches apart. Her body trembles slightly and I bend my head lower. "You know what, Jessie. So, stop playing games with me." I reach up and brush her cheek with my knuckles.

"I'm not playing games, Conor," she whispers. "I thought after last night." She lowers her head.

"You thought what?" I demand.

"That you wouldn't…" She shakes her head and sniffs as though she's about to cry.

Placing my hands on her shoulders, I turn her around until she's facing the mirror. I wrap one hand around her throat, holding her head upright.

"Look at me," I growl in her ear, and her eyes flicker over my face in the mirror until they lock on mine. "Do you think that just because I watched my brothers fucking you, filling you with their cocks, that I don't want you still?"

Her whole body trembles as my hand slides over her hip and down to her panties. "You look so fucking beautiful when you come, Jessie, it only makes me want you more."

She draws in a shaky breath as my hand slides beneath the band of her lacy red underwear and onto her shaved mound. She keeps her eyes locked on mine and my cock throbs painfully. I grow even harder as I look at our reflection. I have one of my hands on her throat and the other one in her panties, and damn if it isn't the hottest thing I've ever seen in my life.

"I want to see you come for me, Jessie. I want to make you come on my fingers, and then my mouth, and then my cock." I say in her ear and she whimpers. "But I'm not as gentle as my little brothers. I know you believe that I'm a pussycat, but that's because you haven't seen the real me, Angel. He is an animal. I keep him safely locked away in a cage, but you make me want to let him loose."

Her throat constricts under my hand as she swallows.

"Conor," she groans.

Sliding my fingers through her pussy lips, I stifle a groan as I find her soaking wet for me. I hope she wants this as much as I do, because I'm edging past the point of no return here. My whole fucking body is screaming to be inside her. My mouth waters at the prospect of tasting her—her mouth, her skin, the sweet cream that she's dripping all over my fingers.

Come on Jessie. Let me in!

I drop my hand from her throat to one of her breasts, tugging on her hard nipple through the delicate fabric of her bra while the fingers of my other hand slide further into her folds, until I'm at the entrance of her hot, wet heat. The only sound in the room is our breathing. Fast and shallow, matching each other's breath for breath.

I pause and close my eyes, savoring the sensation of her in my arms. Our bodies pressed together so closely we're almost like one.

I need her to want this as badly as I do. Because once I get a taste of her, once I get any part of my body inside her, I know I'll never be able to stop. Her heart hammers against my hand and her juices coat my fingers as her breathing grows even faster. Perspiration beads on my forehead as I use every ounce of self-control I have not to drive my fingers into her.

"Jessie?" I hiss against her ear.

"Please, Conor," she gasps.

"Please what, Angel?"

"I want you," she breathes and as soon as the words are out of her mouth, I push two fingers deep inside her and groan as she releases a rush of wet heat.

She places her palms flat on the mirror, her breath fogging the glass as she rocks against my hand while I pump in and out of her dripping channel. Her walls clench around me, sucking me in further and my eyes almost roll into the back of my head as she whimpers my name.

"Fuck, Angel!" I growl in her ear as I finger fuck her. "You feel even better than I imagined you would. I can't wait to feel this hot pussy squeezing my cock."

"Conor," she groans my name as I slide my other hand from her nipple down inside her panties too, until both of my fists are stretching the delicate fabric. I rub the pads of my index and middle fingers over her swollen clit and suck in a breath as they slide easily over the swollen bud of flesh. She writhes beneath me, wriggling so much that I press my body against her until her top half is pinned to the glass. Her pussy squeezes me tighter as she gets closer and closer to the edge.

"Spread your legs wider," I order, and my cock almost busts my zipper as she obeys me without hesitation. I slide a third finger inside her and her body shudders as she rocks against me.

"You like that, Angel?" I growl in her ear.

"Yes," she pants as her head drops low.

"Look at me! I want to see that beautiful face when you come apart for me."

Lifting her head, she looks at me through the mirror and the desire in her eyes matches mine. I need to make her come soon so I can fuck her hard. No more teasing.

I press my fingers hard against her clit, and she cries out as her orgasm hits. Her juices pour over my fingers and my cock weeps in appreciation. When she finally stops shuddering, her body sags against mine as I rub the last tremors from her body with one hand while wrapping my other arm around her waist to steady her.

She tips her head back against me with an enormous smile on her face and I plant a kiss on her neck. When her legs stop trembling and she can stand unaided, I drop my hands to my pants and undo my belt and zipper, pulling down my boxer shorts until my cock springs free. I press against her as I tuck my fingers into the waistband of her panties.

"How many women have you fucked in this room?" she asks as she meets my eyes in the mirror, her face flushed and her eyes dark with desire.

"Plenty. Is that a problem?" I arch an eyebrow at her.

"No. But do you use protection?" she breathes.

"Always," I growl.

"So, do you have a condom?"

"No, Angel," I grunt as I pull her panties over her juicy ass and down her legs. "And there is not a fucking chance in hell I'm wearing one with you."

She blinks at my reflection. "Why?"

"I promise you I'm clean. I know you are. My brothers are. I also know you have that implant to prevent any accidents. And I want to feel your cum on my cock when I make you come apart again. I want you to feel every inch of me, Angel, just like I'm going to feel every bit of you. Okay?"

"Okay," she breathes.

"Good. Now, turn around."

She turns and faces me, snaking her arms around my neck as I slide my hands to her ass. I lift her until her legs wrap around my waist and she's pressed against the mirror. Pushing my hard length against her folds, I coat myself in her slick heat as I press my lips against hers, swallowing her groans as I slide the tip inside her.

Fuck! I'm going to blow my load in her right now if I'm not careful.

"Conor," she gasps as she wrenches her lips away from mine.

"You want this?" I growl as I edge my cock in another inch.

"Fuck, yes!" she pants as she rolls her hips forward.

I have wanted this since the minute I saw her in Nikolai's house. I slide myself all the way inside her. She moans like a porn star while all I can do is growl like an animal. She's so wet that I slide in easily, right to the hilt as her pussy squeezes me.

"Jessie," I hiss. "Stop milking my cock, Angel, or I won't last five minutes."

"I can't help it Conor," she breathes as she leans her head back against the mirror. "You feel so good."

Fuck!

I bend my head and take one of her pebbled nipples into my mouth, sucking on the delicate bud as I thrust in and out of her soaking channel. I'm so fucking close to losing myself in her. But I need to make her come first. I need to know how she feels when I'm buried inside her. I let her nipple go with a wet sucking sound, plant my hands on the mirror beside her head and seal my mouth over hers as I rail into her, driving at the spot inside her that's got her thighs trembling around my waist. She moans, and I swallow the sound.

And then I feel her. Her pussy contracts around my dick and she almost sucks the breath from me as she comes again, taking me over the edge with her while she rakes her nails down my back.

CHAPTER 17

JESSIE

I wrench my lips from Conor's as my legs tremble and the last waves of my orgasm roll through my body.

"Fuck, Angel," he groans as he presses his forehead against mine. "Your pussy should come with a health warning."

I don't have time to reply because we're interrupted by a knock at the changing room door. His head turns toward the noise and he frowns. "Give us five minutes," he shouts. "And we'll be taking everything."

"Everything? I don't need this many clothes, Conor."

He pulls out of me, letting my feet drop to the floor until I'm standing against the mirror. "They all looked good on you. You should have them," he says as he steps back from me and starts fastening his pants and belt. "Now, get dressed."

My hands drop to my side and there is an unexpected lump in my throat at the coldness of his tone after what we've just shared. But then he looks up at me, his eyes burning into mine as he frowns again before lifting his hand to my face and running a finger along my cheekbone. "I need to get you home, so I can take you to bed and fuck you properly, Angel," he growls. "So, move your ass. Now!"

I bite back a smile and stoop to pick up the red panties from the floor.

"Actually, I don't think we should take them," Conor says with a grin as he snatches them from my hand. "I'll tell Callie to put them back in the store."

"Conor!" I gasp as I reach out to snatch them back. "Of all the things we can ask her to put back, those panties are not among them."

"Why?" He grins at me as he holds them out of reach.

"You know why." I glare at him. "Now hand them over."

He holds them to his face and inhales deeply. "On second thoughts, I'm not sure I want random strangers smelling how sweet you are," he laughs as he hands them back to me.

"You have a filthy mind." I flash my eyebrows at him as I begin to dress.

"Says the woman who's been fucked by me and my two brothers in less than twenty-four hours." He arches an eyebrow right back and I can't help but blush.

"You make that sound really bad," I whisper.

He steps closer to me and tucks a strand of hair behind my ear. "It's not, Angel. It's fucking hot. Now get your damn clothes on or I'll carry you out of here in that bra and panties."

CHAPTER 18

JESSIE

*C*onor drove us back to the apartment in record time, flooring the accelerator every chance he got. We take the elevator to the top floor and I'm thankful that none of his brothers are around because he presses me against the wall and starts unbuttoning my jeans as soon as we're in the hallway. His warm hands glide over the skin on my stomach and I suck in a deep breath.

"Didn't you say something about a bed?" I ask with a smile.

"Yes," he growls as he steps back and takes hold of my hand, pulling me along the hallway toward his room. When we reach the door, he pushes me through it and kicks it closed behind us. I turn to face him as I walk backwards toward his enormous bed.

"You are very impatient." I flash my eyebrows at him.

"Impatient? Me?" He grins. "Oh, Angel. You know you're going to regret that, don't you?"

"Really?" I pull my tank top over my head and toss it onto the floor. "We'll see."

He crosses the room and pulls me into his arms before I can

take another step. "Don't tease me, Angel. I've been playing nice with you today."

"Then show me naughty."

"Don't," he growls as he runs his teeth along my jaw.

"I can take whatever you can throw at me, Conor. I'm not made of glass."

He lifts his head and his eyes burn into mine, making the heat sear between my thighs. Then something changes in him. The playful grin on his face disappears. The vein throbs in his temple. "Take off your clothes," he orders, his breath skittering over my cheeks.

Goosebumps prickle along my forearms, but I unzip my jeans and slide them down my legs, kicking my sneakers and socks off with them when I reach my feet. Standing tall again, I look up at him as I unhook my bra and let it fall from my shoulders. His eyes drop to my nipples and a low growl rumbles in his throat.

"The panties too," he snaps.

I swallow hard as I slide the red lace panties down my legs until I'm standing before him, completely naked.

He runs his hands up my arms and then down over my breasts and onto my stomach, sliding one hand between my thighs before bending his head low until his lips are pressed against my neck. "I can smell how wet you are already, Angel. I can smell it dripping out of you while you stand there waiting for me to fuck you. I've waited three long weeks to have you in my bed, and you tell me I have no patience? Maybe I should teach you about patience?"

I shuffle from one foot to the other as he starts to trail soft kisses along my neck. The sound of his belt being unbuckled and the soft leather sliding against the fabric as he pulls it off makes me squirm in anticipation.

"Hold out your hands," he orders.

I hesitate for a moment, until I remember that I asked for

this. I want to see the real Conor, not the mask he wears to protect himself.

As I hold out my hands for him, excitement ripples through my body, and I watch as he loops the belt around them, pulling the leather so tight that it pinches my skin. But I don't flinch. I've experienced so much pain that sometimes it feels like I'm almost immune to it. Certainly, I have perfected the art of masking it, at least.

Conor tugs on the belt and leads me to the bed. "Lie down," he snaps, and I do as he tells me. He tugs my arms above my head and ties the end of the belt to one of the metal spindles of his bed-frame. Then he stands up and looks down at me, licking his lips. "Patience?" he growls.

I feel a flash of panic, but I swallow it down. Surely, he's not going to leave me here naked and tied up? But then he starts to undress and relief washes over me. When he's naked too, he crawls onto the bed, trailing soft kisses up from my ankles to my inner thighs. He blows a cold stream of air over my folds and I lift my hips up to his face.

"Conor," I pant.

He doesn't reply. Instead, he trails kisses over my stomach, up toward my breasts, before sucking one of my hard nipples into his hot mouth. He nips me gently, and I feel the rush of heat between my thighs. One of his hands wraps around my throat as the other one slides up my inner thigh, so close to where I ache to feel him, but stopping before he reaches that spot.

"Please?" I breathe.

He pushes himself up and sits back on his haunches, before grabbing my hips and flipping me over like I'm a rag doll, until I'm lying on my front and my wrists are bound even tighter to the bed. Grabbing my hips, he pulls me up until I'm on my knees with my ass in the air and my head pressed against the pillow. I arch my back in pleasure as he runs a warm hand up my thigh, making me purr with anticipation. Then his hand disappears, and without warning, he brings it down on my ass.

Smack.

I don't flinch.

Smack! Smack!

This time I groan, but only in pleasure.

"You like having your ass spanked, Angel?" he growls.

"By you I do, yeah," I giggle, and he sucks in a deep breath.

He leans over me, pressing his lips against my ear. "If you're laughing, clearly I am not doing this hard enough."

"Oh, you are. In fact, I think you might have bruised my poor ass with that last one."

He leans back and rubs over the burning skin on my ass. "No. Not yet," he growls, but he doesn't spank me again. Instead, he slides one of his fingers into my wet channel before spreading my ass cheeks apart. He takes the same finger and slides it over the puckered hole before slowly pushing the tip inside.

"Oh, fuck. Conor," I gasp.

He pushes two fingers inside my pussy at the same time he slides one all the way into my ass and I moan out loud. He moves them slowly in and out until I'm bucking against him. As I draw closer to the edge, he pulls out of me and I cry out in frustration. I look behind me to find out what he's doing but I'm bound so closely to the bed, I can't quite see him. I close my eyes and feel him instead. His hands on my knees, pulling my legs wider apart. His warm breath on my thighs. Followed by his tongue, his delicious tongue, licking the length of my folds.

"Fuck!" he growls against me and the vibrations go directly to my clit. "You taste so fucking good, Angel."

His fingers dip inside me again and my walls squeeze around him, trying to pull him in deeper and keep him there. A few seconds later, he pulls out again. I don't know how much longer this goes on for; him taunting my pussy and my ass with his fingers and his mouth.

"Conor. Please," I cry out when I can't take his maddening teasing any longer.

"What do you want, Angel?" he growls. "Tell me."

"Fuck me," I'm almost crying in desperation. "Please, just fuck me."

He doesn't. He leans over me and unties my hands before pushing himself back onto his knees. I pull my hands free and rub the skin on my wrists before turning over until I'm lying on my back, looking up at him. Have I completely screwed this up? And if so, how?

He gets up from the bed and turns on a lamp on the nightstand and I realize it's almost dusk outside. My insides feel like they've turned to liquid as I lie here, my legs shaking from the many orgasms he almost gave me. His body is covered in a thin sheen of perspiration, and I can't help but lick my lips as I stare at him. From his thick shoulders and bulging biceps, to his chiseled abs and thick thighs. Not to mention the incredibly impressive erection he's sporting.

"You are freaking beautiful," I say and then I blush, realizing I've said that out loud when I meant to only think it.

He doesn't reply anyway; he crawls back onto the bed and nestles himself between my thighs until his hard length is nudging at my opening. "Wrap your legs around me, Angel," he growls.

I do as he tells me and shudder as he slides himself into me, filling me so completely that it almost makes me want to cry. "You feel that, Angel?" he growls. "Your pussy is fucking made for me. You fit me like a fucking glove."

"Yes," I breathe.

He fucks me slowly and I rake my nails down his back as I feel every bit of him pumping in and out of me.

"You feel so fucking good, Jessie. I'm going to fuck you all night long, because this pussy is so damn sweet."

The tears roll down my cheeks as he slides himself into me over and over again, pushing against the spot deep inside me that makes my insides melt like warm butter. He seals his mouth over mine as he fucks me to a long, intense orgasm that almost makes me pass out. As I release a torrent of wet heat, he sinks his teeth into my neck and drives into me until he finds his own release.

I'm still trembling when he rolls onto his back and pulls me into his arms. "I don't think I have ever fucked anyone like that before, Jessie," he pants.

I place my hand on his chest, right over his heart, where it pounds beneath my fingers. "Like what?"

"Like that. Slow. Soft. With my tongue in your mouth when we both come. Fuck. What are you doing to me?"

I snuggle closer to him, draping my leg over his. "What happened to that animal you told me about?"

"I think you tamed him, Angel," he laughs softly.

"Well, it was amazing."

He hugs me tighter. "Hmm. Amazing."

CHAPTER 19

CONOR

*T*he pins and needles in my forearm wake me from a deep sleep. I flex my fingers to try to bring some feeling back, but there's something heavy on my arm.

Shit! Where am I?

My eyes snap open just as she speaks.

"What is it?" she asks sleepily, and I suck in a deep breath. Jessie fell asleep in my arms and is currently lying on my left one. That's why it feels dead. I'm in my bed. I'm safe.

I shift my arm from beneath her, but I wrap my other one around her even tighter and pull her closer. Her body is so warm and soft, and she smells of vanilla and sex.

"Nothing, Angel. Go back to sleep," I whisper against her ear.

"What time is it?"

I glance over her shoulder at the clock on the nightstand. "A little after 6 a.m."

"Hmm. Too early," she breathes as she snuggles closer to me, pressing her juicy round ass against my groin, making the blood that's just been thundering around my body rushing straight to my cock.

I think about sliding myself into her again, but I spent hours fucking her last night and we could both do with a rest. I close my eyes again and breathe in the scent of her hair as I drift back off to sleep.

* * *

IT'S ALMOST midday by the time Jessie and I finally emerge from my bedroom, both of us freshly showered and dressed, and looking, I hope, like we haven't just spent at least half of the last twenty-four hours fucking.

"Can you make a start on some breakfast while I check on Shane? I want to make sure he hasn't been looking for us," I say as we step into the hallway.

"Sure," she says before she heads off in front of me, leaving me to watch her beautiful figure walking away from me. I catch up with her in two strides and slap her ass on the way past.

"Hey!" she says with a grin and I can't resist grabbing hold of her and giving her a quick kiss on the lips.

I push open the door to Shane's office and find him sitting at his desk, his head bent low and a scowl on his face.

"Everything okay?" I ask as I walk inside and sit down.

He runs a hand over the stubble on his jawline. "Same shit, different day," he says with a sigh as he closes his laptop.

"Anything I can do to help?"

He tilts his head to one side slightly as he looks at me. "You could stop fucking the computer hacker for a start," he offers.

I wince instinctively. "You know?"

"Of course, I fucking know, Con. Your bedroom is right next to mine. I had to listen to both of you fucking all night. And this morning," he snaps.

"Sorry. I didn't think about you being next door."

"No shit! If it's not you shouting the place down because of your nightmares, I have to listen to you and her having a full on fuck-fest. Did you get any sleep at all?"

"Yes. In fact, I slept like a baby. Did I shout in my sleep last night?" I don't think I did, and Jessie never mentioned it.

"No." He frowns at me. "I assumed you'd lost your voice."

"Damn." I smile. "I didn't have a nightmare either, Shane, that's the first time since…"

"I know," he says with a sigh. "And I'm relieved for you, Con, but, I wish you could figure out another cure."

My room is at the very end of the apartment, with only Shane's room nearby. Because for the past eighteen months I've had nightmares that make me shout and sometimes scream in my sleep. I usually wake up covered in sweat and twisted in the covers.

"I promise we'll be quieter tonight."

He scowls at me. "Tonight? What the fuck, Conor?"

"Well, I mean. Unless she's with the twins," I say with a shrug.

"Since when do you share women with Liam and Mikey?"

"I don't know, Shane. This isn't me and you know that better than anyone. But it doesn't feel weird. I've just spent almost the entire night inside her, but I wouldn't care if I walked into the kitchen to find her with either of them. It kind of feels like she belongs to all of us."

"But she fucking doesn't Conor. She could belong to anyone for all we know. She could be a fucking spy."

"She's not a spy. Besides, if you really thought that, you wouldn't have her here."

"I would. Because a spy can be just as valuable as an ally, providing you handle them properly, and you think with your head instead of your dick."

"Relax, Shane. It's not like she's pumping any of us for information or anything."

"Not yet." He frowns at me. "I assumed you had more self-control, Conor."

I close my eyes and take a deep breath. Ordinarily, Shane's

bad moods don't get to me. It's just a part of who he is. It's the way he deals with the constant pressure he's under. A way to keep the world at bay when everybody seems to want a piece of him. But, he has touched a nerve.

"Well, you would know all about that, wouldn't you?" I snarl at him before I walk out of his office.

I feel like shit about what I just said. Shane is only four years older than me, but he's always been more like a father to me and the twins. Much more than our actual bastard of a father ever was, anyway. I know what he's given up for us, and the sacrifices he's made. He even left Ireland for us. It was for the twins mostly. Even though he never wanted to. He would have been happy to live and die in the Emerald Isle. He never asked for any of this, but he took it on anyway. And he's fucking good at it. He made his way straight to the top and brought us along with him. I owe him so much. We all do.

But that doesn't mean he gets to preach to us about our life choices. Jessie is the best thing to have happened to me and my brothers in a long time. And she could be good for Shane too— if only he would let her in.

CHAPTER 20

JESSIE

The apartment is quiet as I walk along the hallway. It's after midnight but I can't sleep. My brain won't seem to switch off lately. I'm not used to having so little to occupy my time. Seeing the light in Shane's office, I wander along and knock lightly on the open door.

"What is it, Hacker?" he asks with a scowl as he looks up from his computer screen.

"I was wondering if Conor or the twins were around, that's all. I didn't mean to disturb you."

He runs a hand over his strong jaw as he glares at me. "They're working. That's what most of us do around here."

"Well, I'd like to be working myself if you'd just let me. I'm bored out of my mind here. Isn't there anything I can help you with?" I ask. So far, Shane has barely given me anything to do and I suspect it's because he doesn't yet trust me fully.

"I'm not sure the kind of work we're doing tonight is up your street, Hacker. Go back to bed."

I don't move. Instead, I stand in the doorway and stare at him. He's so damn prickly, but sometimes I enjoy trying to push his buttons. He's hot when he's angry. "Surely there must be something I can do for you?" I arch an eyebrow at him.

He pushes back his chair so fast that I take a step back in surprise. He stalks across the office toward me. "What do you think this is, Hacker? You think that my brothers are your friends, your fuck-buddies? You have no idea who we are, or what we're capable of. I suggest you remember that the next time you walk around here in the middle of the night looking for trouble," he growls as he pushes his face close to mine.

I tilt my chin up and stare at him. There is no way I'm going to allow him to intimidate me. "I think I have a pretty good idea of who you and your brothers really are."

"Oh, really?" he snarls.

"Yes. Really."

He narrows his eyes at me. "Fine. You want to work for us, Hacker, then it's time you discover what kind of work we really do," he snarls as he straightens his jacket. "Come with me."

I glance down at my bare feet. "Are we going out?"

"We're not leaving the building. You're fine. Let's go."

I follow him to the elevator and we wait in silence for it to arrive. I step in first and lean against the wall while he stands opposite me. For a few painful moments, we wait in complete silence with the air in the small space thick with tension. I steal sideways glances at him as he stands there looking good enough to eat in his exquisitely tailored suit and expensive leather shoes. He wears a distinctive cologne. It's fresh and masculine, and while it's never overpowering, it lingers in the air and makes my mouth water.

When the elevator stops, I let out the breath I've been holding in and he steps out before me, holding the doors open. We're in the basement. The sound of music from the club above and directly next to us thumps through the concrete space. I follow Shane past the line of expensive cars and notice a room that I've never seen before. As we approach, Liam and Mikey are standing outside. They frown at us as we draw near.

"What's up?" Mikey asks as we reach them and he moves to stand directly in front of the door. There's a muffled scream coming from the room, and I look between Mikey and Shane. What the hell is going on here?

"I've come to show Jessie exactly what kind of line of business we're in, boys. Now step aside."

Mikey blinks at him in surprise. "But you know he won't want that. He won't want Jessie to see him in there."

"He's right, Shane," Liam adds.

"It's time she learned the truth. Now step away from the fucking door," Shane snaps and Mikey does so with no further hesitation or resistance.

My heart hammers in my chest as Shane's fingers curl around the metal handle, because whatever is going on behind that door is something that Conor or the twins obviously don't want me to witness. The fact that Shane does makes me wonder exactly what his agenda is.

Shane pushes open the door and steps inside, beckoning me to follow him. I walk into the room and instinctively take a deep breath. As I do, the metallic smell of blood hits my nostrils and almost makes me retch. I stumble, but Shane's strong hand grips my elbow, holding me up. The room is small and dark, with a single lightbulb hanging from the ceiling illuminating the scene before me. There are three men inside, a large wooden table in the middle, and various tools hanging on the walls. It almost looks like a workshop. Except there's a man strapped to the table, and another one on the floor, bleeding out. At least, he looks like he was a man once, but now his face is barely recognizable as human.

The third man is Conor. He stands shirtless and bloodied, holding a sharp scalpel in one hand as he snarls like a demon at the man on the table who screams and pleads for mercy.

Conor barely registers us walking into the room. he's entirely focused on the task in hand—or perhaps he's lost to it. I can't figure out which it is yet. I stand next to Shane who openly watches me rather than the scene unfolding before us, as though this is some sort of test.

Suddenly, the man on the floor, who I assumed was already dead, moves. His hand jerks out, and he grabs hold of Conor's ankle. Conor spins around, raises his foot and brings his boot crashing down against the man's temple, causing his eye to pop out of its socket. Instinctively, I flinch and my hand flies to my mouth to stifle the scream that threatens to come out. I turn to walk out of the room because I don't need to see this. But Shane grabs hold of my arm and pulls me back, forcing me to stay and watch as Conor turns back to the groaning man on the table and starts to pummel his head and body with his fists. Blood spatters everywhere and I shrink back to avoid getting it on my clothes.

I notice the flicker of a smile cross Shane's face as he looks at me before turning back to his brother. "I think he's dead, Con," he says and Conor turns to us as though he had no idea we were there.

His face is so full of rage that I barely recognize him as the man I've come to know. "What the fuck is she doing here?" he snarls as he wipes the blood from his face.

"Our little hacker wanted to see what we did here, and I thought it only fair to show her the kind of men we really are. And, well now she knows."

Conor looks at me, his eyes narrowed. "You need to get out of here, Jessie. Now."

I nod in agreement. Shane has well and truly proven his point. "I think I've seen enough."

I turn to walk out while Shane stays behind. "Mikey, take the hacker back up to the apartment," he shouts through the open doorway.

As soon as I'm out of the door, Shane closes it behind me until only the muffled sounds of his and Conor's voices can be heard coming from the room. Mikey puts his hand on the small of my back, guiding me back through the basement toward the elevator. My insides are churning. The smell of blood stays in my nostrils and makes me want to throw up. I haven't witnessed violence like that for a long time, but Shane Ryan is mistaken if he thinks I haven't seen worse than that before today.

I don't speak until Mikey and I are in the elevator. "Are they the guys from the club? The ones I pulled the footage on?"

He nods. "That's what you've signed up for, Red."

"What did they do?"

"It's a long story. But, ultimately, they disobeyed him. Conor told them never to come back to New York, and they did."

"I thought you and Liam were the muscle?"

"We are." He grins at me. "But when someone really pisses us off, we send Shane in. And when we really want to fuck someone up, we send Conor."

I blink at him. "Conor?"

He smiles at me. "He might lay down like a pussycat and let you rub his tummy, Red, but make no mistake, my big brother is a fucking animal. That's why they took him and not one of us."

"Who took him?"

Mikey winces as though he's said something he shouldn't. "Not my story to tell, Red," he says, shaking his head. "He'll tell you when he's ready."

* * *

I LIE on Conor's bed and stare at the ceiling, listening to the sound of my breathing and the soft ticking of the clock on his nightstand. Shane's little excursion earlier did nothing to ease my insomnia. In fact, since I came back to the apartment thirty minutes ago, my stomach has been churning and my mind has been racing.

I sit up with a start as the bedroom door swings open. Conor walks into the room, covered in blood. He glares at me as he sees me sitting on the bed. "What are you doing here?" he snaps.

"Waiting for you," I say softly.

He sucks in a deep breath and then he just stares at me. After what seems like an eternity, he speaks. "I need to take a shower. Stay here," he says as he stalks toward the bathroom.

I listen to the sound of the water running as I lie back and wait for him to finish. It's at least fifteen minutes later when he finally walks out of the bathroom with a white towel wrapped around his waist, sitting just below his perfectly chiseled abs. Walking over to the bed, he sits down beside me.

"He shouldn't have brought you down there," he snaps. "I never wanted you to see me like that."

"Was that the animal you told me about? The one you keep locked away?"

His eyes lock on mine, so dark they look almost black, but he doesn't answer and there's a pain in them that I know runs deep. It's the same kind of pain that sometimes stares back at me when I look in the mirror.

"You think I didn't already know what type of man you are, Conor? You and your brothers practically run New York. I'm not naïve enough to believe that you get to be where you're at without doing the kind of shit I just saw down there."

"I'm not that man, Jessie," he says softly. "Not up here. But... out there, things are different." He hangs his head low.

"I know that." I sit up and take one of his hands in mine. "Just because you do bad things, doesn't mean you're not a good man."

"I'm not a good man, Angel. Not even close. But I want to be a better one with you."

"I think you might be the best man I know," I say as I reach up and place my hand on his cheek. His beard tickles my palm as he presses his face against it. "You might be a tiger out there, but you're still my pussycat," I smile at him.

He looks up and scowls at me, but his eyes twinkle with wicked deviance. "A pussycat?"

"Okay, a tiger cub?" I offer with a flash of my eyebrows.

He springs up cat-like as he dives on me, pinning me to the bed. He rubs his nose along my jawline and a growl rumbles in his throat. "Shane brought you down there to create some distance between us, Angel. He thinks you're getting too close."

"And what do you think?" I stare up at him as the weight of his body settles against me and I start to experience the familiar fluttering in my abdomen from his touch.

"I think there's no such thing as too close when it comes to you, Jessie," he says as he trails feather light kisses along my throat. Then he looks up at me, his eyes burning into mine. "Do you still want me after what you just saw?"

I curl my fingers through his thick, dark hair. "The more I know you, Conor Ryan, the more I want you."

"Damn, Angel. You surprise the hell out of me every single day. Just when I think I can't be into you any more than I already am," he growls as he nudges my thighs apart with his knee.

"So, you're into me?" I tease him as I bite my lip and flutter my eyelashes.

He grins wickedly. "You know I am, and I'm about to get into you even deeper."

CHAPTER 21

JESSIE

*G*roaning with pain, I sit up in bed and reach for the TV remote. Sleep is not forthcoming for me tonight. I have a hot water bottle clutched against my stomach and I've taken two Advil, but they're doing little to ease the pain. The cramps I get on the first day of my period are completely debilitating sometimes. It feels like someone is pulling out my insides through my navel with a corkscrew.

My bedroom door is open, and I hear footsteps outside. "You okay in there, Angel?" Conor asks as he pops his head inside.

"Just cramps," I say. "They'll go in a few hours or so. I hope."

"You need some painkillers or something?" he says as he walks into the room and comes to sit on the bed.

"I've taken some, but they're not great for cramps. Usually heat works," I say as I lift my cover and show him the hot water bottle. "But even this thing doesn't seem to be helping tonight."

"Heat?" he asks with a flash of his eyebrows.

"Yes." I grin at him despite my pain. Since he and I first had sex a few days ago, we've hardly been able to keep our hands off each other. And if I'm not in his bed, I seem to be with the twins. My period has come just at the right time—an enforced break. Although I doubt a little blood would bother any of them. "Not that kind of heat. I can't be doing anything like that right now."

He laughs softly and brushes a strand of hair from my forehead. "I was *not* suggesting that, Angel. But," he sucks on his top lip in a way that makes him look completely adorable, "I have something that might help. Give me twenty minutes."

"I'll try anything," I say as another intense cramp fires through my abdomen.

He kisses my forehead and then jumps off the bed. "I'll be right back."

A SHORT TIME LATER, Conor walks back into the room, carrying what looks like a small white towel on a tray. As soon as he steps inside, I'm hit by the most awful smell. It only gets stronger as he walks toward me, and I realize the stench is coming from whatever he has on that tray.

He sits on the bed beside me.

"Jesus, Conor!" I pinch my nostrils between two fingers. "What the hell is that?"

"It's magic." He winks at me. "Now lift up your shirt."

"No way. It stinks," I protest.

He rolls his eyes. "Don't be such a baby. Lift it up, Jessie," he orders.

As another cramp crushes my abdomen from the inside, I reluctantly lift my pajama shirt. He removes the hot water bottle and then he places the towel on my stomach instead. The towel doesn't feel overly hot to the touch, but I instantly feel the heat from whatever foul-smelling concoction is wrapped inside.

He gently pulls my top back down and sits back with a smile. "You should feel that in a few minutes."

"What the hell is it?" I ask as I already start to feel the warming effects in my abdomen.

"It's a secret recipe from the old country. You wouldn't believe the injuries that stuff has seen us through."

"Well, I hope it works and I get some sleep, even if I do smell like a skunk who's taken a bath in a garbage disposal truck."

"I hope you feel better soon," he says with a laugh and a kiss on my forehead. "Do you need anything else?"

"You fancy watching a movie with me?" I ask.

"Fuck no, you stink," he says as he screws his face up in disgust.

I blink at him, and he bursts out laughing. "Aw, Angel, I'm just playing with you. Of course, I'd watch a movie with you, but I have to go to work."

"You asshole," I say with a shake of my head.

He stares at me for a second and then he lies down beside me. "I've got ten minutes before I have to leave," he says softly as he wraps one of his huge arms around me.

"You sure you can handle the stink that long?" I nudge him in the ribs.

"Yes. You know I'd still fuck you no matter how bad you smell, right?" he chuckles.

"God, you're such a smooth talker, Conor Ryan."

"Hmm, I know. It's the Irish genes."

* * *

THE FOLLOWING MORNING, I wander into the kitchen looking for Conor. Whatever he made me last night worked miracles, and I slept all night with no cramping. But this morning, my stomach feels like it's in a concrete mixer again and Conor's magic, stinky medicine has lost its healing powers.

Shane is in the kitchen drinking coffee when I walk into the room.

"Morning," I say.

"Morning, Hacker."

"Is Conor around?"

Unable to hide his disdain, he rolls his eyes. "He didn't get in until five. He's asleep."

"Oh. Okay."

Shane must see the disappointment on my face. "Give him a few hours and I'm sure he'll be awake, and you can fuck each other's brains out." He smirks at me.

"That's not why I'm looking for him," I snap and just as I do, a cramp squeezes my abdomen like a pair of hands twisting my intestines, making me wince.

"You okay?" Shane asks, suddenly with a hint of concern in his voice.

"Fine. Just cramps, that's all. Conor made me this foul-smelling stuff last night and it really helped. I was just wondering if he could make me one, or show me how to? I'll just take some Advil instead."

Shane stares at me, and then he sighs loudly. "Go back to bed, and I'll bring some in."

"I can get them," I say, but he's already up off his chair.

"Does it hurt?" he snaps.

"Yes!" I snap back.

"Then go the fuck back to bed and I'll get what you need," he says as he points toward the door.

"You're so bossy sometimes," I snipe like a sulky teenager.

"You have no idea."

IT'S BEEN over twenty minutes since Shane ordered me back to bed and I'm beginning to wonder if he's forgotten about bringing me some Advil. As I'm about to go back to the kitchen and get some for myself, he appears in the doorway—complete with tray and white towel. The smell isn't as offensive as it was last night, and I wonder if it's because I've got used to it, or because Shane doesn't know how to make it properly.

He walks over to the bed and places the tray down. "Lift your shirt," he says as he picks up the white towel filled with the healing poultice.

"I didn't realize you knew how to make this too?" I say as I open the buttons of my shirt and lift it to expose my midriff.

He frowns. "Of course I can. Who do you think Conor learned it from?"

He places the towel on my stomach and presses lightly. His fingers brush over my skin as he positions the fabric correctly, and I experience that familiar fluttering in my abdomen. There is no doubt that Shane Ryan is hotter than hell itself, but his general moodiness ensures that I'm always kept at arm's length. I've never seen this caring, nurturing side of him before, though, and I'm not sure I like it. I know exactly where I stand with asshole Shane. This one makes me feel things I don't want to— not about him, anyway.

"Thank you," I whisper as I lift my hands to fix my clothes, but he's already pulling down my shirt and fastening the buttons with his deft fingers. I can't stop the image of him unbuttoning my clothes instead from popping into my head and it makes me clench my thighs together to stop the throbbing sensation that's starting to build.

"You're welcome," he says smoothly in that low gravelly voice he has, which does nothing to quell my growing need. He picks up the TV remote and flicks it on and I swallow.

Dear God, please don't let him offer to sit in here with me. I couldn't take it. Before I can protest, he hands me the remote. "The twins told me you love watching TV in bed," he says as he picks up the now empty tray. "Get some rest today, Hacker. I have a job for you tomorrow." He flashes one eyebrow at me and then he disappears out of the door.

CHAPTER 22

SHANE

*M*y plane landed in L.A. an hour ago. There was a car waiting for me at the airport, and now I'm sitting in the air-conditioned office of Alejandro Montoya. He's the King of L.A. and an old friend of mine.

I look at the photographs on his desk. One of a young dark haired woman and a little boy, who I know to be his adopted daughter, and her son. I pick up the one next to it. This one is a picture of a woman with brown curly hair holding two chubby babies—his wife, Alana and their twin boys. They all smile for the camera, and I wonder if Alejandro took the photograph.

"Hey, amigo," a voice behind me says and I put the frame back on the desk and stand, pulling my buddy, Jackson Decker into a hug.

"Hey, Jax. Thanks for the car."

"Only the best for you, Shane. You know that," he says with a smile. "Alejandro will be here shortly. He's just dealing with someone real quick."

"Oh?" I arch an eyebrow at him.

"Nothing like that. At least not today."

"So, what did you find out about my house guest?"

Jax takes a seat on the edge of the desk. "Well, you were right about her. She's not who she claims to be. But it blew my mind when I figured out who she really is. No wonder it took me four weeks to get to the bottom of it. I have never seen anyone cover their tracks this well, Shane. You can tell her from me that I'm impressed."

I nod at him while the blood thunders through my veins. I knew Jessie was lying to me. "So, who the hell is she, Jax?"

AN HOUR LATER, Jax puts his hand on my shoulder. "It's been great catching up, Shane, but I have work to do. I hope we can do this again soon."

I put my hand over his. "Yeah, you too. And I appreciate you looking into the hacker for me. Thanks, buddy."

"Any time. Although I think I've left you with more questions than answers," he says with a smile before he turns to his boss, who sits across from us behind his desk. "I'll catch you later, amigo."

"Don't forget. Dinner starts at eight," Alejandro calls out to Jax's retreating back.

I turn in my chair and face Alejandro. He's offered me a suite in his hotel for the night, but after listening to what Jax just told me, I am eager to get back to New York as soon as possible. However, I suppose I can spare twenty minutes to have a quick whiskey with the man who gave me my shot when I came to the States.

"So, how is family life?" I ask him.

Alejandro runs a hand through his hair. "Exhausting! The twins are just starting to crawl and they are literally everywhere. I only come to work for a break," he says with a shake of his head.

"And how is Alana doing?"

At the mention of his wife's name, his face breaks into a huge smile. "She's amazing. She's great with the boys. She's an amazing mom to Lucia. She works full time, but she handles those kids like she's been doing it her whole life. But she's always there when I need her. She blows me away every single day."

I can't help smiling at the change in this man since I last saw him over two years earlier.

"What?"

"I never thought I'd see you of all people like this over a woman, Alejandro."

"Well, my wife is not just any woman, Shane." He arches an eyebrow at me.

"So how does it work, then? Having a family and doing this?" I look around his office. he's the head of the Montoya Corporation, and like me, he has oversight of as many legitimate businesses as he does illegal ones.

He takes a sip of his whiskey and then he shrugs. "We make it work. I used to believe that having a family made me vulnerable, and maybe it does, but they make my life worth living in a way that all of this never could. Why are you asking? Someone special in your life?"

"No," I reply, perhaps a little too firmly and quickly.

"The hacker?" Alejandro asks with a flash of his eyebrows.

I sigh and take a swig of my drink. "There's something about her, that's for sure. But... I can't go there."

"One of your brothers got there first?"

I roll my eyes. "Try all of them."

"Oh! Damn!" Alejandro sits back in his chair and runs a hand over his jaw.

Suddenly, I have an inexplicable urge to defend her that almost blindsides me. "It's not like that," I say, shaking my head. "It's kind of complicated. My brothers adore her. And she seems to care for them too."

"And you?" he narrows his eyes at me.

"I don't know. I think about fucking her all the damn time. Maybe I should just screw her and get her out of my system?"

Alejandro laughs out loud. "In my experience, it doesn't quite work like that, amigo. In fact, I don't think that strategy has ever worked in the history of fucking. If you can't get a woman out of your head, banging her will only make it one hundred times worse."

"So, what do I do? Share her with my brothers? I'm not sure I can handle that. Not even with them? What the fuck would people think?"

"Screw what anyone else thinks. If it works, it works." He shrugs as he downs the last of his drink.

"Well, you've certainly fucking mellowed these past few years. Not so long ago, you'd have told me to fuck her out of my system and then send her packing."

"What can I say? I'm a changed man." He laughs." The love of a good woman will do that to you."

"Yeah well. I'm not sure I want to change."

"Whatever works for you, amigo. You'll get no judgment from me. After all, I bought my wife from a man who I would happily see dead."

I'd almost forgotten about that. Alejandro and Alana are the perfect couple. I've never seen him so happy. But they started out very differently. Alana's father is a corrupt politician, and he sold off his only daughter to a ruthless criminal. Because as much as I respect him, that's what Alejandro is. It's what we both are. "Need any help with that? I'd be happy to end Foster Carmichael for you."

"As much as I'd love to take you up on that offer, he's still my father-in-law. And as much as Alana hates him, I still don't think she'd be thrilled about me bumping him off."

"And you're worried about that?" I challenge him.

"Am I worried about breaking my wife's heart? Um, yeah."

"You really have changed," I laugh as I swig back the rest of my drink and place my glass on his desk.

"Yeah, well, no-one is more shocked by my transformation than me," he laughs too.

I stand up and hold out my hand. "It's been good to see you, old friend."

"You too." He shakes my hand, and then he holds onto it and looks me in the eye. "If you really feel something for this woman, fuck what everyone else thinks, Shane. Life is too short, amigo. Especially for men like us. You need to grab onto any happiness when you can, and while you can."

I nod at him. "Maybe."

CHAPTER 23

JESSIE

Shane got back from L.A. late last night, and this morning Liam told me he wanted to see me. So, once again, I find myself summoned to his office and I'm sitting before him like an errant teenager waiting to be yelled at.

"You seem to be settling in here well?" Shane arches one eyebrow at me.

Heat flushes over my cheeks as I recall him witnessing my encounter with his younger brothers the week before. I'm aware he knows about me and Conor too. His room is next to Conor's and he must have heard us. "I am. Thank you."

"You're certainly a hit with my brothers."

I blush further. *Asshole!* I sit up straighter in my chair. "Well, they're nice guys."

He laughs and shakes his head. "I'm not sure you know them at all, Hacker."

"I think I know them well enough," I reply. "Especially after you introduced me to the kind of work you really do."

He stops laughing, and the change in him is instant. He glares at me, his green eyes burning into my skin. "They don't know you though, do they, Jessica?"

I swallow hard as all the saliva in my mouth dries instantly. I glare back at him. That could just be a lucky guess. Lots of Jessica's shorten their name to Jessie. But my heart starts to hammer in my chest.

Shit!

"Do you really think I would allow someone in my house, in my brothers' house and into their beds, without finding out who they really are?" he snarls.

"I told you who I am."

He stands up abruptly, lunging forward and grabbing my throat with one of his large hands. He squeezes lightly and my breathing grows faster. But I don't move. "Tell me one more lie, and I will have my brothers carve you to pieces and dump you in the Hudson. So, start talking, Miss Romanov," he spits my last name and I shudder at the sound on his lips. I haven't heard that name for over ten years.

"How did you find out?" I croak. No-one else ever has. I learned from my father how to cover my tracks and I am damn good at it.

He releases me from his grip and sits back in his seat. "What can I say? My guy is good. He told me to tell you he was impressed. It's taken him four weeks to find out who you really are. It usually takes him two days."

Despite the circumstances, I experience an unexpected sense of pride at that revelation. But it still doesn't change the fact that my cover is blown, and Shane Ryan knows I've been lying to him and his brothers since the moment I met them.

"As you've already discovered, my real name is Jessica Romanov. And I don't suppose I need to fill you in on my family history?"

"No," he says with a shake of his head.

I sigh with relief at that. My family's story is well documented, and I don't particularly want to relive it right now.

"But, tell me, how did a sixteen-year-old girl escape the Wolf? Or haven't you escaped him at all?"

I flinch at the mention of his name. The man I've been looking for since the night he slaughtered my parents and my twelve year old brothers in front of my eyes. The man who kidnapped me and held me captive for almost two years.

"Of course I escaped. I earned his trust. I spent every single minute of my seven hundred and eleven days with him, learning every single thing about him. I learned exactly what made him tick. His likes. His dislikes. The things that made him get that faraway, glazed look in his eyes. The quickest way to make him lose control."

Shane says nothing, but his eyes remain fixed on mine.

"He never trusted me enough to allow any weapons in the house. He even refused me cutlery. I was only allowed plastic spoons to eat with. But I had a hairbrush with a wooden handle. I was mostly locked in my room, or his room, and that was much worse." I shudder at the memories. "But I was permitted outside in the gardens for one hour every night. Just like in a real prison. Every single night I would sharpen the hairbrush on the edge of a stone step. Do you know how long it takes to sharpen a wooden stake to a perfect point using only a smooth rock?"

Shane shakes his head. "No."

"Seven hundred and eleven days," I say with a snort. "One night, he'd summoned me to his bed, and while he was sleeping, I stabbed him in the throat. I'd figured out his security system. Once he was gone, it was easy enough to get out."

"But you didn't kill him?" Shane raises an eyebrow at me. "Because there's a rumor that he's still out there somewhere?"

My blood starts to thunder around my body. "No. Somehow he survived. The day after I escaped, I panicked. I went back to burn down the house and destroy the evidence that I'd been there, but he was gone."

"And he's been in hiding ever since," Shane adds.

"Yes. But one day, I'll finish what I started."

Shane narrows his eyes at me. "So, Nikolai Semenov didn't find you by chance?"

"No. I set up the whole thing. He was high up in the Russian Mafia. I thought maybe he'd have some information on whoever ordered the hit on my family. Or on the Wolf himself. I never knew why my parents left Russia. Whenever I asked, they would change the subject. What I did know was that we were always running from something. My father was the best at what he did. There was no code, no computer, no system that he couldn't crack. Maybe they killed him because he knew something he shouldn't? Or maybe because he refused to work for them? Whatever it was, eventually, he paid the ultimate price. The Wolf made both of us watch while he slit my brothers' throats and raped my mother before he did the same to her. Then he told my father that he wouldn't kill me, but he would take me as a payment instead, and I would live the rest of my life in pain and suffering. But, from the bits of information he gave away to me while I was his prisoner, I guess he was supposed to kill me too because his employers were furious that he took me as a hostage instead. He said that no-one could ever find me. Everyone had to believe that I was dead. That's why he kept me locked away, and it's probably the only thing still keeping me alive."

"Because everyone believes you're already dead?" Shane says, almost to himself.

I look up at Shane and his face is impassive. He runs his hand across his jaw and frowns at me. "So, where do my brothers and I fit into your plan, Hacker?"

"You don't. I had no idea who you were. I mean, I'd heard of you, obviously, but I had no business in your world. However, when you killed my only link to the Wolf, I needed time to regroup. And you were about to kill me, remember? I figured I could work for you for a few months while I figured out my next move."

He narrows his eyes at me and the heat of his intense gaze penetrates every part of my body. "How do I know that this wasn't all a part of your plan? You could be working for the Wolf right now. Or the Russians. How the hell can I trust anything that comes out of your mouth?"

"I know that I've done nothing to earn your trust, Shane. I get that you don't think you can trust me now. But, I give you my word -"

"Your word means nothing to me. Once you've lied to me, everything you tell me is tainted by that. Even if you spoke the truth now, how would I know it?"

"You must understand why I lied, Shane?" Desperation creeps into my voice, and it annoys me.

"I do," he sighs. "But that doesn't change the fact that I can't trust you. You have lured my brothers into your bed, and you have just admitted to me that you escaped the Wolf by doing the same thing. You used your body as a weapon."

I draw in a breath as my blood starts to thunder around my body and I clench my fists by my sides. "I did not lure the Wolf into my bed! He forced me into his. And yes, I used my body to get what I needed from him. But, as a sixteen-year-old girl held captive by a monster, I had little else at my disposal," I snarl at him.

His face softens. "I know that. And I'm not judging you, Hacker. Simply stating a fact."

"So, what now? You go back to your original plan and kill me?" I narrow my eyes at him, readying myself to launch across the desk if he says yes.

"No." He frowns at me. "I wouldn't hear the end of it if I take away my brothers' new toy."

The sting of his words is like a slap to my face and I blink back the tears. Because that is all a woman like me is to men like him. "Then let me go, Shane, and I can be out of here in five minutes and you never need to see me again. It will be like I was never here."

He glares at me. "Let you go?"

"Yes," I breathe.

"And where would you go, Hacker?"

"I'll figure it out. I've been surviving on my own for ten years. My father taught me everything he knew. I'll get by."

"Do you want to leave?"

I swallow as I try to figure out how to answer to that question. "No," I finally admit.

He stares at me, his eyes searching my face. "Are you sharpening any wooden stakes in that bedroom of yours?"

I blink at him. Did Shane Ryan just attempt a joke? "No. Besides, I wouldn't need to. You have a perfectly suitable set of titanium knives in the kitchen."

A grin flickers across his face. "You can stay for now. As long as my brothers are okay with your deceit. Conor has a particular hatred of the Russians." He flashes an eyebrow at me. "He might just kill you himself, anyway. But, I guess that's the chance you'll have to take."

I ignore his attempt to rile me further. "So, I can stay?"

"For now. My brothers are much better behaved when you're around. But, if you lie to me again…"

"I won't," I say before he can finish his sentence. "Aren't you worried the Wolf will find me eventually? I don't want to put any of you in danger."

"Me and my brothers are always in danger. But, no," he shakes his head, "I don't fear the Wolf. He might have been one of the most feared assassins of his generation, but now he hides in the shadows, no doubt pining for the girl who almost killed him."

I sit forward in my seat. "You know the Wolf? Do you know where he is?"

"No. I don't have any answers for you. Like you said, he's disappeared. I think you might have done your job when you put that stake in his neck. He might not be dead, but he isn't alive either."

"I won't rest until the last breath leaves his body." I spit out the words, surprised by how easily the hatred and venom I hold for him bubbles to the surface. I've kept it hidden for so long.

"I can understand that," he says and for a second, it seems like we have a connection in something, although I can't figure out what or why.

"Thank you for allowing me to stay, Shane," I say, suddenly overcome with gratitude. He may act like a heartless bastard, but there must be one in there somewhere.

"Your brothers were twins too?" he asks.

"Yes." I blink, the question taking me by surprise. "Identical."

"Like Liam and Mikey?"

"Yes. And full of mischief like them too." Tears spring to my eyes and I look down and quickly wipe them away.

"I'm sorry about your family, Hacker," he says quietly.

"Thank you." I look up at him again and my eyes lock with his. My pulse quickens, and something in him calls me, deep in my soul. My breathing becomes harder and faster and I wonder if he feels anything too. But he breaks eye contact, and the moment vanishes. I shake my head. Reliving the past has made me emotional and over-sensitive. Desperate for human connection, I'm seeing meaning in things where there is none.

Shane clears his throat. "You should go tell Conor and the twins who you really are. If they don't kill you, I'll see you at dinner," he says as he stands up.

I stand too. "See you at dinner then," I say with a smile and a confidence I don't feel.

He nods and stuffs his hands in his suit pants as I walk out of his office.

CHAPTER 24

SHANE

I watch her as she walks out of my office and my throat constricts. My cock twitches at the sight of her curvy ass swaying in those skintight jeans, and my veins pulse with need. I consider calling her back in here, bending her over my desk and fucking her until she screams my name louder than she's ever screamed out one of my brothers'.

I close my eyes and imagine slipping my fingers inside her cunt. Tasting her. Filling her with my cock. I lie in bed at night, listening to my brothers making her come over and over again. Sometimes, I imagine what she looks like when she's losing control as I jerk off to the sound of her moaning their names.

Although this is about so much more than the desire to fuck her. I feel her in every fiber of my being. I can't look her in the eye because she sees into my soul. When I was a kid growing up in Ireland, my mother used to warn me of the dangers of witches and fairies who might sneak into my bedroom and cast a spell on me. My father told her she was crazy, and it was the only thing I ever agreed with him on, although I never told her that. But perhaps there was more truth to her fairytales than I ever gave her credit for?

Jessie Romanov has put a fucking spell on me. Even though she lied to me, to all of us, I still want her so badly it fucking hurts. She fills my every waking thought. From the moment she crawled out from beneath that desk in Nikolai Semenov's office and looked me in the eye, I knew she was a warrior. And now I know who she really is, and what she must have endured at the hands of the Wolf, my admiration for her and her strength has grown tenfold. My brothers and I know of monsters and demons, of running from a past that is determined to keep pace with you no matter how far or how high you climb.

Jessie is just like us—and nothing like us.

But I can't give in to this. I can't let her in. Because I don't trust her, and I'm not sure I ever could. I would enjoy nothing more than to walk down that hallway after her and take her to my bed. But how would I ever be sure that she wasn't using that incredible body of hers just to get close to me, to all of us, and then take us down when we're at our weakest?

Sitting back down in my chair, I put my head in my hands and sigh. What the fuck am I supposed to do? How do I protect my family when a pint-sized siren has my fucking heart and my balls in her vise-like grip and she doesn't even know it.

CHAPTER 25

JESSIE

I walk along the hallway toward the gym with my heart pounding in my chest. After I left Shane's office, I headed to my room and packed my small backpack.

Always be prepared to run, Jessie! Another of my father's lessons.

How will Conor, Mikey, and Liam react to the news that I've been lying to them? I don't know why Conor hates the Russians, but Shane was keen to remind me of that fact. The sound of footsteps behind makes me spin around as I reach the door.

Shane!

I frown at him. "You making sure I tell them the truth?" I snipe.

He smirks at me before reaching in front of me and grabbing hold of the door handle. His hand brushes mine and I bristle at the touch of his skin as goosebumps prickle along my forearm.

"After you, Hacker," he says as he opens the door wide.

I step inside. The music is loud in my ears now that we're inside the soundproof room. Conor is spotting Mikey on the bench press, while Liam does pull-ups in front of the mirror. The three of them are shirtless. Their hard, muscular bodies covered in a thin film of sweat. My ovaries ache in response to the testosterone and pure sex confined in this room. The thumping bass of Snoop Dog's *Sweat* pounds in my ears and the three of them move as though they're perfectly in tune with the music. I swallow as I try to focus on the reason I've come in here.

Suddenly, the music stops, and I realize Shane has turned it off. His brothers turn to us in surprise.

"What's up?" Liam asks as he lowers himself to the ground and wipes the sweat from his eyes with a nearby towel.

"Our little hacker has something she'd like to get off her chest," Shane says as he sits on one of the nearby weight benches and stares at me.

Conor frowns and walks toward me. "What is it?"

I look at Shane and then back at his brothers before I take a deep breath. "My name is not Jessie Heaton. It's Jessica Romanov," I blurt out the words.

Conor frowns at me for a few seconds until he realizes why he knows that name. "No," he shakes his head. "She's dead."

"Definitely not," I say as I look down at myself. "I'm right here."

"Who the fuck is Jessica Romanov?" Mikey asks.

I swallow hard and the tears spring to my eyes. I'd assumed they'd all know, and I wouldn't have to explain. Closing my eyes, I'm preparing to tell them my story when Shane answers for me. I smile at him, grateful for his intervention.

"Jessica Romanov is the daughter of Peter Romanov. There were some rumors he was former KGB. Some said he was the head of the Russian mob. But what is known, is that he was one of the best hackers in the world. Ten years ago, him, his wife and two sons were slaughtered in their home, and their sixteen-year-old daughter, Jessica, disappeared, presumed dead. The case was all over the news and there was a nationwide manhunt for Jessica, but she was never found. You two were only sixteen

117

yourselves at the time, and you paid even less attention to the news back then than you do now. It's well known, in our circles at least, that an assassin named the Wolf carried out the attacks. He is, or he *was*, the Bratva's finest and most experienced hitman. The hit fitted his MO. But he disappeared afterwards. And as no-one had ever met him and lived to talk about it, he was impossible to find. Whoever paid him and ordered the hit, and why, has never been revealed."

"Fuck!" Mikey says.

"And you're her? The missing daughter?" Liam asks.

"Yes," I nod.

"How did you disappear? Where have you been? Are you working for the Russians?" Conor scowls at me as he bombards me with questions.

"The Wolf was supposed to kill me too, but he kidnapped me instead. He kept me prisoner for nearly two years until I almost killed him and escaped. No, I am definitely not working for the Russians. But I want to find out who paid for the hit on my family and why, and I want to finish the Wolf for good."

Liam walks over to me and wraps me in his arms. "Fuck, baby, you really are a warrior," he says as he plants a kiss on my temple.

"You're safe here with us, Red," Mikey adds. "We'll help you find who was responsible. Won't we, Conor?"

I look up at Conor who frowns at me. "I fucking hate the Russians," he spits. "Present company excluded."

"I hate them too," I breathe. "Not the entire people, obviously. I hate the Bratva. But, I can find them on my own. I just need somewhere to lie low while I do. If you'll still have me here?"

"Of course we will," Conor nods as he walks over and kisses the top of my head, and then he straightens up. "I'm going for a shower," he adds as his eyes glaze over and he walks out of the gym.

* * *

AN HOUR LATER, I've answered as many of Liam and Mikey's questions as I can. They've asked me about my family, particularly interested in my twin brothers after I told them how much they remind me of them. Eventually, Shane intervened and told them to give me some space for a while. They dutifully obeyed him and have left me alone. Shane has left now too, and I should probably go to my room and have some quiet time to myself. Reliving the worst time of my life has left me mentally and emotionally exhausted. But I can't stop picturing Conor's face when he walked out of that gym.

I go to his bedroom and knock quietly.

"Come in," he shouts.

Opening the door, I step inside to see him lying on his bed in his boxer shorts with a book in his hand.

"What is it?" he asks.

"Can we talk?"

"What about?" He frowns at me.

"About what I told you earlier?" I say as I walk over to the bed and sit beside him.

He puts the book down beside him and holds out his hand to me. When I take it, he pulls me down to lie next to him and wraps one of his huge arms around me. "You can tell me when you're ready, Angel," he says softly.

I place my hand on his stomach, my fingers flexing over his hard abs. "My parents came to the US when my mom was pregnant with me. I never knew what my father did in Russia – whether he worked for the KGB or the Bratva, but I do know that he spent the rest of his life running from it. He thought he could build a better life for us here in the States. But he was always on the move. Always looking over his shoulder. We never settled anywhere for long. I never went to school, or made friends like regular kids did."

119

Conor runs his warm hand over my arm, and I press myself closer against him. "But we always had a really happy home. My mom home-schooled us and made sure we always had everything we needed. She was an incredible woman," I say as I recall her beautiful face and her soft hands. "She always made wherever we were feel like home. And my dad, well, he was the smartest man I've ever known. He taught me so much. All about computers and how to cover your tracks. He taught me how to fight too. He used to tell me that one day our pasts would catch up with us and that I would need to be strong. I always got the sense there was something he wasn't telling me, but I never got the chance to find out."

"You have no idea who ordered the hit on them?" Conor asks as he brushes my hair from my face in that way that makes me feel completely cherished.

"I've figured out plenty of people that it wasn't, and I suppose that's a start. I also suspect that there is a lot more to it than my father simply refusing to work for them or a fear that he would reveal their secrets."

"Hmm?" Conor pulls me tighter to him. "What happened to your family is almost like an urban legend. And the Wolf disappearing with the daughter, well, you," he says quietly. "You must have been terrified."

"I was. I've buried it all so deep that I wonder now if my memories are reliable anymore. And I promise I'll tell you anything you want to know, Conor. I'll never lie to you again. But can we stop talking about me for a while?" I press my cheek against his chest.

"Of course, Angel."

We lie in comfortable silence for a few minutes and then Conor draws in a shaky breath. "You've never asked why we killed Nikolai Semenov and his men?"

"No. I figured you'd tell me if you wanted me to know." I whisper.

"The Christmas before last, they kidnapped me and kept me chained in the basement of that house where we found you, for four weeks."

My head snaps up and I look at him. Bile surges from my stomach, burning the back of my throat as I think about this man I've come to care for so much being at the mercy of Nikolai Semenov. Because I'm aware of exactly what kind of man Nikolai was, and what he did to his enemies. "What? Four weeks? Why did they take you?"

"They figured me and my brothers had something to do with some deal they had that went south. It was another family, but Shane is the head, so Semenov held him responsible. And he took me as payback."

"Did they hurt you?" I ask, the tremor in my voice clearly audible.

"What do you think, Angel?" he breathes, and I feel kind of dumb for asking such an obvious question. "But mostly it was psychological torture. Sleep deprivation. Hardly any food or water. No contact with anyone. No light, and no idea of time or space."

"Is that why you don't like the dark?"

"Yup. Or small spaces. Or Russians," he laughs softly. "Present company excluded," he adds.

"You do know that Leo Tolstoy is Russian, don't you?" I nod toward the tattered copy of Anna Karenina beside him.

"Yes," he says with a dramatic sigh, making me laugh too.

"How did you get out?"

"My brothers found me. Shane had to pay Semenov off so as not to cause an all-out war. Then we bided our time until we could exact our revenge cleanly and walk away with no reper-cussions."

"You knew they would come for you, though?" I say as the sob catches in my throat.

"Yeah. I had no doubt about it. It was what kept me going."

"That must have been some comfort to know they were looking for you."

He places his hand under my chin and tilts my head up so I can look into his soft brown eyes. "I'm sorry you never had that, Jessie."

"Well, I'm glad that you did." I smile at him.

He wraps both arms around me and pulls me tighter to him. "You have it too now," he says quietly as he strokes my hair. "I will always come looking for you, Angel, and I would burn the whole world down to find you."

I don't reply because I'm scared I might tell him how much he means to me. Instead, I lie there in his arms. "Will you read me some Tolstoy?"

He picks up the book with one hand and opens it where he left off. I listen to the soft, velvety tones of his voice, and it soothes every nerve and every frayed edge in my body.

CHAPTER 26

JESSIE

I stand near the elevator with Conor, Liam, and Mikey. Nervous energy sizzles in my veins. I have hardly left this apartment since I arrived here six weeks earlier. And when I have been out, it's been to the store. There has been nothing exciting. Well, except for that day Conor took me to his friend's boutique, the memory of which will keep me warm when I'm a lonely old woman.

Today, I'm accompanying the Ryan brothers on a job and I couldn't be more thrilled.

"Remember. Be discreet. I need this sorting quickly and quietly," Shane says as he hands me a slip of paper. "This is the information I need. But, if you have time, get anything else you think might be helpful."

"Aren't you coming with us?" I frown at him.

"No. I've got a meeting." His tongue darts out and he licks his lower lip. It's a habit he has that drives me crazy because it makes me think of what else I'd love him to do with that mouth.

"Erin stopping by, is she?" Mikey says with a laugh, earning him a glare from Shane. Liam and Conor chuckle quietly behind me, while an acute pang of jealousy strikes me out of nowhere. Who the hell is Erin?

"Just get the job done. I'll see you back here later," Shane growls before turning around and walking down the hallway and out of sight.

"Who is Erin?" I whisper once he's out of earshot.

Conor chuckles softly. "I'm sure you'll find out soon enough."

I want to ask more questions, but the elevator doors ping open and we step inside. Once the doors close, Conor and the twins begin to go over the plan for the job we're headed to, and I listen intently. I don't want to screw up on my first time out.

* * *

WE ARRIVE at Balthazar's bar over an hour later. Liam drapes his arm over my shoulder as we walk through the doors and I can't help but notice the many admiring glances he and his brothers attract.

After we select a table near the back, Conor orders us some drinks from the waitress.

"We all clear on the plan?" he asks when she walks away from the table.

"Yes," I say, and the twins nod their agreement.

"Let's do this, baby," Liam says with a grin as he holds out his hand. I take it with a smile and he pulls me up from my seat. He makes a show of grabbing my ass and kissing me deeply in front of the customers and then we stumble to the back of the bar toward the toilets. When we reach them, he takes his arm from around my waist and we walk toward the office at the rear of the building. He tries the handle, and as we suspected it would be, it's locked. Taking out a small multi-tool from his pocket, he picks the lock in a matter of seconds.

"You're up, baby." He grins at me as he opens the office door. "I won't let anyone else in here."

I nod at him, just before I slip inside the door and fire up the computer. It doesn't take me long to guess the password and I'm in within five minutes. Ten minutes after that, I've got all the information Shane asked me to retrieve. I'm about to switch off the machine when I see the file titled Romanov and my breath catches in my throat. Why the hell does this guy have a file with my family name on? My heart starts to pound against my ribcage as I move my fingers over the mouse and click on the tab. The sound of the door opening startles me and I turn to see Liam's face.

"We might have some trouble out front. We need to go."

I look back at the screen and then at Liam. "Can I have just one more minute? Please?"

He rolls his eyes. "One minute. I need to check on Conor and Mikey. I'll be back in sixty seconds. Do not leave this office until I come get you."

"I won't. Thanks," I say as I turn back to the screen and open the document. It's a Russian marriage certificate, but it doesn't relate to the name of the family on the file. I scroll further until I'm disturbed by the door opening again.

"It hasn't been a full minute," I say as I turn around, but it's not Liam's face I'm looking at. Instead, there is a tall man with a shaved head and a tattoo of a raven on his neck.

"Who the fuck are you?" he snarls as he advances toward me.

My instincts kick in and I spring from the chair and flash him my best smile. "I was just looking for the restroom…" I say, but as I'm speaking, he stops in his tracks and stares at me, his mouth hanging open as he blinks at me. I don't know what the hell has him so spooked, but I need to get out of here, and fast. Glancing behind him, I mentally plan my route out of here, but I'm hampered by the fact that he's blocking the whole doorway.

I hear the commotion in the hallway outside, making me wonder where Liam and his brothers are.

The bald-headed man continues staring at me while my heart keeps pounding in my chest. After what feels like an eternity, he finally speaks. "Nataliya?" he breathes. "I've found you."

I blink at him, but I don't have a chance to tell him that he's mistaken because I see the figure of Liam looming behind him as a large hand wraps around his throat. The glint of a blade flashes before my eyes as the bald man's head is pulled back. I close my eyes as his blood sprays my face and body, and when I open them again, he's on the floor clutching at his throat while his blood pours through his fingers and onto the ground. Liam holds out his hand to me and I grab it.

"Let's get out of here," he says as he pulls me out of the room. I stumble after him, wiping the blood from my face with the back of my hand. It's in my mouth and my nose, and the copper tang makes me want to retch. As we round the corner, two more men with tattooed necks almost crash into us. They see me covered in blood and draw their weapons. Liam pushes me behind him. He knocks the gun from the hands of the one closest to us before slicing his throat with the blade, while Conor steps seemingly out of nowhere and snaps the second man's neck.

We run past them and into the bar where Mikey is holding off two more men who look like they were trying to make their way into the back.

"Let's go," Liam shouts and Conor pulls a gun from the waistband of his trousers and aims it at the head of one of Mikey's attackers. That seems to stop everyone in their tracks and the two assailants back off, allowing the four of us to run out of the bar to the car parked outside.

Liam bundles me into the back along with Conor and then jumps into the passenger seat while Mikey climbs into the driver's seat and starts the engine. The car wheel spins out of the parking lot as he floors the accelerator.

"Jessie," Conor snaps as he pulls me toward him. "Are you okay?" he asks as he starts lifting my clothes and rubbing his hands over my body.

Looking down, I remember that I'm covered in blood and I grab hold of his hands. "It's not mine. I'm fine."

"Thank fuck!" he sighs as he wraps his arms around me and kisses the top of my head.

"What the fuck happened?" Mikey shouts. "Why the fuck is Jessie covered in blood?"

"Some guy walked in on her in that office. He had a gun in his hand. I had to make a split-second decision."

"It was my fault," I add. "I asked Liam for more time. I should have left when he told me to."

"But how did he get into the office? Why weren't you there? Why didn't you stay with her, Liam?" Conor snaps.

Liam puts his head in his hands and groans. "I heard the noise in the bar and recognized the Russian accents and knew that we didn't have much time. I only left her for a few seconds to see how many of them were there. I don't know where the other guy came from. He must have already been in the building."

"Which is why you were supposed to stay with Jessie and divert anyone who tried to get in there, Liam," Conor says in exasperation. "Now we have three dead Russians. Cleanly and quietly, Shane said."

"It was my fault," I say again.

"It wasn't, Jessie," Liam snaps. "I know the drill. I should never have left you."

"He could have fucking killed her," Conor says as he punches the back of the passenger seat so hard that Liam jolts forward.

"Don't you think I know that," Liam shouts. Then he turns in his seat and looks at me. "I'm sorry, Jessie."

"There's no need to be. I'm completely fine, and you saved my life."

"Shane is going to go fucking nuclear when he finds out about this," Mikey says with a shake of his head.

"Fuck!" Liam says with a sigh before he puts his head in his hands and stays quiet for the remainder of the journey home.

CHAPTER 27

JESSIE

*S*tepping out of the shower, I wrap myself in a towel before walking back into Conor's bedroom. He sits on his bed, as his eyes roam over my body.

"Are you okay?" he asks, his face full of concern.

"I'm fine." I smile at him and how much he cares about my welfare.

"Good," he says with a sigh. "Because Shane wants to see us. Like, right now."

"Okay. Let me go get changed."

"Here," he says, handing me a white shirt and a pair of black lace panties. "I grabbed these for you from the laundry. He's pissed, and you know he doesn't like to be kept waiting."

"Fine," I reply with a roll of my eyes. I put the clothes on, eyeing Conor as I do. I've never seen him looking so nervous. But then, I suppose we all just made one huge clusterfuck of epic proportions. Deep down, he and the twins want nothing more than to impress Shane. I'm learning that he's much more like a father to them than a big brother.

A few moments later, Conor and I walk out of his bedroom to find the twins waiting for us outside.

"Ready?" Conor asks.

"Fuck, no!" Liam groans with a shake of his head.

"Hey. This is on all of us, not just you," Mikey says, placing a reassuring hand on his twin's shoulder.

"He's right. Now let's get this over with," Conor adds with a sigh.

I follow the three of them down the hallway toward Shane's office and the tension hangs in the air as though it is something tangible I can reach out and touch. I've seen Shane Ryan pissed plenty of times. It seems to be his default setting. But I have never experienced this level of anxiety from his brothers before. It's coming from them in waves. I swallow as I wonder just what the hell we're walking into.

Shane is pacing up and down his office when we walk in, the four of us sticking close together as though it offers some sort of protection.

He looks up as he hears us come in. "Sit!" he barks at us with a scowl.

Like naughty kids who have been summoned to the principal's office, we do as he tells us. I sit between the twins, taking some comfort from the warmth of their bodies pressed against mine on the small sofa. I place my hand on Liam's thigh and squeeze, and he gives me the faintest hint of a smile. Shane sees it too, and he scowls at me.

"Who's going to tell me what the fuck happened?" he snarls, his teeth bared like a rabid dog.

Liam sucks in a breath beside me, but it's Conor who answers. "We fucked up, Shane. One of them was already in the bar when we got there, but, we didn't know. Then, when the others came in, they saw us and got suspicious. When one of them walked into the office and pulled a gun on Jessie, we had to act. We were sloppy and we got distracted."

"Who was supposed to be Jessie's lookout?" Shane snaps.

"I was," Liam says quietly.

"So, why the fuck weren't you doing your job?" Shane snarls as he walks toward where the twins and I are sitting, leaning down so his face is close to Liam's.

Liam opens his mouth to speak, but I act first. "It was my fault, Shane," I say, my voice trembling. "Please don't blame your brothers. This is all on me."

Shane's head snaps toward me and he frowns. "You?"

"No, it wasn't," Liam adds. "I was the lookout."

"It's on us, not Jessie," Conor says with a sigh.

"Yeah," Mikey agrees with a nod beside me. "Jessie was just doing what we asked her to."

"No. I was the distraction. You were only looking out for me, and if you hadn't been, none of this would have happened," I say as I glare into Shane's dark green eyes and my pulse thrums against my skin. I swallow as he narrows his eyes at me as though he's trying to see into my soul.

"Are you lying to me, Hacker?" he snarls.

"No," I snap. "Your brothers messed up today, but it was because of me. I was the one who created the problem, Shane. I take full responsibility."

"No," Liam says, and Mikey and Conor voice their agreement, but Shane holds a hand up to quiet us all, and like obedient little puppy dogs, we do as we're told.

He walks back to his desk. "Did you at least get the information I asked for?"

"Yes," I whisper.

He chews on his lip and sits down. "I've spoken to our contacts in NYPD and they're dealing with the fallout. This is being pegged as a robbery that went wrong. Our names won't be connected to anything. Fortunately, the hacker did something right and at least disabled the CCTV before you lot had your little party."

We all sit there nodding at him and I'm wondering whether this is it. Is this what his brothers have been so worried about?

But I sneak a look at their faces and realize it's not the telling off they were worried about, it's the fact that they've let him down. He asked us to handle this quietly, and we did the exact opposite.

"It really was my fault, Shane," I say again. "Your brothers were protecting me because I was distracted. I'm sorry. It won't happen again."

Liam shakes his head and places his hand over mine.

"Enough!" Shane snaps. "It's done. And it better not happen again. Ever."

"It won't," Conor says, and the twins nod their agreement.

"Good. Now, you all look like shit. So, get out of here," he snarls and we all stand.

"Not you, Hacker. Come here," he growls as we all start to file out of his office.

I glance at his brothers and swallow. Conor winks at me reassuringly and Liam kisses my cheek before the two of them walk out of the room.

"Uh-oh, you're in trouble now," Mikey says quietly with a grin before kissing my forehead and following his brothers.

Heat is searing between my thighs as I walk to Shane's desk and stand directly in front of him. Goosebumps prickle along my forearm beneath the cool cotton of the shirt I'm wearing. He pushes his chair back slightly and nods at the small amount of room he has created between him and his mahogany desk. I slide into the tight space, perching myself on the edge of the cool wood.

"Why did you do that?" he asks, rubbing a hand over the stubble on his jaw.

"Do what?"

"Try and take the fall for them. They're grown men. They take responsibility for their own actions."

"I know that. But I also know how much they hate to disappoint you. And they really were just looking out for me," I say with a tremor in my voice as the heat of Shane's gaze makes the warmth pool between my thighs. "They've had a rough day, and I wanted to protect them. The way they protect me. You know?"

"You care about them?" he asks matter-of-factly.

"Of course I do," I can't help but frown. "I care about all of your brothers."

He eyes me suspiciously, and I glare at him. He is as hot as hell, but he's also a moody asshole. "Is that all?" I ask before I suck in a breath.

His tongue darts out of his mouth and he licks his lower lip, making my inner walls clench at the sight. Jesus! Being so close to him is maddening. He makes me want to wrap my legs around his waist and beg him to fuck me.

"No," he growls, lifting one hand and fingering one button of the shirt I'm wearing. "Why are you wearing my shirt, Hacker?"

I look down and swallow. Shit! This is his? Conor said he'd just grabbed it from the laundry, but I assumed it must have belonged to him. "I'm sorry. I didn't realize. Conor gave it to me," I whisper.

"Hmm?" he narrows his eyes at me as though he doesn't believe me.

Asshole!

He obviously gets off on making me feel uncomfortable. Let's see how he responds when the tables are turned. I lift my hands to the collar. "Would you like me to take it off?" I purr.

"Yes. Right now," he growls, taking me entirely by surprise.

Shit!

I draw in a deep breath as I unbutton it slowly. My fingers tremble, making the task more difficult than usual. When I'm done, I slide the cotton over my bare skin until I'm sitting in only my panties, my almost naked body just inches from his. My nipples pebble under his gaze and heat creeps over my neck and cheeks. Why the hell didn't I wear a bra?

His eyes linger on my hardened nipples, and he shifts in his seat slightly. Dropping my eyes to his groin, I can't help but notice the bulge in his pants and bite back a smile.

"Here you go," I breathe, handing him the shirt.

His eyes burn into mine as he takes it from me and tosses it onto the floor. Without breaking eye contact, he palms his dick through his suit pants and wet heat rushes between my thighs. "Those panties belong to me too," he growls.

"What?"

"I paid for them. So, that makes them mine."

I open my mouth to protest, but nothing comes out. So, he wants my panties, does he? "Fine," I breathe as I hook my fingers into the black lace fabric and slide them down my legs.

He holds out his hand, and I place my embarrassingly damp panties into his outstretched palm. He closes his fist over them and just as I expect him to toss them aside too, he holds them to his face and inhales deeply.

Fuck! Me!

"I wonder, little hacker. Do you taste as good as you smell?" he growls, and I feel another rush of wet heat.

"You'd have to ask your brothers about that," I reply with a pop of one eyebrow.

"Will I?" He stuffs the panties into his pocket and then rubs a hand over his jaw. Those hands. I imagine him running them over my body and touching that place where I am aching to feel him.

I swallow as my pussy starts to throb with need. "Or you could see for yourself," I add. Damn, this man has me a hot, trembling mess.

His eyes narrow and my pulse quickens as his green eyes burn into mine. Reaching out his hand, he slides it up my inner thigh, leaving a trail of fire in his wake. My legs part for him of their own accord, and the low rumble in his throat seems to reverberate through my whole body. His hand reaches the apex of my thighs and I draw in an expectant breath before he palms my pussy possessively. I shudder at his touch, pressing my hips forward as he slides his index finger through my wet folds.

"Shane," I pant with need as he reaches my hot entrance and pushes the tip inside me.

"Why are you so wet?"

"I live in a house with four men who are as hot as hell," I bite back before staring into those incredible green eyes.

He narrows them at me. "Do you want this, Hacker?" he asks as he pushes his finger deep inside me and I moan loudly, my head tipping back between my shoulder blades.

"Well?" He curls the tip of his finger, pressing against my G-spot and my hips almost shoot off the desk.

Then he slides his finger out of me and leans back in his chair. "I guess not," he growls, and I realize I didn't answer his question.

I stare at him while I practically drip onto his desk. I need to take back some control here. Because Shane Ryan is too much. He's going to unravel me. Break me apart and leave me in pieces.

I sit up and lean forward, pressing my face close to his neck and inhaling his incredible scent—expensive cologne and raw sex. "I wonder, Shane. Do you taste as good as you smell?"

His eyes blaze with fire, and he pushes his chair back a few inches. "Why don't you see for yourself?" he growls as he looks down at his impressive erection straining at the seam of his suit pants.

I don't need any further encouragement and I drop to my knees and unzip his fly, letting his hard cock spring free.

God, he's huge!

I lick the bead of pre-cum from his tip and then suck him into my mouth as far as I can take him, pressing my tongue flat against the underside of his shaft and sucking to the tip as his hands fist in my hair and he curses in Gaelic.

I take him as far back into my throat as I can. Until my eyes are watering. I expect he's going to start fucking my mouth, but he allows me to stay in control and pleasure courses through my body at the guttural sounds he makes as I suck and lick his beautiful cock.

I can feel him on the edge, and I work faster.

"Stop!" he orders suddenly as he pulls my head back by my hair. I look up and blink at him, thankful that my eyes are already watering as tears spring to them.

I wipe my mouth with the back of my hand. "Is something wrong?"

"Stand up," he growls, ignoring my question.

I do as he instructs, my legs trembling as he places his hands on my hips to steady me. His fingers dig into my soft flesh as he grips me tightly. "I haven't fucked a woman without a condom for a very long time," he says as he stares at the space between my thighs.

"Really?"

"My brothers assure me you're clean?"

"I am. I was tested when I had my checkup when I first got here."

"And you're on birth control?"

"Yes," I pant as I stand here, literally dripping for him.

He nods as though he's satisfied with that answer and then he leans forward. His hands slide up to my waist and he lifts me as though I'm made of air, before pulling me onto his lap and impaling me onto his huge, thick cock in one swift movement.

"Jesus, Shane," I hiss as he stretches me wide open. My feet can't touch the floor, so I have no leverage to work with and I'm completely full of him. I shift my weight to try and get a more comfortable position, but he holds me tight to him, letting my body adjust to his size.

"Fuck! Hacker," he growls in my ear. "You feel so fucking good."

My insides are on fire as his hard length throbs inside me. I

136

draw in a shaky breath as my walls clench around him. His warm hands slide up to my back and he rubs over my skin, soothing me.

"Your cunt is so hot. You're dripping all over me. Does sucking my cock make you wet?" he leans forward and breathes against my ear.

"Yes," I groan as I tip my head back, allowing him easier access to my neck.

He runs his teeth along my sensitive skin before sucking on a spot just below my ear, and a rush of my arousal coats him. I breathe deeply as my body finally adjusts to his size. He knows as soon as I'm ready, and he moves his hips slightly, making me moan out loud as I cling to his neck.

"Shane,"

Chuckling against my skin, he places his hands on my hips again and rolls me over his cock. The friction and the angle are perfect and he reaches the sweet spot deep inside me so easily that I am panting for breath and teetering on the edge of oblivion. As if I could possibly take any more, he bends his head low and sucks one of my hard nipples into his hot mouth, licking and nibbling me gently until my whole body feels like it is on fire.

"You going to come all over my cock already, Hacker?" he mumbles, and I want to call him an arrogant asshole. But I can hardly form a coherent thought in my head, never mind speak. Besides, he's right.

I run my fingers through his hair as my orgasm crashes over me like a freight train. I shudder against him, my walls squeezing and clenching around him until he throws his head back.

"Fuck," he grunts as he fills me with his own release.

. . .

I PRESS my forehead against Shane's as we both pant for breath. He lifts me slightly until he has enough room to pull out of me, and then he shuffles me backwards while he fastens his zipper and belt. I watch his Adam's apple bob as he swallows hard, and I wonder if he's going to tell me to leave now. He has resisted this thing between us for so long, perhaps he has taken all he needs from me.

But then he stands up, with my legs wrapped around his waist, and walks us out of his office, right past the den where his brothers are watching TV.

They all voice their approval as he carries me past them. Me completely naked, and him still in his suit. I blush as I bury my face in his neck.

"Don't forget, you can't have her all to yourself, Shane," Conor shouts as we pass by.

Shane stops and turns to them. "You three have had your fun for the past four weeks. Tonight, it's my turn," he growls, and my insides melt like warm butter. I'm getting him all to myself, for tonight at least.

WHEN WE REACH HIS BEDROOM, Shane throws me onto the bed, making me giggle as I bounce into the middle. I stop laughing when I look up at his face. he's so serious and fierce. I swallow as he undresses, his deft fingers making easy work of his shirt buttons. It's only seconds before he's sliding the crisp white cotton over his thick, tattooed biceps, exposing his muscular torso. I have only snatched glimpses of it before now, so I take the time to appreciate his hard, toned chest and abs. Not to mention those incredible arms, inked from wrist to shoulder.

I lick my lip unconsciously, earning me a smirk. Shane is an arrogant, self-entitled asshole, but right now I don't care. I want him naked and inside me again, and I want him now. He slows his movements, unbuckling his belt and pulling it off in deliberate, unhurried strokes. By the time he reaches his zipper, I am trembling with need.

"Spread those legs wide for me, Hacker. I want to see you."

Heat flushes over my cheeks as I do as he instructs and his gaze drops to my pussy. "Your cunt looks beautiful with my cum dripping from it."

"You think I'm beautiful?" I can't help but tease him.

"I said your cunt is beautiful. And that is the only part of you I'm interested in," he snarls.

"Oh really?" I challenge him, unable to stop myself from trying to push his buttons.

"Really," he snaps as he pushes off his pants and boxer shorts and crawls onto the bed. He places his large, powerful hands on my inner thighs and presses them flat to the mattress, spreading me wide open before bending his head low. He inhales deeply and growls his approval and the animalistic way he does it makes me pant with need. Leaning down, he presses the flat of his tongue against my opening. The warmth sends a shiver down the length of my spine and I whimper shamelessly as he works the tip inside me. But it's when he licks the length of my pussy that I almost come undone again.

"Shane," I pant as he swirls his tongue over my clit and I experience the rush of wet heat between my thighs.

"Your cunt is so fucking sweet, Hacker," he growls against me. "Even full of my cum. Now I know why my brothers can't keep their fucking hands off you."

Heat sears through me at his words as he sucks my clit into his mouth and pushes two fingers inside me at the same time. My back arches off the bed in pleasure and then I raise my hips, grinding myself on his mouth and his fingers. My climax runs from me in a hot, wet rush, making my whole pussy and thighs slick with my arousal as he tips me over the edge.

I rake my fingers through his hair and try to pull his head away. "Stop," I pant as he keeps on sucking. "Shane. Please, I can't," My legs tremble violently as he keeps his tongue and his fingers working me into a frenzy until I'm cresting another wave. The intense pressure builds in my core as I realize I'm going to lose all control and I'm not sure I want him to be the one I lose it with. I have less of a connection with him than any of his brothers, but damn if he makes me come as hard as I ever have in my life.

"I want more. I want it all," he growls as he increases his efforts and I press my head back against the pillow, powerless to resist him. I cry out his name as the next orgasm rips through my body like black powder. Wet heat gushes from me, soaking the bedsheets and Shane's face. I pant for breath as my whole body convulses. That has never happened before. He looks up at me with a look of pure deviance in his eyes. "Damn, little hacker. Did you just…?"

"Stop," I say, throwing my hands over my eyes. "I don't know how that happened."

He crawls up the bed, not even bothering to wipe any of my cum from his mouth, and takes hold of my wrists, pulling my hands from my face and pinning them either side of my head. "How the fuck am I supposed to keep out of this sweet little cunt of yours now?" he growls.

"Well, you don't have to," I whisper.

"Isn't it enough that you have my brothers wrapped around your little finger? You don't need me too. Besides, I'm not sure you'll survive me *and* my brothers. And I don't share well with others."

"Well, maybe you need to try and learn?" I say with a grin as I place my hands on his face and pull him toward me for a kiss, but he pulls back.

"All I need to do, Hacker, is fuck you tonight. Just one night. In fact, I'm going to fuck you so hard neither of us will ever forget it, and then you can go back to my brothers."

"Whatever you say, Shane," I smile at him to hide the

gaping hole he just tore through my chest. He might be right that I already have his brothers, but he's wrong if he thinks that I don't need him too. I need all of them. Each of them makes me feel something completely different, and I want it all. I know that makes me selfish. I know that I have no right to any claim on any one of these men, let alone all four of them, but it doesn't stop me longing for it just the same. I feel something here that I haven't experienced since I was a kid. On their own, they make me feel cherished, desired, wanted, even loved, but together, they make me feel like home. And I haven't had that for such a long time that I'd forgotten what it was like, and how good it is to belong somewhere, or to someone.

"You ready?" Shane growls, snapping me from my thoughts. He's holding himself up on his forearms. His breath skates over my cheek. I can smell my arousal on his face and it makes my stomach contract with the need for him. But I don't even have a chance to answer as he pushes himself deep inside me, forcing me a few inches up the bed.

I feel every single inch of him as he buries his face in my neck and nails me to the mattress. He gives me everything he has, and I know it's because he wants this to be it for us. I clench my walls around him, pulling him in deeper as I rake my nails down his back. If this is going to be all I get from him, then I want it all too.

"Your cunt is fucking perfect, Hacker," he groans against my skin. "I can feel you squeezing me and dripping all over my cock. How the hell am I supposed to keep my hands off you?"

"Shane. You can't. You fuck me too good," I pant in response, and he growls in Gaelic in my ear as he doubles his efforts.

I LIE in Shane's bed with his arm draped over my stomach as we both catch our breath. It's almost 3a.m. and he has fucked me over and over again for hours. He is a machine, but I'm not sure my body can take any more of him.

He curls his arm tighter around me. "Has anyone ever made you squirt twice in one night before?" he growls.

I swallow hard as his words vibrate through my core. "No-one has ever made me do that before," I whisper.

He sucks in a breath. "Fuck, Hacker," he grunts.

"Don't tell your brothers that," I say. "They'll only view it as some sort of challenge."

"I won't," he says softly before he stretches and yawns.

"Shall I go back to my room?" I ask, the words catching in my throat.

He wraps his arm back around me and pulls me to him until I'm pressed against his chest. "I said one night, Hacker. That means the entire night," he says, pressing his lips against my hair. "Now get some sleep."

I close my eyes and lean into him. Our bodies fit together so easily that I wonder how I will ever live without sharing his bed again. I only hope that he feels the same.

CHAPTER 28

JESSIE

*T*he sound of the shower running wakes me from my sleep. I stretch my limbs and smile as the dull ache in my muscles reminds me of the previous night's endeavors. Shane Ryan is a machine in the sack. Climbing out of bed, I walk to the bathroom and find him standing in the huge walk-in shower; the water running over his perfectly chiseled body. He looks up and grins as he sees me.

"Come here, Hacker," he says, holding out his hand.

I lick my lips. My pussy is tender, and he fucks hard. I'm not sure I can take another session with him right now. But I can't resist him either. I step closer and take his hand, allowing him to pull me under the water with him. He runs his hands over my hips to my behind. I lean forward to kiss him, but he dips his head low, kissing my neck instead before trailing his soft lips over my hard nipples. Suddenly, I realize he has never kissed me, at least not on the lips. He has slipped his tongue into the most intimate parts of my body, but he won't kiss me? What the hell is that about?

I'm stopped from thinking about it any further when one of

his hands slides between my thighs and through my slick folds. I can't help but wince.

"Are you sore?" he asks softly.

"A little," I admit.

He closes his eyes and draws in a breath as he slips one finger inside me. "You're already wet," he growls. "How can I not fuck you?"

"You can, Shane. Please do," I whimper as he pulls out and circles my swollen clit.

"I can't do gentle," he breathes.

"Then don't. I don't want gentle. I want you."

"Fuck," he grunts as he lifts me by my ass cheeks until I wrap my legs around his waist. Then he presses me against the cool tiled wall and fucks me again. I moan his name when I come and he presses his face into my neck as he grinds out his own release. When we're done, he lowers my legs and presses his forehead against mine as the water continues running over both of us.

"Do you still feel me inside you, Hacker?" he growls.

"Yes," I say as my pussy throbs.

"Good. Then I think my work here is done."

I force a smile even though my heart breaks a little bit more.

WHEN I'M SHOWERED and dressed, I make my way into the kitchen. Conor turns as I approach, placing his cereal bowl onto the counter before he pulls me into his arms. He presses his body against mine until I can feel his growing erection against my abdomen. "Morning, Angel. Listening to you and Shane all night made me so fucking hard. I jerked off twice listening to him make you come. So you're staying in my room tonight."

He doesn't give me a chance to respond as he seals my mouth with a kiss. At this point, Shane walks up behind me and smacks my ass, and I giggle into Conor's mouth.

"Morning, Jessie," Mikey and Liam say as they walk over to me, both of them dressed in only boxer shorts. I'm still in Conor's arms when Mikey presses himself against my back and plants a kiss on my neck. Despite mine and Shane's marathon fucking session, the wet heat sears between my thighs. These boys make me so horny. Conor slides his hands between me and Mikey, and down the back of my jeans, beneath my underwear, until he's cupping my bare ass cheeks. Some gentleness might be just what I need tonight. The twins can be gentle, but there are always two of them to please. Conor, on the other hand – he is always all about me. I wrap my arms around his neck and kiss him deeply as Mikey's hands run over my hips, before sliding into the front of my jeans and my panties as he continues nibbling my neck.

I feel the heat from Liam as he approaches too. "You look so fucking hot being felt up by my brothers, Jessie."

Shane loudly clears his throat from the other side of the kitchen and we all stop and turn to him as warmth flushes over my cheeks. I'm turning into a complete sex addict. The more I get, the more I need.

"Thanks to your fuck up yesterday, we have plenty of work to do today. So, take your hands out of her fucking panties and go get ready," he barks. We untangle ourselves and the three of them each give me a soft kiss on the cheek before they walk out of the kitchen.

I walk to the breakfast bar and pick up a clean mug, holding it out to Shane as he fills up his own mug from the pot of coffee.

"You *are* a distraction," he says with a flash of his eyebrows as he pours me a drink too.

"Sorry," I whisper. "But they distract me as well."

"Do *they*?" he frowns at me and I'm not sure why. "Can you behave yourself if we leave you here alone for the day?"

"Can't I come with you?" I blink at him.

"No. It's not the kind of work I want you involved in.

145

Besides, haven't we already established that you are far too much of a distraction for my brothers?"

"But not for you?"

He sighs and rolls his eyes, avoiding my question. "Do I need to get a babysitter in here for you, Hacker?"

"No," I shake my head. "I'll behave, I promise."

"Good," he says with a nod of his head and then he walks out of the kitchen, leaving me standing alone.

CHAPTER 29

MIKEY

I lean against the back seat of the car as Conor drives us through the streets of New York.

"Where the hell did you say we're going?" Liam asks from beside me.

I can't see Shane's face, but I know without a doubt that he just rolled his eyes. Liam has a habit of asking the questions that we all want the answers to, but aren't stupid enough to ask.

"To sort out your epic fuck up from yesterday," he snaps.

"Yeah, I know. You told us that part. But where exactly is that?" he replies. "It's kind of hard to get psyched up when you don't have any idea what the plan is, bro."

"Do you even know what the plan is, Shane?" Conor laughs, earning him a punch in the arm from our oldest brother.

"We're going back to the bar. You three left too many loose ends, and I don't need a war with the Russians right now."

"What if they've already talked?"

"They haven't. They're small time. They don't have a direct line to the top men. My sources tell me they've not spoken to their handlers yet. Nobody there recognized any of you. But it's only a matter of time before one of them says something or sees one of you somewhere one day and realizes who you are."

"You know we're sorry, right?" Liam says.

I put an arm around my baby brother's neck. He hates it when I call him that though, and I suppose I am only older than him by sixteen minutes. Liam is always the one who is most desperate for Shane's approval. Not that he needs to worry. He already has it. Everyone knows that except Liam himself. Shane respects the hell out of him, out of all of us. But Liam will never measure up to his own expectations. he's always so damn hard on himself. Then we all have our demons. I suppose it was hard to get through our childhoods without some scars.

"So? You and Jessie?" Conor asks, changing the subject completely, and making me lean forward in my seat. I have wondered if this would be a thing between the two of them. Liam and I have always shared everything, including women, and we're more than happy to share Jessie. Knowing that she cares about Liam and Conor doesn't make me feel any less cared for by her. I'm not big on relationships, and Jessie gets that. She makes time for me whenever I need her, and I like it that way. But Conor and Shane never share. They love each other deeply. They only had each other for eight years until me and Mikey were born, and they share a bond as close as me and my twin do. But they do not share women. Until now.

"What about us?" Shane snaps.

"I knew you wouldn't be able to resist her," Conor chuckles softly.

"Well, I'll admit she has a certain appeal," Shane nods. "You okay with that?"

Conor turns to him and smiles. "I am actually. Go figure."

"Go figure," Shane agrees.

"Hey. Let's not forget, we liked her first. No-one asking if we're okay with this arrangement?" Liam interrupts the bonding going on in the front.

Shane turns in his seat and just as I'm sure Liam is going to get a slap across the face from our oldest brother, Shane speaks instead. "This okay with you two?"

"Fine by me," I nod.

"Of course. It's just nice to be asked, that's all," Liam nods too.

"Good," Shane snaps and then turns back to the road, before he quietly adds. "Because I wouldn't give her up if it wasn't."

"You're an asshole." Conor shakes his head.

"You know, that's what she said," Shane bursts out laughing and suddenly the four of us are laughing like we haven't done in a long time. Not since before they took Conor eighteen months ago. Jessie Romanov might just be the best thing that's ever happened to the Ryan brothers. Our little red-haired ray of sunshine.

CHAPTER 30

LIAM

*W*alking behind Conor and Shane back into that bar where we fucked up so badly yesterday, I still feel guilty. Shane asked us to do a job and we completely let him down, and that was mostly because of me. But even worse than letting him down, Jessie could have been killed. A minute later and things could have been so much worse. And I would never be able to live with myself.

Mikey steps up behind me, placing a reassuring hand on my shoulder. He knows exactly what I'm thinking.

Shane turns to us as we reach the doors. He speaks to all of us, but for some reason, I can't shake the feeling that it's mostly aimed at me. "This place is closed to the public right now. So, anyone who is in here is a target. No shooters unless absolutely necessary. I want this to seem like amateurs were here. Like a bust up between two rival gangs. And no loose ends. Okay?"

"Okay," I nod, just before Shane opens the doors. The four of us walk inside and bolt the doors behind us. There are at least a dozen men in the place. Most of them sit around two tables that are pushed together in the corner, as though they're having a meeting and the others are near the bar.

"Jesus, Shane," Conor hisses through clenched teeth. "You sure we can't use our shooters?" he asks, referring to the handguns each of us have tucked into the back of our waistbands.

"Not unless they do. Besides, I thought you three were always up for a fight?"

"But this is one of my favorite shirts," Conor feigns his protest, although his grin gives him away.

The men in the room start standing up or making their way toward us, and Mikey leans close to Shane's ear as "You do realize if we beat and, or, stab all of these fuckers to death, it will still look like a professional job though, right?"

Shane shrugs. "Less professional though than if we just shoot them all in the head."

"Whatever you say," Mikey laughs as he rocks back on his heels, ready to spring into action. Conor cracks his knuckles and then his neck. He was an undefeated bare-knuckle boxing champion back in Ireland, and he loves any excuse for a good punch-up. It's why he enjoys working in the club so much.

"Three each? Give or take?" Shane suggests.

"Does the one who kills the most get a prize?" I ask.

"No," Shane snaps. "Just get to work."

The four of us split off into the room and within seconds, I no longer have any idea what my brothers are doing because the giant bastard who has been sizing me up since we walked in launches himself at me, barreling into me with such force that he almost knocks me on my ass. I steady myself and push back against him, making him stumble. I am six foot four; I work out hard to keep in shape, and I'm the biggest out of my brothers, but this guy must have at least four inches and eighty pounds on me. And not only that, he can fight too. I hit him with an uppercut just as he throws a right hook that catches me right on my left cheekbone. Both of us stagger backwards but then we're back at it again. We keep going, landing blow after blow, until he catches me with a knee to my ribs, which completely takes the wind out of me and knocks me flat on my ass.

I lie on the floor, glaring up at him. Since I came to New York at the age of sixteen, the only other person who has ever knocked me on my ass is Conor in a sparring session. My head spins as I look around the room and watch my brothers making easy work of the rest of this misfit's crew. Shane and Mikey wield a knife each, while Conor is snapping someone's neck with ease. I have a knife strapped to my calf. I could pull it out now and use it, but this has become personal. I will take this fucker down in a fair fight if it fucking kills me. If he's only using his fists, then so am I.

Launching myself back up, I throw myself at him like a caged tiger. I don't know how long we go on fighting but every part of my body starts to hurt. It becomes an all-out brawl. Each of us punching and kicking the other one. Landing blow after blow that seems to do little more than temporarily wind the other. I'm vaguely aware of the room around us growing quieter and soon my three brothers are standing around me, having wiped out at least eleven men between them while I'm still grappling with this huge fucker.

My ribs ache so much it hurts to even breathe. There is blood pouring down my face from a cut above my eye. And now I carry the shame of being the weak link. I was the only one who didn't pull my weight today. The anger wells up through my chest and I launch myself at him again, finally knocking him to the ground. I dive onto him, straddling his chest while I punch him in the face. Over and over and over. One of his eyes pops out of his socket and blood spatters my face, but I keep going until a pair of arms wrap around my chest.

"Jesus, Liam. He's dead, kid," Shane says in my ear. "Come on," he pulls me backwards until I'm sitting on the floor. Looking, down, I realize I'm covered in blood. My brothers eyes are on me, burning into my skin.

"What the hell are you three looking at?" I snarl.

"Nothing, bro. Come on. Let's go," Conor says.

I look up just as Mikey whispers something in Shane's ear.

"Go wait for us in the car," Shane says to my brothers. "We'll be out soon."

I watch Mikey and Conor walking out of the bar, and I swallow hard. I've let them all down again.

Shane crouches down, sitting back on his heels so he can look me in the eye. "He was one tough motherfucker, kid," he grins at me. "You did good."

"No, I didn't," I shake my head. "Three each it was supposed to be, and I just about handled one."

Shane looks back at the huge man lying lifeless on the floor. "He's a fucking giant, Liam. Why do you think we left him for you? He would have used my face as a boot-scraper. Conor might have got the better of him, but I knew you would be the best match for him. Why didn't you use your knife?"

"I wanted it to be a fair fight," I shrugged.

Shane smiles, and then he stands up, holding out his hand to me. I take it and allow him to pull me up. "You always insisted on fighting fair. Even when you were a little kid," he says as he reaches up ruffles my hair, taking me back to all the times he looked out for me or stood up to our father for me. "You did a good job today. I mean that. I know I don't tell you enough, but I'm proud of you."

"But, yesterday, I fucked up," I shake my head.

"We all fuck up sometimes, Liam," he wraps an arm around my neck. "No matter what you do, no matter how many mistakes you make, you will never disappoint me. Do you understand me?"

"Yes." I blink at him as I wipe the blood dripping into my eye.

"Good. Now, don't tell your brothers this, but you're my favorite," he pulls me closer, until he almost has me in a head-lock, and kisses the top of my head.

I laugh because I know that's not true. He doesn't have favorites. I wish I could tell him how much I admire and respect him. How he's more like a father than a brother to me. But, I can't find the words.

"Come on. We need to go to the club and get cleaned up before we go home, because Jessie will have you all wrapped in cotton wool if she sees the state of us all."

"Well, I wouldn't mind a little Jessie TLC," I smirk at him.

"I bet you wouldn't," he grins back before we walk out of the bar, leaving the room full of dead bodies behind us.

CHAPTER 31

JESSIE

I switch off the laptop and lean back against the chair with a sigh. Seeing that document on the computer at the bar yesterday has made me remember what I'm supposed to be doing with my life. I've been so distracted by the Ryan brothers – distracted being happy for a change, that it was easy to forget that I'm supposed to be tracking down the Wolf.

That day when I finally escaped, I was convinced that I'd killed him. I stuck that wooden hairbrush handle right into his throat. I have never seen so much blood. But when I went back the next day to torch the place, he was gone. So, I ran, and I kept on running until I reached civilization two days later.

The Wolf didn't have a car, or I would have stolen it. So, where the hell did he go to? Maybe he is dead after all?

But maybe he's not. And until I know for sure, I'll never be able to rest.

THE BOYS HAVE BEEN GONE all day and I've kept myself distracted with some more work and a workout in the gym. I showered and put on one of Liam's huge baseball shirts. The soft cotton feels good against my skin, and it's so big that I can wrap my whole body in it when I'm sitting on the sofa. Walking into the kitchen, I look in the refrigerator for something for dinner. I wonder if the boys will be hungry when they get back or whether they will have eaten while they were out.

The sound of raised voices makes my heart skip a beat as I realize they're home. I had thought I'd enjoy some time to myself, but I've missed them.

A few seconds later, they walk into the kitchen carrying pizza boxes and the delicious aroma makes my stomach growl. Liam and Mikey reach me first. Putting the takeout onto the counter, they press me into a hot man and Jessie sandwich as Mikey kisses me, while Liam pulls my hair aside and rubs his nose along my neck. "We've missed you, baby," he breathes.

When the twins let me go, lured away by the smell of the tempting food, Conor pulls me into his arms, lifting me onto the kitchen counter and kissing me deeply. I wrap my legs around his waist. "Come take a shower with me, Angel," he groans. "I need inside you."

"Sorry, Con. I need Hacker to check out that security system for me. She's coming with me," Shane says as he reaches us and places a hand on Conor's shoulder.

"As soon as you're done, then," Conor groans as he brushes my hair back from my face.

"She'll still be with me," Shane says matter-of-factly and my insides contract at the thought. He said just one night, didn't he?

Conor turns to him with a scowl. "I had to listen to the two of you fucking the whole of last night."

"And I've listened to the four of you for the past four weeks. It's still my turn," he says with a wink as he reaches for my hand and pulls me from the counter, picking up a pizza box with the other. "But, first, we have work to do."

I kiss Conor softly before following Shane into his office.

He sits at his desk and fires up his computer while I take the pizza from him and open up the box. My stomach growls again as soon as the aroma of pepperoni hits me, and I take a slice.

He holds out his hand to me. "I need you to hack into the security system at Balthazar's. I want you to wipe any footage from today."

I nod as I take a bite. He doesn't usually let me use his computer. "Sure. Shouldn't take me long," I say as I take a step toward him. I wait for him to stand up and let me sit down so I can get to work, but he doesn't move, and I realize he is my seat. I sit on his lap and open up the page I need.

He pulls my hair back and kisses my neck and I wriggle on his lap. "This would go a hell of a lot quicker if you weren't distracting me," I say with a grin.

"Fine," he says as his hands drop to my lap. "But, you're sexy when you work."

"So are you," I reply as I watch the footage of him and his brothers wiping out the entire room.

"You don't have to watch it all, Hacker," he says as his hand slides between my thighs and his fingers edge dangerously close to my panties. "Just wipe it."

"Okay. I can fast forward, but I need to make sure I wipe it all."

"Fine," he answers as his fingertips brush over my folds and I suck in a breath.

"Why do you insist on walking around the house in nothing but panties and a t-shirt?" he growls as he presses his lips against my ear.

"What can I say? I enjoy wearing yours and your brothers' clothes," I shrug. "Besides, it's easy access for you, isn't it?" I chuckle, and he nips at my neck.

"You are far too much of a distraction, Hacker," he says as he tugs my panties to the side and slides a finger through my wet folds, making him groan out loud. "You're dripping wet. Have you been enjoying yourself while we've been out?"

"No," I breathe. "I've been busy." I shift in his lap, but he holds me tight to him. "Now let me finish my work."

"A good hacker should be able to work well under pressure," he breathes in my ear as he pushes one finger deep inside me.

"Shane," I groan.

"Hurry up and finish what you need to do," he growls.

I try to focus as I forward through the footage while he gently pumps his finger in and out of my channel. Then I come to the end. Conor and Mikey leave the bar, and it's just Shane and Liam.

He isn't watching the screen. Instead, he's nuzzling my neck and fingering me to distraction, but I watch as Shane wraps an arm lovingly around his younger brother and kisses the top of his head. "What did you say to Liam?" I ask.

He looks up at me. "Nothing. Just delete it."

"It doesn't look like nothing."

He pulls his hand from between my thighs. "It's none of your business. Now delete the footage."

"Fine," I snap, and press delete. "There. All done. Can I go now?"

He frowns at me as he lets out a long, slow breath of exasperation. "You are fucking infuriating."

"Well, so are you."

"Fine. Do you want to go, Hacker? Would you rather be with one of my brothers tonight?"

I swallow, realizing that I've offended him. He has every right not to tell me about the details of a private, and quite obviously meaningful conversation with his brother. "No," I whisper. "I'd rather be right here with you."

"Here?" he growls. "You'd like to be fucked on my desk?"

"I just like being fucked by you," I breathe as his hand slides back to where I'm already aching to feel him again. "Anywhere is fine."

He moves the computer keyboard out of the way, pushing it beneath the monitor before he stands up, lifting me with him and sitting me on the edge of his desk with Liam's t-shirt up around my waist. "I've been dreaming about fucking you on my desk. Especially when you're wearing these pretty pink panties," he looks down at my underwear. "You realize they're wet already?" He arches one eyebrow at me as he runs his finger over the damp patch.

"Well, this really hot, moody guy has just had his fingers inside me. So, what do you expect?" I bite on my lip and look up at him.

He grins as he lifts the edge of Liam's t-shirt and pulls it over my head before tossing it onto the floor. Then he trails his fingers down over my stomach and to the edge of my panties. He tugs the band roughly and shoves his entire hand inside them. It makes me gasp, but it's so freaking hot, I experience the familiar rush of wet heat. He chuckles as my skin flushes with warmth too. His other hand reaches for my hair, wrapping it around his fist as he tips my head back slightly and licks from my collarbone up to my jaw. "You smell so fucking sweet, Hacker."

I push my hips against his hand as he slides his fingers through my soaking wet folds before pushing two of them inside me.

"Shane," I cry out.

"Fuck, I love the way you say my name," he growls as he kisses and sucks on that perfect spot on my neck, right below my ear, at the same time as he begins to finger fuck me. His thumb knuckle grazes over my clit and my legs almost buckle until I wrap them around his waist.

The pressure builds and my thighs begin to tremble as the skin on my neck and chest burns with heat.

He moves his lips to my ear. "Come for me, Hacker. I want to feel you creaming on my fingers."

His filthy talk is my downfall and my orgasm bursts through me and I shout his damn name – again. He smiles against my skin, holding me in place as he rubs the last tremors from my body. "Good little hacker," he chuckles.

CHAPTER 32

JESSIE

*M*y eyelids flutter open as Shane stirs beside me. "Hey, Hacker," he says in the low, smooth tone he has that turns my internal organs to melted chocolate.

"Hey. What time is it?" I purr as I stretch like a cat.

"Four a.m. You were talking in your sleep," he says as he raises one eyebrow at me. "Who is Volk?"

That name is like a knife through my heart. I realize I'm staring at him with my mouth open when his face pulls into a frown.

"Who is it?" he snaps.

"Volk is Russian for Wolf," I reply before drawing in a long, shaky breath. I don't remember dreaming about him. Why was I calling his name?

"Are you okay?" he asks as he reaches out and dusts the back of his knuckles across my cheek.

"I'm fine. I'm sorry if I woke you."

"I'm used to people shouting in their sleep around here," he says softly. "I've never heard you do it before, though. You sure everything is okay?" he stares at me with such concern in his eyes that it makes me want to cry.

"I've been thinking about things since the day at the bar," I say with a shrug.

He sits up and looks down at me. "What things?"

"My family. The Wolf," I shake my head. "I saw something on Dmitriy's computer. It was a file titled Romanov. When I opened it, there was a marriage certificate."

"Was is something to do with your family?"

"I don't know. I didn't think so anyway. The names were unfamiliar. I didn't recognize them. Alexei Ivanov and Nataliya Vasiliev. But Nataliya had the same birthday as my mother. A different year, but same month and day."

Shane narrows his eyes at me. "Was it a recent document?"

"No. It was from twenty-eight years ago."

"So, you *didn't* think it was anything to do with your family? But now you do?"

"I'm not sure." I look at him and swallow. "Why was it kept in a file marked Romanov?"

"Romanov is a common name, right'" he asks.

I nod. "Yeah. But there's something else. When that guy came into the room... he was about to make a grab for me, but then he stopped. And then he called me Nataliya. Like he recognized me. So, maybe I'm related to this Nataliya in some way?"

"Did your parents have any siblings?"

I shake my head. "Not that I know of, anyway. They told me they were only children."

"Perhaps it's their marriage certificate? And they changed their names?"

"But my parents married when I was three. I was there. That document is dated two years before I was born."

"Why didn't you tell us any of this before?"

"With everything else that happened, I didn't get the chance. Besides, I was still trying to work it out myself. It could be a coincidence, couldn't it? That I see that on Dmitriy's computer right before one of his men calls me Nataliya?" I look up into his beautiful green eyes, hoping that he'll tell me that of course it is, because if it's not that I might not know who my parents were at all.

"Do you look like your mother?" he asks instead.

"Yes," I swallow. "Who is Dmitriy, Shane?"

He shakes his head. "No-one of note. He used to work for the Semenovs. He was running a gambling racket in Brooklyn, though. That's why I was interested in him."

"So, why did he even have that document on his computer?"

"I don't know. But, I don't have the time for a war with the Russian right now."

"I know. I won't do anything stupid. I have enough information to start a new search. And it could be a coincidence. I've been chasing these leads for eight years, Shane, and they all lead me down the same dead end road. This could be nothing at all," I insist, although I don't quite believe it myself.

"Okay," he nods. "But it might also mean that your mother or your father aren't who you think they were. And that could be the reason your family were killed. You shouldn't have kept this from me. You promised me no more lies."

"Shane." Reaching out my hand, I take hold of his. "I didn't try to hide this from you, I swear. To be honest, I wasn't sure..." I swallow the lump in my throat.

"Wasn't sure of what?"

"I wasn't sure that you would be interested. You're only interested in one part of me. Remember?"

His jaw tenses. "If there is any threat to you, then there is a potential threat to me and my brothers too. Don't you understand that?"

"Yes," I whisper. "I've been used to only looking out for myself for so long, I swear I didn't think of how this might affect you all too. I was going to tell you as soon as I figured out what there was to tell."

"So, what are you planning on doing now that you have this information?"

"I'll look into Nataliya and Alexei and see where to go from there."

"Do not do anything to draw any more attention to us right now," he warns.

"I won't. I'll do it all from the comfort of my laptop. Promise."

"You are going to be my downfall one day, Hacker. I can already feel it," he whispers as he crawls over me.

"I won't. Because we're only about one thing, you and me. Aren't we?" I bite my lower lip as I stare up at him, trying my best to be completely irresistible and seductive.

"Yes, we are. Would you like me to remind you again just what that is?" he growls before bending his head and sinking his teeth into my neck.

"Shane," I half squeal, half groan, and he chuckles against my skin.

"You want my mouth on you?" he breathes as his head sinks lower.

"Yes," I pant as the tingling between my thighs skyrockets.

"You have such a sweet tasting cunt, I don't know how any of us get any fucking work done around here anymore."

"Well, it's a good job there's four of you," I groan as his lips skate over my breasts and my stomach until his head is settled between my thighs.

"Only I can make you squirt though, can't I?" he growls as his lips are pressed against my skin and his words reverberate throughout my entire body.

"Stop talking and put that hot mouth of yours to work," I say with a wicked grin. If this is all we are, then I might as well embrace it.

He laughs again, and his hot breath dances over my slick folds, making me writhe beneath him. Then his magical tongue licks me from my opening to my clit, where he settles his mouth and begins to suck gently while rimming either side of the tender nub of flesh. I push my hips further against him as he tortures me with his incredible oral skills. This man is a magician with his tongue. And as my orgasm builds and threatens to wash over me, he pushes two fingers inside me, causing me to almost shoot off the bed.

"Shane," I cry out and he continues his relentless pace until I'm screaming his name. I haven't recovered from the earth shattering orgasm when he's moving back up the bed and pressing his hands against the inside of my thighs, until they're flat against the mattress.

I reach out for him, clawing at his neck as he drives his huge cock deep inside me. "Fucking you is like my kryptonite, Hacker. This sweet cunt gets you anything you want, doesn't it?"

I close my eyes and try and ignore the hurt from his words. he's intent on pushing me away. Instead, I concentrate on the feel of his hard body on mine. The flex of his muscles as he takes exactly what he wants from me.

CHAPTER 33

JESSIE

*W*hen I wake the following morning, Shane is gone. Glancing at the clock, I notice it's a little after nine am. I wonder what time he left as I rub my hand over the side of the bed where he slept. It's cold and I can't help being a little disappointed by the fact that he didn't even wake me.

Rolling out of bed, I make my way to the shower and step inside. I turn the temperature up as high as I can stand it and enjoy the hot water running over my body, easing my aching muscles. These Ryan brothers are certainly keeping me active. I smile to myself because I wouldn't have it any other way.

I ALMOST BUMP into Conor a little later as I step out of my own bedroom.

"You know where his office is," he says to the person standing out of my view.

"Yes. Thank you," a soft Irish voice says, immediately followed by one of the most beautiful women I have ever seen in the world striding past me and walking confidently down the hallway in pumps that must have at least a six-inch heel on them. She's dressed in a cream, fitted suit and her long, wavy blonde hair is styled perfectly. She looks like she just stepped out of some fancy magazine shoot.

"Who the hell is that?" I whisper to Conor as I watch after her with my mouth hanging open.

He leans against the wall, his arms crossed over his broad chest and his legs crossed at the ankles. "Erin. Our family lawyer," he replies. "Don't be fooled by her ladylike exterior. She's vicious," he laughs.

"She's stunning," I say, experiencing an unexpected pang of jealousy. So, this is Erin?

He pulls a face as though he disagrees with that statement before he adds matter-of-factly. "She's also Shane's ex. They almost got married."

"What?" I stare at him, my mouth hanging open in shock. "How could you not lead with that?" I push him playfully on the arm.

He grins at me. "Not jealous are you, Angel?"

"No," I snap back a little too quickly. "But Shane? Married?"

"Almost," he says as he stands up straight and steps toward me. He wraps an arm around my waist and we walk toward the kitchen.

"What happened? Which one of them broke it off?"

"No idea." He shakes his head.

"Liar." I smile.

"I'm not," he laughs. "It's a closely guarded secret. Shane never talks about it. But two days before their wedding, they suddenly called everything off. He never told us why."

"But aren't you desperate to know?" I ask, my eyes wide as we walk into the kitchen to find the twins sitting at the table eating cereal.

"Not as desperate as you are, it seems," he grins at me. "If Shane wanted us to know, he would have told us."

"So, you've met the Ice Queen then?" Mikey asks with a flash of his eyebrows.

"Don't let Shane hear you calling her that," Liam warns him.

Mikey shrugs. "She broke his fucking heart. And she hates us. I'll call her whatever I want."

Conor shakes his head as he picks up a box of muesli and pours himself a bowl. "You don't know that she broke his heart," he says with a sigh.

"No. But he was a miserable bastard for fucking ages after," Mikey says.

"Still is," Liam adds, and the twins burst into laughter.

"I'm spot on about her hating us though, bro," Mikey says when he stops laughing.

"Yeah, well, you might just be right about that," Conor agrees.

I put on a pot of fresh coffee while the boys chatter amongst themselves. The subject of Shane's ex-fiancée isn't raised by them again, but I can't help thinking about it. Shane Ryan almost married. And to that goddess?

Well, of course, if he was going to marry someone, it would be someone who looked just like Erin. I look down at my five foot four frame. My thick hips and my curvy thighs. How the hell do I ever compete with a woman like that?

I turn and look at the boys and remind myself that I don't have to. I have the Ryan brothers' attention for now, and I should enjoy it while I can. Although I care for them all deeply, I know this can't last. It's not like I'm going to marry any of them. Especially not Shane who has made it abundantly clear that he's only interested in me for one thing. I knew that this was just a temporary thing when I signed on, didn't I? As soon as I figure out where the Wolf is hiding, I'll be moving on anyway. That's if this thing doesn't fizzle out before then all on its own.

"What's the ETA on that coffee, Angel?" Conor asks and I'm snapped from my thoughts.

"Coming," I smile sweetly, and take the pot over to the table. As soon as I set it down, Mikey wraps an arm around my waist and pulls me to him. "You fancy a movie and a sleepover with me and Liam tonight, Red?" he asks as he nuzzles my neck.

"Sure. Sounds good," I smile at him, but I'm still distracted by the blonde goddess currently in Shane Ryan's office.

I HANG around the enormous living room when the boys and I have finished breakfast, under the pretense that I'm tidying up. But you have to walk past the huge open plan area to get to the elevators, and I hope to catch another glimpse of Shane's guest before she leaves. If she leaves. What if she spends the night? Or longer? The thought makes me shudder just as I hear voices coming along the hallway.

"Thanks for this, Erin," Shane says as he escorts her past the room.

I stand up, blowing a strand of hair from my face. "Hey," I say as breezily and naturally as I can, as though I haven't been loitering here waiting for them to make an appearance.

"Erin, this is our house guest…" Shane says.

"Jessie," she interrupts him.

"Yes," he nods as his eyes linger on her face, and jealousy gnaws at my insides. *Get a grip, Jessie.*

I walk over and extend my hand, seeing as Shane offers no further introduction.

"I'm Erin. Shane's lawyer," she says with a curt smile as she takes my outstretched hand.

"It's lovely to meet you," I lie.

"Well, it's been lovely to see you, as always, Shay," she says as she turns back to him. "But I need to get going. I can show myself out."

Shay!

"Of course. It's always a pleasure," he says softly as he kisses her cheek. I glare at the two of them. I bet he used to kiss her on the mouth.

"I'll be in touch." She gives him a last lingering look before turning around and walking to the elevator.

He looks at me as I stand there with a bottle of furniture polish in one hand and a cloth in the other.

"Cleaning?" he arches one eyebrow at me.

"Shay?" I snap back.

He glares at me. "Don't ever call me that."

"Fine. Are you two dating or something?" I frown at him.

He steps closer and wraps one arm around my waist and slides his free hand onto my ass. "No. She's my lawyer. Nothing more. Do you think I'd be fucking you with no protection if I was seeing other women?" he growls in my ear, and my insides tremble as his voice vibrates through my body.

"No," I whisper.

"So, don't ask me stupid fucking questions, Hacker."

"Okay," I frown and then he releases me and stalks off toward his office.

Asshole!

CHAPTER 34

JESSIE

*I*t's been two days since I first learned about Shane's ex-fiancée and he has mostly avoided me since. Who would have thought it would annoy him so much that I called him Shay? He didn't seem to mind when Erin purred it in his ear.

I sit in the den, looking at his office door, wondering whether to just go in there and clear the air with him because I can't stand this constant tension between the two of us. I seem to be always pushing his buttons lately, and not in a good way either.

I put the magazine I've been reading down on the sofa and stand up as voices approach from the hallway. Straining my ears, I'm sure it's Erin's voice. What the hell is she doing back here again?

Sure enough, a few seconds later, she glides gracefully past the living area in her impossibly high heels and heads straight to Shane's office. I sit down, picking up my magazine and flicking through it, but I can hardly focus on anything.

I stand up and make my way into the kitchen. I need to stop

obsessing about Shane and his ex. She's his lawyer and nothing more. And even if she isn't, it's no business of mine.

AN HOUR LATER, I'm in the kitchen stirring the sauce I'm making for tonight's dinner, when that now familiar, soft Irish voice speaks out behind me.

"Something smells nice."

I turn around and wipe the sauce from my hands on a towel as I come face to face with Erin. "Oh, thanks. It's just a recipe I found online."

She tilts her head and stares at me, sizing me up. No doubt she's scrutinizing the woman who is living in the same house as her ex-fiancé. I wonder if she still loves him?

"Can I help you with anything, Erin?" I say with a smile as I size her up right back. God, she really is beautiful. She's dressed in a navy suit today and she looks stunning.

"I was just looking for Conor," she says as she looks around the kitchen, as though he might jump out from a cabinet somewhere.

"I think he's asleep. He was working really late last night," I say. I don't add that he came to my room when he got home at six am and then he didn't leave to go to his own bed until two hours later. "Can I give him a message?" I ask, trying to be helpful.

She smirks at me and shakes her head. "I'm sure I can get the message to him myself. But thank you for your kind offer."

I suck in a breath. *Don't offend her, Jessie. She's their lawyer.*

"Okay." I force a smile and then I turn back to my sauce.

"What exactly do you do around here, Jessie?" she asks.

I close my eyes and count to five before turning back to her. "What did Shane tell you I do?"

She narrows her eyes at me. "If you think he might be the one for you, you're sadly mistaken."

"Is that so?" I snap.

"Shane will never put you before his brothers. He will never, ever make you a priority. He will never leave them to fend for themselves."

"Well, maybe I don't want him to," I frown at her.

She sucks on her top lip as she looks me up and down. "Hmm. You're not really his type, though. Maybe Conor's?" she laughs. "Perhaps you could do me and Shane a favor and take one of his brothers off his hands for him?"

"Perhaps you could do everyone a favor and get the hell out."

She walks across the kitchen, towering over me in her heels while I'm in my bare feet. "Don't make an enemy of me, Jessie," she snarls.

"Ditto." I snarl back.

She flicks her long blonde hair over her shoulder before she walks out of the kitchen. I stare after her, wondering what the hell that was about. Clearly, she does still love Shane. Does he still have any such feelings for her?

I turn off my sauce and make my way to his office. The door is open, and I walk straight in.

"Hacker. Come here," he growls as soon as he sees me.

I walk over to his desk. "Erin just left," I snap.

"I know," he stands up and walks over to me.

"What is the deal with you and her?"

He ignores my question and slides his hands over my hips and onto my ass, squeezing hard as his head drops to my neck.

"Shane. Are you even listening to me?" I groan as I lean my head back.

"No. Because I don't want to talk about Erin," he snaps as he walks me backwards across the room until I'm pressed against his filing cabinet.

"I only -"

"I just told you I don't want to talk about her, Hacker," he interrupts me. "I only want to fuck you." Then he spins me around until my front is pressed against the metal cabinet and he is pressed against my back. His cock is rock hard, and he pushes it against the seam of my ass. Erin left his office not less than five minutes ago and now he has a massive hard on for her that he intends to relieve using me.

"Shane," I gasp as he reaches beneath my oversized t-shirt and tugs my panties down my legs.

Then, he opens his zipper and bends his knees before he pushes his cock deep inside me.

"Fuck, you feel good," he grunts in my ear and I groan out loud. I resent the hell out of him fucking me as a poor substitute for Erin, but damn if his body doesn't feel good inside mine. I place my hands on the cabinet and lean into him as he reaches in front of me and rubs my clit to the same intense rhythm that he thrusts in and out of me.

"Shane," I moan out loud as he nails me to the cabinet while sucking on that sweet point on my neck. I wish he would say my name. Just once. Just so I know that it's me inside his head and not her.

He increases his pressure on my clit and a few moments later, I am coming apart around him and a rush of my cream coats his cock. Shane increases his pace further and a few seconds later he curses in Gaelic as he spurts inside me, hot and heavy.

He pulls out of me and steps backwards, and I take the opportunity to pull my panties back up. We both stand there panting for breath, but as the waves of my orgasm ebb away, the tears prick my eyes. Shane has always been an asshole to me, but he has taken his assholery to new heights today.

"Is there anything else?" I ask.

He looks up and frowns at me. "What? Well, not right now."

"Good. I'll leave you to your work then," I feign a smile before I walk out, leaving him standing in his office.

CHAPTER 35

SHANE

I sit in the armchair and watch Jessie with my brothers. So easy and relaxed. Liam has his arm casually around her shoulder while Mikey has one hand on her thigh and the other holding a bowl of popcorn. Whenever a funny part of the film comes on, she laughs and looks between the two of them. My little brothers smile back at her and I'm not sure I've ever seen them so happy before.

Conor sits on the armchair opposite and he rarely takes his eyes off her. My broken right-hand man who had been a shell of his former self after what happened with the Semenovs, with a contentment on his face that I haven't seen for a very long time. She looks over at him too, reminding him she's there, and that all he needs to do is say the word and she's his. Because she would do that for him. If he held out his hand to her now, she would leave the comfort of the sofa and the warmth of the twin's bodies against hers and go to him. She would do the same for Liam or Mikey too. They give her everything she could ever want or need, and she does the same for them.

Yet, she can barely stand to look at me. My heart races as I recall the last time I touched her. It was two days ago, and she has barely acknowledged me since. I miss her when she's not in my bed, but I accept she can't spend every night with me and I can live with that. Usually, she calls into my office at least once a day, and more often than not, I fuck her on my desk. So, to not touch her at all, to not feel the brush of her lips on my skin, or the perfect weight of her ass in my hands, I fucking hate it, and I miss her.

I was rough with her the other day, but then I often am. So, what the hell have I done to make her so pissed at me? If I called her name right now, would she come to me too? And if she did, would it be because she wanted to, or because of something else?

The film credits are rolling over the screen and I watch her stretch and yawn. Liam curls her hair around his fist and pulls her face to his, pressing a soft kiss against her temple. I wonder if she's planning on spending the night with the twins. If I have any say in it, she won't be.

I stand up. "Jessie," I growl, and all of their heads snap toward me. I have never called her by her name before. "We're going to bed."

She blinks at me, and Mikey squeezes her thigh reassuringly.

My heart pounds in my chest as I wait for her response. I have never felt this vulnerable in front of my brothers before. What if she says no? I'll have to walk over there and carry her out of here. But then she stands, and a wave of relief washes over me.

"Night, boys," she says before leaning down and kissing Mikey and Liam on the cheek. She walks toward me, her head slightly bowed, and as she reaches Conor, she stops to kiss him too. He's not satisfied with a peck on the cheek though and he pulls her into his lap, places his hands on either side of her face and kisses her deeply. She closes her eyes and leans into him and there is a connection between them that is so tangible, I could almost reach out and touch it. It makes me feel something I don't like feeling. After a few seconds, she pulls away.

"Goodnight, Angel," he whispers before giving her a slap on the ass as she stands up. She giggles, but then she stops again when she looks up at me. I turn and walk toward the hallway and she follows close behind.

CHAPTER 36

JESSIE

I walk along the hallway behind Shane, watching the powerful muscles in his back flexing beneath his white shirt. Did that really just happen? Did he just order me to bed like I'm a teenager? What the hell is that about? I obeyed him though, didn't I? Without question. Because he can play me like a six-string.

When we reach his room, he holds open the door and I step inside. I walk toward the middle of the room as the soft click of the door signals it closing behind us.

"Take off your clothes and lie on the bed," he says softly. His voice is as smooth as hot chocolate and it sends a shiver through my body.

My pulse thrums against my pressure points as I turn to face him and peel the oversized t-shirt over my head before dropping it onto the floor. Hooking my fingers into the side of my panties, I look him in the eye as I peel them down my legs and kick them off, so they land on top of the t-shirt.

He doesn't speak, but he rubs a hand over his jaw as his eyes roam over my naked body. My nipples pebble under his gaze and although I'm still mad at him, a rush of wet heat sears between my thighs.

Stepping backwards, I reach the bed and lie down on it. I look up at him as he walks toward me.

"Why have you been avoiding me, Hacker?" he asks as he begins unbuttoning his shirt.

My pulse quickens. The sight of Shane Ryan removing his clothes could be a Broadway show. I know I would pay good money to see it. "Because you're an asshole," I say with a smile.

He doesn't reply, but simply cocks one eyebrow at me as he shrugs off his shirt before his hands drop to his belt and he unbuckles it. My abdomen flutters at the sight of his powerful hands working the soft leather, pulling it through the metal buckle and letting it hang loosely. I lick my lips as he unzips his fly and pushes his suit pants and his boxers down his thick thighs in one swift movement before bending and pulling them off his feet along with his socks. When he stands up straight again, his cock is rock hard, glistening with pre-cum. I swallow at the sight as my body thrums with the anticipation of what is about to happen.

"So, why have you been avoiding me?" he asks again as he takes a step toward the bed.

I flash one eyebrow at him. "You're an intelligent man, Shane. I'm sure you can figure it out."

He narrows his eyes at me. "Well, I can only assume it has something to do with my refusal to talk to you about my past? But I have been one hundred percent clear with you from the start about what this is." His eyes drop to the space between my thighs, that is already starting to throb with need, as though to emphasize his point. "So, why, Hacker? And don't make me ask you for a fourth time."

I have to stop myself from rolling my eyes at him. "It's not that you wouldn't talk to me. It was what happened after," I say, suddenly feeling vulnerable in front of him in a way that I never have before.

"I fucked you?" he snaps with a frown.

"Did you?"

"I'm pretty fucking sure I did."

I lean up on my elbows and tilt my head as I stare at him. "Well, it kind of felt like it was Erin you were really fucking."

The fire flashes in his eyes. Is that for her? Does he feel that heat and anger simply at the sound of her name? He steps toward the bed and crawls over me, holding himself up on his forearms until our faces are only a few inches apart. "I was most definitely inside you, not Erin. So, what the fuck does that mean?"

I glare into his blazing green eyes. "I get that sex is all you want from me. But I don't appreciate you screwing me when you've got a hard on for another woman."

His nostrils flare as he glares back at me. "You think that was for her?"

"Wasn't it? She had literally just walked out of the room and your dick was almost busting through your zipper."

He gives a subtle shake of his head. "I don't like sulking, Hacker," he says with a snarl. "But just this once I will indulge you. I told you that I don't want Erin and I am not a liar. But I can't help the fact that she still wants me. She sat on my desk and then she crossed her legs to make sure I got a good view of her panties."

I suck in a breath and blink at him. Is this supposed to make feel better?

"But all I could think about was you sitting on my desk the other day in those damn pink panties that were soaked with your cream. That was why I was hard, Hacker." Pushing his knee between my thighs, he nudges my legs apart and then settles himself between them. He pushes his hips against mine, and his erection presses against my opening. "*You* make me hard."

"I thought..."

"I told you I have no feelings for her like that. Not anymore," he interrupts me.

I want to ask him if that means he has feelings for me, but I don't dare.

"So, the next time you doubt me, do me the courtesy of speaking to me about it instead of sulking like a spoiled brat. Okay?"

"Okay," I whisper.

He narrows his eyes at me and my heart lurches into my throat. He presses his lips against my collarbone and then slowly moves down my body, covering my breasts and my stomach in kisses.

"Shane," I moan his name as I rake my fingers through his thick hair.

"You smell so good, Hacker," he mumbles against my skin before his head dips lower and he settles between my thighs. He slips his tongue inside me and I reward him with a rush of wet heat. A few seconds later, his tongue is replaced by two of his thick fingers and I groan out loud, arching my back off the bed in order to take more of him. My walls clench around him, sucking him deeper inside. He licks the length of my folds and sucks my clit into his mouth, swirling his tongue over the sensitive bundle of nerve endings until I'm writhing beneath him. He curls his fingers inside me, pressing against that sweet spot while he sucks and licks and it's not long before I am shouting his name out loud as my climax tears through my body.

He stays there until the last of my orgasm has trembled through me, before sliding his fingers out of my channel and moving up the bed so we're face to face. "You taste so fucking sweet too," he grins at me.

I place my hands on either side of his face, which glistens with my arousal. "Show me," I breathe.

"You want to taste yourself?" he growls.

"Yes," I pant. I want him to seal his mouth over mine and kiss me the way that I have imagined him kissing me since the first time he summoned me to his office. But he has never kissed me, and I realize he's not going to as he slides one hand back down my body and slips one finger inside my slick channel.

A few seconds later, he lifts his finger to my lips. "Open," he commands.

Opening my mouth, I allow him to push his wet finger inside. I suck on it, tasting my sweet, salty arousal on his skin. His eyes burn into mine and his Adam's apple bobs as he swallows hard.

"Fuck. Jessie." he growls as he moves his face closer to mine. Then he slides his finger from between my lips. I'm about to protest, but before I can utter a sound, he seals his mouth over mine, pushing his tongue inside and flicking it against my own. I groan into him as I taste myself again on him. There is something so hot and intimate about his kiss. And as his tongue claims my mouth, he drives his huge cock into me, swallowing my moans with his own.

I melt into him as he nails me to his bed. Our bodies pressed together so closely I can hardly tell where one of us ends and the other begins. I know I will probably pay for this. Shane will punish me for getting too close to him. For being vulnerable. For making him kiss me. But right now, I don't care. All that matters is me and him and the things he makes me feel.

CHAPTER 37

JESSIE

*I*t's been almost two days since Shane kissed me, and as I suspected he would, he's been doing his best to avoid me since. I'm walking past his office on my way to the library when he calls my name.

"You need something?" I ask him as I pop my head inside.

"Yes," he growls.

I step into the room and resist the urge to roll my eyes. "What is it?"

"Come over here."

I walk to his desk, and he pulls me to him, wrapping an arm around my waist. "I'm having a shitty day. And I missed you last night, Hacker."

I smile at him. So much for one night. That was what he said when we first had sex a few weeks ago. "I'd say that I missed you too, but Conor kept me pretty occupied," I grin at him.

"I know. I heard you moaning his name."

"Did it make you hard?" I purr.

He grabs my hand and places it over his stiff cock. "Yes. And it's been like that ever since."

"Sorry."

He narrows his eyes at me and I bite my lip nervously under the heat of his intense gaze. "Turn around," he says eventually.

I do as he asks, and he bends me over the desk in one swift movement, pulling my t-shirt up over my ass until it's bunched around my waist. I already feel the familiar heat pooling between my thighs from his touch. He pulls my panties roughly to one side and without warning he slips two of his fingers inside me.

"Shane," I groan out loud.

"Why are you always soaking wet? You make it far too easy for me to slide my cock into you whenever I want to."

He pulls his fingers out of me, and the sound of his zipper opening makes me suck in a breath. A few seconds later, he's filling me with his cock instead and nailing me to his desk.

"This cunt is so fucking hot and tight," he groans as he leans over me. "You think I can make you drench me with your cum again, little Hacker?"

"You can try," I pant as my walls squeeze around him.

Shane is still fucking me over his desk when Conor walks into the room a few moments later. He flashes his eyebrows at us, but he doesn't make any attempt to leave. "You just can't keep out of that sweet pussy, can you?" Conor says with a shake of his head as he takes a seat on the sofa.

I turn my head to Shane, assuming he's going to stop, or at least tell Conor to leave, but he places his hand on my back between my shoulder blades, pressing me against the desk as he carries on pounding me.

"Did you get the information we needed?" he growls as he slips his hand between me and the desk, pressing on my swollen clit and rubbing firmly until my legs start to tremble.

I groan out loud as my eyes lock with Conor's. He reaches down and palms his cock, rubbing it through his trousers as he watches his brother nail me to his desk.

"I'm still working on Chester," Conor replies, his eyes never leaving mine. "He should have something for me by the end of the day."

"Shane," I pant.

"Well, see that he does," Shane growls as his hand reaches for my hair. Wrapping it around his fist, he pulls my head up slightly and leans over me, pressing his lips against my ear. "If this is going to work, you're going to have to get used to being fucked in front of all of us. If you're a really good girl, maybe one day we will all fuck you at the same time. So, I want you to look at my brother while you come all over my cock," he growls as he presses down on my clit and I come apart around him, my knees trembling and my cum spilling out of me. "Shane." I groan as he grinds out his own release while my eyes remain locked on Conor's.

"That's my hacker," he says against my ear as he leans over me and gives me a soft kiss on the cheek. He stands up, pulling me with him and onto his lap as he sits down. His arms circle around my waist as he holds me against his chest.

"Oh, Erin says she needs to meet with you again," Conor says.

"Fine," Shane nods. "Tell her I'll stop by her place tomorrow at eleven."

My whole body tenses at the idea of him being alone with her. Shane feels it too and his hand slides up my inner thigh. "I've told you she means nothing to me, Jessie," he says in my ear, but loud enough for Conor to hear. "Now, what is it going to take for you to believe me?"

"I do believe you," I whisper as he pulls my panties to the side again and runs his fingers over my slick folds.

"Shane," I groan. "Don't."

Shane looks at Conor and nods toward the door. Conor stands and winks at me before walking out and closing the door behind him. "Why not?" he says as he slides two fingers inside me and I can't help but clench around him as he rubs against that sweet spot.

"You are the only woman I have any interest in. I can barely keep out of your sweet cunt. I've just fucked you, in front of my brother, and my cock is already weeping for you again. So, why do you have a problem with me meeting with my lawyer?"

I shake my head. "Shane, please," I beg as he brushes the pad of his thumb over my clit. "Let me go."

"Tell me why you don't believe me," he insists as he keeps thrusting his fingers in and out of me. My orgasm builds slowly until suddenly it comes out of nowhere. I let it crash over me and then I cling to the collar of his jacket as the tears start to run down my cheeks.

"Jessie?" he says as he frowns at me. "What the hell is wrong?"

I scramble up off him and swallow. "Nothing," I say as I head for the door.

he's up off his chair and blocking my way before I can escape. "Jessie," he snarls.

I look up at him through my tear-filled eyes and feel like a complete idiot for what I'm about to admit, but he's not going to let me go. "I know you don't want her now," I choke down the tears. "And I know that you want me. At least a part of me. But you loved her, Shane. You wanted all of her. You loved her so much that you were going to leave everything you knew for her, and I can't help it, but I hate that," I sniff.

He steps back, blinking at me, allowing me the space to leave and I take my chance and walk out of his office. I head toward my room, where I plan on staying for the rest of the night. Shane has always made it clear that he and I are only about sex, and I have just gone and made a complete fool of myself. At least I never told him I love him, and I want him to love me too. That would have been completely disastrous.

. . .

186

I'M LYING in bed watching TV when my bedroom door opens. Looking up, I am about to tell my visitor to leave me alone. I've had about enough of the Ryan brothers for one day, but despite that I can't help but smile as Mikey and Liam shuffle into the room with huge grins on their faces. Mikey is holding a tub of Ben and Jerry's in one hand, and a bag of candy in the other.

"Need some company, baby?" Liam asks.

"We heard Shane's being an asshole," Mikey adds with a grin.

"Where did you hear that?" I flash my eyebrows at them, sure that Shane wouldn't have mentioned our encounter.

"Okay, well, we didn't exactly hear about it, but Shane is in a foul mood and being with you is the only thing that cures his bad moods lately. So, if he's not with you…" Mikey says with a shrug.

"I must be the reason for his foul mood?" I offer.

"Exactly," Liam says as he slides onto the bed and lies next to me. "And we know you're not an asshole, so it must be him."

I can't help but laugh. "I'm not sure about your logic, but I appreciate you having my back."

"And your front," Mikey grins as he slides onto the bed on the other side of me until I'm sandwiched between them. Liam hands me the bag of candy while Mikey rips the top from the ice cream and hands me a spoon.

A FEW HOURS LATER, I wake with a start. The room is in darkness, but I'm sandwiched between the warm, hard bodies of Liam and Mikey. I must have fallen asleep watching the movie we chose earlier. Smiling as I snuggle against Mikey's hard chest, I pull Liam's arm tighter around my waist. I am safe and warm and content. Suddenly, I understand why cats purr.

Liam stirs behind me. "Are you okay, baby?" he breathes in my ear.

"Yes," I whisper. "Better than okay. I'm not sure I've ever been happier."

He rubs his jaw over the soft skin on my neck. "Hmm. Me too," he replies sleepily.

CHAPTER 38

JESSIE

*D*ropping the weight bar onto the floor, I stand straight and flex my shoulders before pulling out my earbuds.

"That's an impressive weight for a short-stack like you," a low voice says behind me. "What is that. One ten?"

"One twenty actually," I say, wiping the sweat from my brow with the back of my hand. "What can I do for you, Shane?"

I turn around to find him already dressed in one of his impeccably tailored suits, despite it being only 8 a.m. He looks damn near good enough to eat and he knows it. I'm so glad that my cheeks are already flushed from my gym session as I remember what I said to him last night. I'm aware that it's ridiculous to be upset about the fact that he once loved Erin, but I can't help it. He's so closed off from me. He reminds me at every opportunity that I am nothing more than sex to him. I have asked myself what is so special about Erin that she was able to capture his heart, but I suppose I know the answer. She's smart and successful, and she looks like some kind of blonde goddess.

"Finish your workout. Grab a shower and get dressed. We're going out," he says coolly.

"Where?"

"You have such an issue with me going to see Erin. You can come with me."

"What? No, thanks. I'd rather not."

"It's a pity you don't have much choice then. We're leaving at nine-thirty. Don't keep me waiting," he smirks before turning around and walking back out of the gym.

I stare after him and shake my head. Arrogant asshole! What the hell does he want me to go see Erin with him for? So I can watch her fawning all over him and calling him Shay? Is this part of my punishment for telling him how I felt about her?

AN HOUR AND A HALF LATER, I walk down the hallway toward Shane. He's glaring at his watch, but I can't help but smile at the undisguised look in his eyes when he sees me. My usual attire is skinny jeans and tank tops, pajamas, or more often than not, one of the guys' shirts and my underwear. I checked my wardrobe after my shower and was suddenly incredibly grateful for Conor's excellent taste and his insistence that I try on some sexy dresses when he took me shopping a few weeks earlier. I've chosen a knee length, skin tight green dress that shows the perfect amount of cleavage to be classy while still showing off my assets. To top it all off, I've paired it with some six-inch heels, or fuck-me pumps, as Conor's friend, Callie, called them.

I strut along the hallway, enjoying the expression on Shane's face as I make my way toward him. Conor and Liam were just starting their workouts when I was leaving mine earlier, and they're walking along from the other end of the apartment in just their gym shorts, with a towel each slung over their shoulders.

Liam wolf whistles so loudly that it echoes all around the room.

"Damn, Jessie!" Conor says appreciatively as they reach me. He pulls me into his arms and tries to kiss me.

"Conor. You're a sweaty mess," I squeal as I untangle myself from him. "But it is nice to be appreciated, boys."

From the corner of my eye, I notice Shane shake his head.

"You make sure you come find me when you get back from wherever you two are going," Conor winks at me.

"Not if I find her first," Liam nudges him on the arm.

"If you're quite done, we have to go," Shane says with a sigh.

"Bye boys. I'll see you both later," I smile, turning back to Shane as the elevator arrives. I step inside first and stand with my back to the wall. He follows me inside and steps toward me. He leans close, his breath skittering over my cheek. "You clean up good, Hacker. I'm going to fuck you in nothing but those heels later."

The breath catches in my throat, but I glare at him. "We'll see." I flash him my best smile and he chuckles and steps back, leaning against the wall, fully aware that I would let him fuck me any way and anywhere.

WE ARRIVE at Erin's office building over an hour later. I glance around as I step out of the elevator. "This place is fancy," I say as I struggle to keep pace with Shane in these damn heels.

"It should be for the money I pay her," he growls and then a few moments later, he stops outside a huge solid oak door, with a small glass window that has the name Erin McGrath, Managing Partner, stenciled onto it.

Shane knocks, and Erin smiles widely as she opens the door to let him in.

"Shay. It's lovely to see you," she says, placing her hands on his arms and kissing his cheek.

"Hi, Erin," he says. "I hope you don't mind that I brought Jessie along today."

She looks behind Shane and at me and the disappointment is clear on her face, but it's quickly replaced by her huge, fake smile. "Of course not. Come on in both of you."

I walk into Erin's office. It is enormous, with floor to ceiling windows and a huge glass desk in the center of the room. There's a large chrome bookcase at one end of the room crammed full of law texts and journals. The whole place is polished chrome and glass and the height of sophistication. I sit in a black leather chair and don't move, afraid to touch something that might cost a few thousand dollars and break it.

I listen intently as Shane and Erin discuss the legalities of the Ryan brothers' business and the transferring of ownership of some property in Ireland to Shane. They talk business for over half an hour, and I'm beginning to wonder why Shane bothered bringing me here. It seems like they're wrapping things up when Shane throws me for a curveball.

"You did some work with the Russians a few years back, Erin?"

"You know I did, Shay," she purrs. "I stopped working for them when we got engaged, at your insistence."

"If I remember rightly, you did some work with the Ivanovs?"

"What if I did?" She sits up straighter in her chair now and frowns at him and suddenly, I am much more interested in this conversation.

"You ever hear of one of them named Alexei? Or a woman named Nataliya Vasiliev who married into the family?"

She stares at him and then at me.

"You can trust, Jessie," he assures her. "She hates the Russians as much as we do."

"You trust a woman who you barely even know, Shay? That's so unlike you." She flashes her eyebrows at him.

"Do you remember, Erin?" he sighs.

She doesn't answer him, but she looks directly at me. "Is this something to do with you?" she asks, her lips curling back over her teeth, making her beautiful face look strangely unattractive.

I lick my lips. "I am interested in finding out about the Ivanovs," I whisper. "Anything you can find out about them might be useful."

"Why?" she snaps.

"I... I have an interest in them," I stammer. I wasn't prepared for this change of direction at all and my usual lies don't trip off my tongue quite so easily.

"An interest?" she snorts.

"Erin," Shane snaps. "Why we want the information isn't important. Can you answer the damn question?"

"That was all so long ago. The Ivanovs are one of the oldest families in Russia. they're not easy people to work with. I'd have to pull some of my old personal files, but, I'll have a look when I have time to, if it's important to you, Shay."

"Thanks, Erin," he says as he stands to leave.

I stand too, and Erin walks toward me, looking me up and down like she's just found me stuck to the bottom of one of her Louboutins. "You must have a magical pussy or something, girl, to have this one fighting your corner."

I blink at her and step back. I'd like to slap her in the face, but she's important to Shane, and she could be a big help in finding out who Nataliya is.

"Enough," Shane intervenes for me and Erin smiles sweetly at him. He still kisses her cheek before we leave the office though. Asshole! "I'll be in touch," he says smoothly.

We walk out of Erin's office and I take a deep breath, relieved to be out of there. Shane turns to me and scowls as we walk along the hallway. I frown back at him. What the hell have I done now? I was perfectly nice to Erin, even when she was being a complete bitch to me.

As we pass the ladies' room, he stops and grabs my hand, pushing open the door and pulling me inside. He closes the door behind us and turns the lock with a loud click.

"Shane? What are you..." I start to say but before I can finish my sentence he's on me, pressing me against the tiled wall with the weight of his body. He lifts one hand to my face, dragging his thumb across my lip before he cups my cheek. He rubs the pad of his thumb along my jawline and stares at me so intently, the warmth spreads through my core.

"You know that she means nothing to me?" He frowns.

I swallow hard. "Yes. You told me that."

He bends his head low and seals his lips over mine, forcing his tongue inside my mouth and kissing me roughly. Just as suddenly, he pulls back from me, leaving me wanting more. "So, why don't you believe me, Hacker?"

"I do," I protest.

"Does she intimidate you?" He narrows his eyes at me, and I swear sometimes this man can read my mind.

"A little, I guess," I admit.

He takes hold of my chin and tilts my head up, so I have no choice but to look at him. "You know that no-one can make you feel inferior without your permission, right?"

I roll my eyes at his pop psychology and he squeezes my jaw tighter. "Don't roll your eyes at me. Why do you let her talk to you like that?" he scowls at me now. "You're like a different person around her. Where is my little firecracker?"

"I don't know. She's just so damn perfect, she seems like she has her shit completely together. I mean has she ever made a single mistake in her life?" I flash one eyebrow at him.

"Believe me, she's made plenty."

"Why don't you let me call you Shay?" I whisper.

"Because I fucking hate it. She calls me it because she knows it's one of the few ways she has left to push my buttons."

"Oh." I chew on my lip. I hadn't even considered that. "You

and her just look so good together," I say as the emotion wells up in my chest. "She's perfect for you."

"Perfect? You've said that twice now. And if she was perfect for me, we'd be together, wouldn't we?" he growls and suddenly I'm aware of his free hand reaching down and lifting the edge of my dress. The soft fabric glides over my thighs as he gently pulls it, raising it higher.

Pressing his lips against my ear, he whispers. "You want to know what's perfect?"

"What?" I pant as his hand skims over the bare skin on my thigh and between my legs.

"This sweet cunt," he growls as he pulls my panties to one side and pushes two fingers straight into my hot, wet entrance.

"Shane," I groan as the pain and pleasure burns through me.

"Perfect the way it is always soaked with your cum, Hacker. Always ready for me. The way you squeeze my cock when you're desperate to come. How fucking sweet you taste. It's so damn perfect that I think about being inside it all fucking day," he growls as he pulls his fingers out of me and drops his other hand from my face. The familiar jangle of his belt being unbuckled causes a sudden rush of wet heat between my thighs.

I wrap my arms around his neck as my cheeks flush with fire. He is about to fuck me in this restroom, which to be fair is possibly the fanciest one I've ever been in in my life, in his ex-girlfriend's office, and I am desperate for him to.

The sound of his zipper opening makes my insides melt like warm butter and I spread my legs wider apart to allow him easier access. "Eyes on me, Hacker," he snaps, noticing that my eyes have dropped down to his hands to watch as he takes his stiff cock out.

I look up at him again. His green eyes hold mine captive as he pulls my dress up around my waist and slides my panties aside once more. I'm thankful I chose to wear these fuck me pumps because without them he's almost a foot taller than me.

He grabs one of my thighs, pulling it up and wrapping it around his waist before bending his knees and driving himself into me.

"Is this what I have to do to prove to you that you're the only woman I'm interested in?" he groans as he nails me to the tiled wall.

"Don't pretend this is all about you making me feel better," I pant.

"There's my firecracker," he chuckles. "And yeah, this is also about me not being able to keep my fucking hands off you," he growls as he hits that perfect spot, releasing a rush of my arousal. My walls squeeze tighter around him, drawing him in as deep as I can.

"Stop squeezing me, Hacker, or I'm not going to last five minutes."

"Well that could be good thing, seeing as we're in your ex-girlfriend's restroom."

He growls in frustration as he thrusts into me harder than before. "But you'd love her to catch us though, wouldn't you?"

"You're an asshole."

"Maybe. Now stop talking and let me fuck you. The only word I want to hear from your mouth is my goddamn name when I make you come."

CHAPTER 39

JESSIE

*I*t's been almost a week since our trip to Erin's office. She still hasn't provided Shane with any information about the Ivanovs, but I suppose she's a busy lady. I've spent so little time digging into them myself that I can hardly blame her. Finding the Wolf used to be my only goal in life. It occupied my mind constantly. But, these days I find myself almost permanently distracted by the four fine-ass men who are currently sitting eating dinner with me.

Conor looks up at me as he licks his fingers clean. "That was some meal, Angel." He grins.

"It sure was," Liam adds while Shane simply winks at me, but I know that is the equivalent of his seal of approval.

"Thank you. Mikey has been teaching me," I blush. "I'm glad you all liked it."

Mikey walks up to me and kisses my cheek. "It was perfect, Red. You're a natural."

"I think our talented new chef deserves a treat for working so hard in this kitchen all day." Conor says with a flash of his eyebrows.

"Oh? Like what?" I grin at him.

"How about a night out?"

"At the club?" I ask with a huge grin.

"Anywhere you want, Angel," Conor replies.

"You sure you want to go to the club?" Shane asks.

"Yes. I love dancing. I haven't been out dancing for as long as I can remember." In fact, I've done it about four times before in my life.

"Then let's get our asses in some showers and get ready," Mikey says with a big smile on his face. "You want any help getting ready, Red?" he says to me.

"No. Everyone to their own showers, or we won't get out this side of midnight," Shane snaps.

A LITTLE UNDER two hours later, I walk out of my room and down the hallway to where my four guys are standing, chatting with each other. they're dressed in suits, but not their usual work ones. No, these are both more casual and somehow even sexier. Each of them has their shirt open at the collar and my ovaries almost explode at the sight of them. Do I really get to have my pick of these guys?

Mikey sees me first and he wolf whistles so loudly, I blush to the roots of my hair. I pull the hem of my dress down nervously. "Is this too short?" I say, referring to the black leather and mesh mini dress that I've chosen.

"No," Mikey says with a vigorous shake of his head as he walks toward me, taking one of my hands in his before he twirls me around while Conor and Liam loudly voice their approval. Shane is quiet as usual, but his eyes linger on the exposed skin of my thighs as I walk toward the elevator where he's standing with his two brothers. When I reach them, Shane grabs my hand and spins me around until I'm facing the doors.

"Let's go," he growls, but he slips his hand around my waist and holds me tight against his body before his other hand slides between my thighs and up my dress. He palms my pussy possessively. "Don't forget who this belongs to, Jessie. If anyone gets even a glimpse of these panties tonight, I'll spank your ass so hard you won't be able to sit down for a week."

His brothers chuckle softly beside us while I stand there biting my lip and wondering why I find Shane's sudden possessiveness so damn hot. A hard spanking from Shane Ryan makes me hot and wet and needy.

"They won't," I breathe. "Promise." Despite how much I would like him to deliver on that promise, I'm not in the habit of flashing my panties, or anything else, in public.

We walk through the crowded club toward the VIP area. There are scantily dressed clubbers everywhere, men and women, bodies pressed up against each other in the dark space, but none of them get close to me as I'm flanked by my four hot, protective bodyguards. I step into the booth and the Ryan brothers follow me. I'd have to be blind and stupid not to notice the attention they draw when they walk through the crowd - the attention that I draw. I can feel the eyes on me and almost hear the questions buzzing through people's heads. Who is she? Is she with one of them? Which one?

I'm not used to drawing attention to myself. In fact, I've done my best to avoid it for the past eight years. But as I sit down, and Shane and Liam sit either side of me, draping their arms around me possessively, I can't help but feel a sense of satisfaction, and a massive fuck you to all the people who ever told me I wasn't pretty enough, or good enough.

Shane turns his body toward mine, placing his warm hand on my thigh, and sliding it up the edge of my dress. "You look incredible, Hacker," he mouths against my ear as his hand slips between my thighs again and up toward my panties. "I want to fuck you right here in this booth."

I bite on my lower lip as his words cause a rush of wet heat in my core. "You wouldn't, though, right?" I breathe.

"Oh, yes, I would. But I'd clear this club out first. I don't want any of the assholes in here who have been drooling over you since we walked in seeing you being fucked, do I?"

I suck in a breath. God, his filthy mouth is in overdrive tonight. Maybe I should wear sexy mini-dresses more often. "No. So can we just enjoy the music for now?" I smile at him.

"Okay," he growls. "But I'm warning you I will shut this place down without a second's hesitation and spank your ass right here on this table before I fuck you, if you keep biting that lip and driving me crazy."

Liam must hear him because he laughs softly beside me. "Okay. No biting my lip," I reply just before I look up to see two young, tall blondes making their way up to our booth. They make a beeline for Conor and Mikey. "You want to dance?" One of them asks with a smile.

"No. I don't dance," Conor replies.

"Me neither," Mikey adds.

She shrugs her shoulders and then looks up at Liam and Shane. "How about you two?" she says, licking her plump red lips.

Shane scowls at her while Liam starts to laugh out loud. Shane opens his mouth to speak, but I put my hand on his thigh, squeezing to let him know I've got this. I have to shout to be heard over the music. "I think I've got them all pretty tied up here, girls, so do us all a solid and go back to your dates. I'm sure they'll need to get you home soon, so you don't break your curfew."

"Bitch," one of them snaps before they turn around and head back to the dance floor.

"Ouch," Liam laughs.

I shrug. "Hey. I'm not the jealous type, but I'm sitting right here. The nerve of some people."

Liam grabs my face and turns my head before kissing me softly just as *Ride it* by DJ Regard starts playing, and I pull back from him. "Oh, I love this song."

"Me too," Conor smiles as he holds out a hand to me. "Come dance with me, Angel."

"I thought you didn't dance?" I arch one eyebrow at him.

"I'll dance with you," he grins as he pulls me up from my seat and I follow him to the edge of the dance floor to a spot where we're still in view of the booth and the rest of the Ryan brothers. I can't fail to notice that almost every woman we pass by gives him the once over. He is incredibly handsome, and I imagine most of the people in this club know he owns it. There is something incredibly intoxicating about power, and the Ryan brothers have that by the bucket-load. The fact that they're all as hot as hell makes them completely irresistible to a lot of women, including me, it seems.

We stop near a stone pillar and Conor slips his hands over my hips and onto my ass, pressing his groin against mine as our hips sway to the music. He dips his head to my neck and rubs his nose along my jawline. The bass thumps in my ears and vibrates through my body, making my insides thrum with energy. I'm hyper aware of the warmth of Conor's body pressed against mine, his hands squeezing my ass, and his hot breath on my neck as we grind against each other.

He whispers the lyrics in my ear as one of his hands slides up my body, caressing me softly until he reaches my throat. He brushes his hand beneath my hair and palms the back of my neck as his lips skate across my skin. I wrap my arms around his neck and tilt my head back, and he opens his mouth and presses his teeth against my skin. I lean into him. I like it when he bites.

"You think anyone would notice if I fuck you right here?" he breathes.

"Yes," I purr as I roll my hips, dragging my body over his hard length. "Because every woman in this club is watching you."

"Maybe they're watching you, Angel? Dancing with you is dangerous, Jessie," he says before he takes my earlobe between his teeth and tugs lightly.

"I thought you lived for danger, Conor Ryan," I reply with a smile.

He lifts his head and stares at me, his eyes narrowed. I think he's about to say something, but then he seems to change his mind. Bending his head low, he presses his mouth against mine, licking the seam of my lips until my mouth opens for him, allowing him to push his tongue inside as his other hand slides up my body and they both fist in my hair while he holds my head still so he can claim me completely. We continue moving in perfect sync, grinding to the music as it vibrates through my whole body and the rest of the world falls away.

CHAPTER 40

JESSIE

*A*ll five of us step out of the elevator and into the apartment. Mikey and Liam each give me a kiss on the cheek before they head off to bed while Conor keeps my hand firmly grasped in his. He squeezes, and goosebumps prickle along my forearm. Ever since we danced to that hot song about three hours earlier, I knew that I'd be spending the night in his bed.

The club was amazing. I haven't had that much fun, well ever. I danced all night. Mostly on my own, but up there in the booth with the boys' eyes on me the entire time.

"Night," Shane growls as he steps out of the elevator and stalks down the hall toward his office.

I stare after him. He has been watching me like a hawk all night, but for the last hour he has barely spoken to me. I know I didn't put a foot wrong and I wonder if I will ever understand his mood swings.

"What's crawled up his ass tonight?" I whisper.

Conor laughs softly. "You don't know?"

I turn and look up at him. "No."

He cups my chin in his hand and narrows his eyes at me.

"He's pissed because his sexy little hacker was very well behaved, and so no-one got even the tiniest glimpse of her panties."

"So?"

"So, he's got no reason to drag you into his office and spank your ass." He arches an eyebrow at me and I feel an unexpected rush of wet heat between my thighs as I recall what he said before we left for the club.

I bite on my lower lip as I stifle the groan that threatens to escape my lips at the idea of Shane Ryan spanking me.

Conor frowns as he leans his head closer to me. He brushes the pad of his thumb along my jawline before dipping his head lower and pressing his lips against mine. I push up onto my tiptoes as I kiss him back, but just as I deepen our kiss, he pulls away.

"Go on," he nods his head toward Shane's office. "Go to him."

"What?" I blink. "But I'm staying with you tonight."

He sighs softly as he stares at me with those dreamy, dark brown eyes. "I'm not sure I can give you what you're looking for tonight, Angel."

"You can always give me what I want," I breathe.

"Yeah. And I can give you what you need too. That's why I know what you need isn't me. Not right now. You're looking for some pain to take the edge off. And I get that. But I can't do that with you." He drops his hand.

"But, Conor," I start to say. The last thing I want to do is hurt him.

"And that's okay," he adds with a smile. "I don't want to be that for you, Angel. Maybe one day, but not now."

I stretch up, placing my hand on his jaw and running my fingertips over his beard. "How do you understand me so well?" I ask softly.

"Because we're the same, Angel," he whispers. "Now, go get yourself some punishment and I'll see you in the morning."

I smile at him and I almost say the words, but for some reason, they stick in my throat. Telling Conor Ryan that I love him is the last brick in the wall. Once I do that, my last line of defense is gone.

"Thank you," I whisper instead as I push my body against his and pull his face to mine. I kiss him softly and he groans into my mouth. "Go, Jessie, before I change my mind and carry you to bed."

I pull back, rolling my lips over my teeth as I savor the taste of him. "Night, big guy." I say before I walk down the hallway to Shane's office.

WHEN I REACH the door to Shane's office, it's open, and I step inside. He's sitting at his desk staring at his computer even though it's clear that it's not switched on.

"Everything okay?" I ask him.

He looks up at me and blinks. "I assumed you were with Conor?"

"I was. But then I remembered something, and I thought I should tell you about it," I say as I walk toward his desk.

"What's that?"

"You remember when I was dancing earlier?" I step closer.

"Yes?"

"And Mikey dropped his little pocket-knife, and I bent to pick it up for him?"

"Yeah," he scowls at me as he runs a hand over the dark stubble on his jaw.

"I think that one of your bouncers might have seen my panties," I breathe.

His eyes darken in an instant and his eyes roam over my body, making my nipples pebble beneath the fabric of my bra.

"Hacker," he growls as he holds out his hand. I take it and he pulls me toward him. "You think? You'd better be sure because if

I punish you, it will hurt." I know that it will but my pussy clenches in anticipation anyway. "Not to mention that my bouncer is fired," he adds.

"What? You can't fire someone because he got a glimpse of my panties," I say. Shit! I hadn't considered that.

"I can, and I will, Hacker," he scowls at me.

"Then maybe I got it wrong. He didn't see them. Please don't fire him, Shane."

"So, you just came in here and straight up lied to me?" He arches one eyebrow.

"I was just trying to…" I don't finish the sentence. But I don't have to because he knows exactly what I was doing.

"You thought you'd come in here looking for some fun, looking for me to punish you? Which obviously I'm going to do now because you've just lied to me. But you could have cost a man his job."

Well, shit! This escalated quickly. "I'm sorry. I didn't think about it like that."

"What have I warned you about lying to me?" he snarls and goosebumps prickle over my entire body. Fear shivers along my spine, along with a tingle of excitement.

"Not to," I whisper.

"You could have simply walked in here and asked me to spank you," he says as he stands up from his chair.

"I know," I breathe.

"And you must also know that the punishment for lying to me is going to be a damn sight worse than any I'd have given you for inadvertently flashing your panties?"

The heat throbs between my thighs at that realization. "Yes," I almost whimper.

He nods. "Turn around."

I do as he says until I'm facing his large mahogany desk. He places one hand on my hip and his other one between my shoulder blades, pressing me down against the cool wood. I lie there with my face against the mahogany, wondering how the hell I let this happen.

Shane is pissed - for real. His fingers trail down my ass and over my outer thighs until he reaches the edge of my minidress, skimming over my hot skin as he lifts it gently. He pushes it up over my ass until it's bunched around my waist, and I suck in a deep breath as he grabs my panties in his powerful hands and tears them roughly over my skin.

My heart races and I'm hyper aware of my breathing becoming faster and heavier with each passing second. The metallic jangle of his buckle as he unfastens his belt reverberates around the room and my insides contract. The whisper of the soft leather sliding against the fabric of his suit pants makes my skin prickle with fear.

Shane Ryan is about to spank me with his belt. Fuck!

There is no warning. No prep spanking. Just the sound of leather cutting through the air before it lands on my ass with a loud, satisfying thwack.

It hurts like hell and I almost cry out, but I won't give him the satisfaction. I suck in a breath and brace myself for the next one. It lands even harder than the first.

"Will you ever lie to me again, Hacker?" he growls before the third blow slices across my ass cheeks.

"No," I say as I imagine the red welts that must be striping my ass right now.

"Your ass is a beautiful shade of pink, Hacker," he says as though reading my mind.

"I barely even felt it." I grind out the words and he draws in a sharp breath.

"Really?"

"Really," I snap.

"Well, it must be true because you just promised never to lie to me again. So," he growls as he lands the fourth one even harder and the tears spring to my eyes. My skin burns like a million tiny, fiery needles are dancing over my ass, but the wet heat still rushes between my thighs. Because Conor was right. Sometimes, I need to feel the pain, so I can give myself permission to have the pleasure too. I focus on my breathing. I have dealt with much more intense pain than this before. It's nothing really. My body is just not as used to it as it once was.

"You feel that?" he growls.

"Fuck you," I snarl.

"Fuck me?" he says as he lands the fifth blow and now the tears are streaming down my cheeks.

Damn! I'm not crying, but the sting of his belt makes my eyes water like hell. I don't want him to think he's made me cry, though. He's standing over me and he can't fail to see, but it doesn't make him falter and I love that. Because I would hate him to believe that I can't take this. I need this from him.

Shane brings the belt down on my ass another seven times and by the last one, my skin is on fire and I start to get a slight queasy sensation in my stomach. I close my eyes as I prepare for the next one, but his belt drops to the floor as he breathes heavily. I lie still, waiting to be dismissed, but then his firm hands run softly over the skin of my ass. I can't help pressing myself back against him slightly as his touch soothes the fire burning through my flesh.

"You like pain, Hacker."

It's a statement rather than a question, but I answer anyway. "Sometimes."

He slides one finger through my dripping folds and into my hot entrance.

"You must really like pain," he groans. "Because you're fucking soaking."

Heat flushes through my chest and onto my cheeks and my pussy is throbbing along with my ass. It aches for him. But he pulls my dress down, smoothing it over my ass, before grabbing me by the elbow and pulling me up.

"Go to bed. Your own bed."

Blinking up at him, I have to force myself not to cry for real. I want to call him an asshole, but I bite back the retort. I'm fed up of trying to second-guess his moods or figure out what he wants from me.

I give up.

Shane Ryan can go fuck himself.

CHAPTER 41

CONOR

I sit on the sofa in Shane's office watching him flick through some of the paperwork on his desk. As well as our more nefarious business dealings, we have plenty of legitimate ones too. I manage the club mostly, and Liam and Mikey take care of the illegal stuff, but that leaves the bulk of it to Shane. He works at least twelve hours a day and I wish he'd cut himself some slack sometimes.

"You need me to do anything with that?" I ask.

He looks up at me as though he'd forgotten I was even in the room. "What?" he frowns.

"I said, do you need any help?"

He sits back and runs a hand over the stubble on his jaw. "No. It's fine."

"Why don't you ask Jessie to help out with some of the admin stuff? Anything on the computer would take her half the time, and I know she'd be happy to be more useful around here."

"I'm not sure allowing her even more access to our businesses is a good idea."

"Why not? She lives in our house, Shane. If she wanted to

look at our business records, I'm pretty sure she'd just freaking hack her way in."

I watch as he sucks in a breath. "You need to be careful with her, Conor."

"What the fuck is that supposed to mean?" It's my turn to frown now.

"I mean. I was watching you in the club with her last night -"

"We were dancing," I interrupt him.

"You were almost fucking her in the middle of the club. You think with your dick when she's around."

"And you don't?" I snarl at him as anger begins to bubble beneath my skin.

He shrugs. "Maybe. But I don't look at her the way you do, Conor."

I scowl at him. Part of me is so annoyed because he's right. Last night she told me she thought I lived for danger, and that used to be true. But now, it seems like I live for her. For every touch, every smile, the way she laughs, and I almost told her so too. "Just what the fuck are you trying to say?"

"I'm saying she's getting too close. And no, not just to you, to all of us."

"What happened between you two last night?" I frown at him.

He frowns right back. "Why?"

"Because our girl was so fucking hot for you, I'd have assumed you'd be in a much better mood than this one today. In fact, it surprised me to see either of you out of bed before midday. And I didn't hear you either."

"You listening out for us, were you?"

"No," I snarl. God, he's being an asshole today. "But, usually. Well, she's not exactly quiet, is she? And when I sent her down that hallway to your office, she was after the spanking of her life. I thought you'd be at it all night after that?" I raise one eyebrow at him. We shared a much smaller apartment than this when we first came to New York and spanking is definitely Shane's thing. I also know that it's Jessie's too, and she sometimes needs a little pain to get off. And last night was one of those nights.

"Why did you send her to me?" he frowns. "She was supposed to be staying with you."

"I didn't exactly send her. She wanted you, so I told her to go to you."

His Adam's apple bobs as he swallows and I wonder what the hell stupid shit he pulled. I'm not going to ask him. What he and Jessie do in their private time together is between the two of them.

"Just be careful, Conor," he snaps. "She's not one of us."

My heart sinks in my chest. "Promise me you won't do anything stupid, Shane," I say with a sigh as I lean back against the sofa.

He doesn't answer. Instead, he glares at me silently.

"I mean it, Shane," I warn him. "She is not the fucking enemy."

"Okay." He holds his hands up in surrender.

I WALK along the hallway to Jessie's room. Her door is open and I step inside. She's lying on her bed working on her laptop. When she looks up and sees me, she gives me the most incredible smile and it makes my heart jump into my throat. How the hell did we ever live without this girl?

"Hey, big guy," she says as she closes her laptop.

"Hey, Angel," I say, walking over to her and sitting beside her. "I'm heading to bed. I've slept about five hours in two days. But, if you fancy curling up next to me later tonight, then you know where I am." I run my hand over her ass and she winces slightly before she rolls over so she's lying on her back, looking up at me.

"You got your spanking, then?"

"Yes," she breathes.

"Feel better now?"

"It's complicated," she rolls her eyes.

"You mean Shane is complicated?" I laugh.

"You could say that," she sighs.

"He's not really," I say as I run my hand up her thigh to the button of her jeans and open it. "If you remember one thing."

"And what's that?" she purrs as I lift her shirt up, exposing her stomach.

"The more he wants you in his life," I lean down and kiss her soft skin, right above her waistband. "The more he will push you away."

"Then he must want me real bad," she chuckles.

I flash my eyebrows at her. "Exactly, Angel," I growl as I pull down her zipper. Who needs sleep? She lifts her ass up and I wiggle her jeans and panties down over her hips and thighs. I can smell her sweet juices already, and I place a soft kiss on her mound.

"And of course, I will come and curl up with you later. I don't like sleeping on my own. And I love that I always know exactly what you want from me," she says as I work her jeans and underwear off and down over her legs. Pulling them over her ankles, I toss them onto the floor.

"That's because I always want the same thing." I chuckle as I spread her thighs apart and run two fingers through her slick folds.

"Don't say that," her voice trembles, forcing me to look up at her.

"Say what?"

"That you only want me for one thing." She blinks and I notice the tears pricking her eyes.

I move up toward her and wrap a hand gently around her

throat. "That's not what I said. And you *know* that's not true, Angel."

She bites on her lip and it trembles. I have never seen this girl cry. Not even when she had a semi-automatic stuck in her face. Or when that Russian was about to murder her and she ended up covered in his blood. I could throttle Shane for pushing her away.

"You must know that I love you, Jessie?" I breathe.

She blinks at me. Shit. She didn't know that. How the fuck could she not? The few seconds before she speaks again stretch out in an eternity as I wait for her to say what I need to hear. Fuck. What if I've read this completely wrong?

She reaches out her hand and rests it on my cheek. "I love you too," she whispers, and I let out the breath I've been holding. She reaches between us and slides her hand into my sweatpants, pulling out my cock and rubbing the pad of her thumb over the tip as it pulses in her grip.

"You want that?" I arch an eyebrow at her.

"Yes, please." She smiles that incredible smile again as I pin her wrists to the bed on either side of her head before I slide myself deep inside her.

CHAPTER 42

JESSIE

*P*ulling my hair out of my ponytail, I look in the mirror and watch as it falls over my shoulders in long, rolling waves. It hasn't been this long for years. I always used to cut it short when I first escaped the Wolf. He would constantly tell me how much he loved my hair. Once I was convinced that he wasn't coming looking for me, and I felt like I had changed enough from the seventeen-year-old girl he'd last seen, I let it grow again. I take hold of a small section and lift it to my face, inspecting the ends. It's still in good condition, but I could do with a trim, and I need to speak to the brothers about making myself an appointment at a salon.

I can't help smiling at my reflection and how much the twins love my long hair. Liam likes to curl it around his fingers and Mikey sometimes likes to brush it. It kind of reminds me of being a kid when my mom would sit and comb the tangles from my hair for hours. Conor and Shane seem to love it too, although thinking about what they do with it makes the heat sear between my thighs. Both of them have a habit of wrapping it around their fists, Conor to make me more compliant when he's kissing me, and Shane when he fucks me from behind.

Conor eventually went to bed a few hours ago and I plan on joining him shortly, as he suggested. Although, just to sleep. I could do with catching up on some myself.

A loud knock makes me jump. "Yeah," I shout and spin around as Shane opens the door. I haven't seen him all day. I've been avoiding him. I suspect he's been dodging me too, but I couldn't give a shiny rat's ass.

"What can I do for you, Shane?" I say, my voice dripping with sarcasm.

"I have something to show you, Hacker," he says and holds out his hand.

"I don't have time right now." I glance at my watch. "I was just going to have a soak in the tub and then head to bed."

"I think it's something you'll be interested in," he replies with that cocky smile of his that practically sets my panties on fire. "And you might want to put on some shoes."

I sigh and roll my eyes, as though being in his company isn't going to be excruciating no matter what we're doing. He ignores the eye roll, which isn't like him, and waits expectantly for me at the door while I slip my sneakers back on.

A FEW MOMENTS LATER, Shane and I are in the elevator headed to the basement. I stare at him, looking for clues as to where he's taking me, but he avoids my gaze and suddenly I get a strange feeling of dread in the pit of my stomach. Why won't he look at me?

"Where are we going? Can I have a clue?"

"You'll see soon. Stop being so impatient," he snaps, still avoiding eye contact.

The elevator doors finally open and he steps out into the basement garage and walks toward a large Mercedes SUV. I follow him and we both stop in front of the car and I look around. It's a beautiful car, but this garage is filled with incredible cars. If I was going to choose one to stand beside and admire, it would be the Bugatti Veyron or the Aston Martin Vulcan.

"What's so special about this?" I ask him.

"It's yours," he says calmly and my heart almost stops beating in my chest.

"What? You're giving me a car?" I frown at him. "What's the catch?"

"Not just a car, Hacker. There are papers in the glove compartment, giving you a new identity. Social security number, passport, birth certificate – the works. And there's a half a million dollars in the trunk too."

I blink at him. "What?" I get a sudden sickening feeling that I know where this conversation is headed and I don't like it at all.

"It's all yours, Hacker. You get into it right now, and you drive. Your new life awaits."

"Just like that?" I snap.

"Just like that." He turns to me and nods. "You will never get a better offer than this, Jessie. This is me offering you your freedom. No strings. No catch."

"Except I don't get to say goodbye? And I don't see any of you ever again, right?"

"Well, that's kind of the point of a new life, isn't it? To leave the old one behind?" he frowns.

"Fuck you, Shane," I snap as I start to walk away from him.

He grabs hold of my arm and pulls me to him, bending his head low so his face is close to mine. "Think about what you're giving up here," he snarls. "I am giving you everything you need to start over. I could just toss you out onto the street instead."

"Your brothers wouldn't let you."

He laughs softly. It's not a pleasant sound. It's mocking and cruel, and it echoes around the concrete basement. "And how exactly do you see your future playing out with us, Hacker? We just go on passing your around between the four of us until we get bored? Until someone else with bigger tits and a smaller ass takes your place?"

I stumble back from him, reeling so hard he might as well have slapped me in the face. I try to wrench my arm free and move away from him, but he holds me firmly in place. "Why are you doing this?" I say as tears spring to my eyes. I hate myself for crying in front of him, but he's tearing out my heart.

"We're no good for you. And you're not good for us either. You distract us, Hacker. You make my brothers vulnerable, and that makes them weak."

Blood pounds through my veins, thrumming beneath the skin on my wrist where he holds me tightly. I suck in a deep breath and wipe my tears away with my free hand. Planting my feet squarely on the ground, I look up at him, glaring into his fiery green eyes.

"You can say what you want about your brothers and me, Shane. But I love them. And despite what you think, they love me too. I feel it in every part of my being. You think that love makes you weak, and so you run from it. Men like you will never know true strength, because you are too afraid to feel. Love does not make you weak, you jackass. Don't you see that it's the most powerful force in the world? So, you can stick your car, and your money, and your new identity up your goddamn ass! Now take your hands off me and let me go back to my room."

He stares at me, his jaw working overtime and that vein pulsing in his temple. Then he releases my wrist. I draw in a few shaky breaths and then I turn and walk back to the elevator and leave him standing alone.

CHAPTER 43

JESSIE

$\mathcal{I}$ push open the door to Conor's bedroom. The soft glow of the lamplight illuminates the vast space. He hates the dark.

As I look over at the bed and his sleeping form, a wave of disappointment washes over me. I was hoping to talk to him about his asshole big brother, but I shouldn't wake him. I kick off my sneakers and begin to undress when I hear him groan in his sleep as he thrashes his arms.

"No," he shouts and I rush over to him, sitting beside him on the bed. I place my hand on his cheek and he stirs. "Jessie," he blinks at me.

"Sorry," I whisper. "You were shouting in your sleep."

He rolls his eyes. "Weird dreams." Then he holds up the duvet. "Jump in, Angel."

"Thanks," I say with a smile as I hop in next to him and press myself against him. He wraps his arms around me and plants a kiss on the top of my head. He smells of expensive soap and fresh sweat and I feel the familiar fluttering in my abdomen as I inhale his scent and press my cheek against the skin of his hard chest.

"Everything okay?" he asks softly as he smooths my hair back from my face.

"No. Your brother is a complete asshole, do you know that?"

He laughs softly, and the sound rumbles through his chest and into me. "Did he test his little hacker?"

I look up at him. "Yes. How do you know?"

Conor shrugs. "He tests us all. I knew yours was coming. I could sense it in him. What did he do?"

"He offered me a brand new SUV, half a million dollars and a new identity if I left. He said it was my freedom."

Conor lets out a low whistle. "I didn't realize he was going to go that far. What did you say to him?"

"I told him to stick it all up his ass," I reply and Conor laughs again.

"I wish I could have seen his face."

"He wants me gone, Conor. How long before he gets his way?" I snuggle closer to him.

"He doesn't want you gone. I get that he has a fucked up way of showing it, but, I told you, him trying to make you leave is really about him wanting you to stay."

"That's some twisted logic right there."

"That's Shane, Angel."

"He said I make you all weak. And vulnerable. Do you think that?" I whisper.

Conor places his index finger under my chin and tilts my head up. He stares at me with those incredible brown eyes. "Do you?"

"No," I swallow.

"Good. Because you make us all stronger, Jessie," he replies, and then he bends his head low and seals my mouth with a kiss. I drag my fingers through his thick hair and pull him closer as I grind my hips against his.

His hand slides down to my ass, and he squeezes hard, making me groan into his mouth.

I pull back. "I need you, Conor," I pant.

"I know, Angel," he growls as he rolls on top of me, pinning me to the mattress. His hand slides down my body and between my thighs before he tugs my panties to one side and slides two of his fingers through my slick folds.

"Conor," I gasp as I press myself against his hand.

"You want my fingers in you first, Angel?" he soothes as he starts to trail soft kisses over my neck and toward my breasts.

"Yes," I breathe. Him and his magic fingers are exactly what I need.

He sucks one of my hard nipples into his mouth at the same time as he pushes two fingers deep inside me. My hips shoot off the bed as pleasure courses through me, and he chuckles softly. "You are so fucking tight."

"Conor," I moan again as I release a rush of wet heat and my walls clench around him.

"Damn," he grunts. "I need to taste me some of that sweet pussy."

"Don't stop," I pant. "Please."

"I won't, baby. I know you like a good finger fucking," he growls as his head sinks lower until he's so close I can feel his breath on my wet folds. He continues working his fingers inside me as he settles his warm mouth over my clit and begins to suckle. It's not long before I'm coming apart around him as my orgasm rolls over me, making my entire body tremble.

CONOR WRAPS me in his arms, and I lay my head on his chest, listening to the sound of his heartbeat thumping gently against my ear.

He curls my hair around his fingers and I sigh contentedly.

"You realize if you'd got into that car and driven off, I'd have come find you and brought you straight back here, don't you?" he asks softly.

"You would?"

"Yes. Don't ever make me do that, Jessie," his voice cracks. "I told you, I would burn the whole fucking world down to find you, Angel."

"I won't. I promise," I say as I wrap my arms tighter around him.

CHAPTER 44

JESSIE

J spent the entire night with Conor and this morning I avoided the kitchen and the living area because I didn't want to bump into Shane. I can still hardly believe what he did last night. Conor has done his best to try to convince me that Shane testing me means that he's finally ready to accept that I'm staying. And I suppose I can kind of understand his twisted logic - pushing a person away before you're willing to let them in, to see how far they're willing to go. But I can't forget the things he said about him and his brothers passing me around until someone better comes along. It stung like hell. It still does.

As the day goes on, I keep replaying his words over and over in my head, and each time I do, I find myself becoming angrier by the minute. How dare he speak to me like that. As though I'm some gold-digger who manipulated my way into their lives. As much as I wanted each of them, I never made a move. I didn't cross that line first. Not with any of them. They pursued me.

I would have been content to spend a few months here working for them, and then moving on. They changed the rules of the game. Not me. And now I'm in too deep to walk away.

Now, they've given me a taste of something that I never want to lose.

I walk along the hallway from my bedroom toward Shane's office. His door is open, and I storm inside. He looks up at me as I enter the room. Sitting behind his desk in suit pants and a white shirt open at the collar, he also has a light dusting of stubble. He looks so damn good. I remind my treacherous body that we're not speaking to him.

"What can I do for you, Hacker?" he asks smoothly.

I scowl at him. So, he's just going to sit there and pretend everything is fine, and that he didn't insult me on almost every level last night.

I stalk toward his desk and plant both of my hands on it as I steady myself. My thighs are trembling, but thankfully his desk hides them from view. I glare at him and he simply leans back and looks at me with a mild look of amusement on his face, which only infuriates me more.

"I've decided that I do want my freedom after all," I snap.

He frowns at me. "You do?"

"Yes. But on my terms."

He leans forward in his chair, resting his elbows on the desk, his hands steepled under his chin. "Go on?"

"You can keep your money, and your fake ID. I'll borrow the car occasionally. But, I want my fingerprint added to the security for this apartment."

"Really?" he arches one eyebrow at me.

"Yes. I want to come and go from this place whenever I please. Just like you and your brothers do."

He narrows his eyes at me. "I'll think about it."

"You'll think about it?"

"I believe that's what I just said, Hacker."

"Well, while you're thinking about that, you can also think about the fact that if you ever make me feel like a cheap whore again, I will slap that arrogant grin off your face, Shane Ryan. I don't care how tough you believe you are."

He doesn't answer me. He just sits there, staring at me.

"And if you think you're going to *pass me around* with your brothers any longer, you're sadly mistaken. So, now might be a good time to go find yourself one of those women with bigger tits and a smaller ass that you're so fond of. I hear Erin is unattached."

He still doesn't speak. Instead, he glares at me, and I wonder if any woman has ever spoken to him like that in his life.

I smile triumphantly, and then I turn on my heel and walk out of his office with my heart pounding in my ears. I'm pretty sure I'll pay for that, but right now I don't give a damn, because it felt so good to put Shane Ryan in his place.

CHAPTER 45

JESSIE

I walk out of the bathroom to find Shane standing in my room with his hands stuffed in his trouser pockets. He looks as fierce as ever and I wonder if he's still mad at me for what I said in his office earlier. But I don't even care anymore. The things he said to me last night cut me deeply and I'm not sure I will be able to look at him the same way again.

"What do you want, Shane?" I ask with a sigh as I cross the room and stand in front of him. As usual, he smells incredible.

He holds out his hand to me, and I look down at it hesitantly. "Come with me," he orders.

"Again? And just what are you planning on doing tonight? Driving me to the state line and kicking me out of the car?" I arch an eyebrow at him.

"Stop being a brat and come with me." He grabs my hand now and my pulse quickens at his touch. I dutifully follow him out of my bedroom, down the hallway, and to the elevator.

"Where are we going, Shane?" I demand.

"Wait and see, Hacker," he says, and I roll my eyes in annoyance. Thankfully, he doesn't see me, or he'd probably reprimand me for it.

We step into the elevator and take it to the ground floor. Shane steps out first and I follow him. He walks straight to the SUV he offered me last night and the car beeps to life as we approach.

I stop in my tracks and pull my hand from his, crossing my arms over my chest. "I already told you, I'm not leaving."

He sighs deeply in frustration and frowns at me. "I know. Just get into the car."

He pulls the passenger door open for me, and I shake my head in annoyance before climbing inside. I suspect that if I don't get in voluntarily, he'll just pick me up and throw me in anyway.

I STARE out of the window as we drive away from the city and my heart races in my chest as we get further and further away from the place I've come to call home. "Why won't you tell me where we're going?" I turn in my seat and ask him.

"It's a surprise."

I chew on my lip nervously, and he reaches out his hand and brushes my cheek with his knuckles. "Don't you trust me, little hacker?"

I stare at him. I'm not sure how to answer that question. "I thought I did. But then last night..."

"Last night, what? I didn't force you to leave, did I?"

"No. But now I know that you want me to, I feel like I'm on borrowed time. I don't know what you're planning on doing or where you're taking me, Shane," I admit, the tremor in my voice clearly audible now.

"I would never hurt you, Hacker," he says softly. "Well, not unless you want me to. What happened the other night. You wanted that, right?"

"I did. But..." I shake my head. There is no use reasoning with him.

"But what?" he frowns.

"After. You just dismissed me. I wanted more than…" Damn. Why do I keep speaking in half sentences?

"You wanted me to fuck you," he finishes for me. "You wanted me to make you feel better. But that's not the point of a punishment, is it? The real punishment is you going to bed alone with your cunt dripping wet."

I roll my eyes and he sighs.

"You're never honest with me, Jessie. You are with Conor and the twins."

I turn in my seat and glare at him.

"If you had come to me the other night and told me what you needed, then I would have given it to you – the pain and the pleasure. But, instead you lied because you can't be honest with me."

"I… Damn." I don't even know what to say.

"You think it was easy for me to send you away? I was as hard as fucking stone for you. You could have asked me to let you stay. You could have asked me to come with you, Jessie. You could have been honest about how you were feeling instead of walking out and hating me."

"God, I wish I hated you." I snap at him. "Besides, you make it hard to be honest with you, Shane. You're completely unreadable. I think you might be the most difficult person I have ever met in my life!" I cross my arms over my chest and sit back in my seat.

"At least that was honest," he says with a faint laugh.

"Anyway, none of that matters considering what you did last night," I breathe as the memory cuts a fresh welt across my heart. "You said you'd never hurt me, but you did. Those things you said…"

"I know," he whispers. "I was way out of line, and I'm sorry."

"How much further is this place?" I say, looking out of the window.

"Not much. We're almost there."

LESS THAN FIFTEEN MINUTES LATER, we pull off the highway and onto a dirt track leading into the hills. I glance at Shane, but he keeps his eyes fixed on the road ahead, seeming to know exactly where he's going. Finally, we come to a spot near a lake and he stops the car and unclips his seatbelt.

"Where are we?" I ask as I peer out of the window. There is nothing here but the lake and trees.

"Come and see," he says as he climbs out of the car. He walks around to my side as I'm opening my door and takes my hand. I grab onto it as I step out, wondering what I'm stepping on. It's so dark out here, I can barely see. He keeps hold of my hand and leads me closer to the water. When we reach it, he stops and looks out at the water with a strange look of contentment on his face. Meanwhile, my blood is thundering in my ears. What the hell is going on here?

"Would you look at that?" he says, nodding toward the lake.

I turn and look. It is a beautiful sight. The water is almost black, but the reflection of the full moon ripples on the surface, illuminating the lake and the surrounding trees.

"It's beautiful," I admit.

"It's yours," he says softly.

"I'm not sure about that, Shane," I smile. "As powerful as you are, I'm not sure a lake and the moon are within your gift to give."

He turns to me, his face full of emotion. "If you're going to stay with us, then you'll need this."

I frown at him, not understanding what he means.

"I know my brothers can be a bit much," he says.

I raise my eyebrows at him.

"And I know that I can too," he adds. "I used to come to this spot at least once a week. Just to have some quiet and some space from them and their constant noise. It's hard being the one who always has to have the answers, Jessie," he says with a sigh and despite him being a complete asshole at times, my heart aches for him. He puts himself under so much pressure.

"I suppose I get that. But if you give this spot to me, then where will you go?"

He smiles at me. "Wherever you are." My breath catches in my throat and my pulse quickens. What the hell is happening here? "I realized this morning that I haven't been to this place for over two months. Not since you came into our lives. You bring us all into balance somehow, Hacker. You take the worst parts of each of us and make them softer and more tolerable. I want you to have a place to run to when you need some space – and some peace. When you need to get away from my brothers, or from me."

"Shane, you don't have to do this."

"I want you to have this place, Jessie," he says, his voice thick with emotion. "Because if I'm going to let you in, I need to know that you will never leave. If you're going to be one of us, then you always will be. So, this is the place you can run to when we get a bit too much. If only for a little while."

I blink away the tears. This might be the nicest thing anyone has ever done for me. "Shane, I can't take this."

"Yes, you can. And if you're worried about privacy, I own this land. I've always planned to have a cabin built here someday."

"Wow, that would be incredible. A cabin out here," I say as I take another look around. "I would love to spend time here with you and your brothers."

"You would?" he smiles at me.

"Of course," I whisper.

"I know what you said today, and you had every right to say it, but tell me you didn't mean it. Jessie. Tell me that I still get to touch you. Tell me that I still get to have all of you."

"I don't know, Shane. You made me feel completely worth-less. Like I was some whore. You talked about me like I meant nothing to any of you."

He reaches up and tucks my hair behind my ear. "You mean more to me than you will ever know, Hacker."

"You expect honesty from me, Shane, but that's a two-way street. Where is my honesty?"

"I've never lied to you," he frowns at me.

"Maybe. But you have never let me in either. You never tell me what you want from me. You don't share any of your life with me."

"What do you want from me, Jessie?" he shakes his head.

"Something real, Shane. Anything real?" I plead with him.

He licks his lips and stares at me. "I called the wedding off."

"To Erin?" I ask.

"She's the only woman I've ever been engaged to, so yeah," he frowns, and I bite back the retort that's on the edge of my tongue.

"Why?"

"She had a pregnancy scare," he says with a sigh and I blink at him.

"It's not like that," he shakes his head. "I'm not a complete asshole, Jessie."

"I know," I whisper as my pulse thrums against my skin.

"She wasn't pregnant. I'd always told her from the start, I was clear that I never wanted kids. And she said she felt the same. Then, she had this scare, and I found out she hadn't been taking her birth control properly and she was just so fucking laid back about it, like she hadn't completely lied to me. She admitted she thought I'd change my mind one day. But I had never, ever give her any indications that I would. I do not want to carry on my bastard father's bloodline," he snarls, and I reach out and take his hand in mine. "The plan was we were going to live in the apartment for a few years, and then convert one of the other floors for ourselves. But, after the whole baby thing, I found out she'd put a deposit on an apartment overlooking Central Park. Without even telling me."

"Haven't you ever told your brothers about this?"

He shakes his head. "No, because besides all of that shit, she blamed them for us not working out. She said that they were too dependent on me. Conor and Mikey and Liam think I was miserable because we'd broken up, but I wasn't. I was miserable because I knew that she was right. I would never leave my brothers, Jessie. My family is everything to me."

"So, why did that make you miserable?" I frown.

"Because, I realized I would always put them first. Above everyone else. I don't want kids, because I feel like I already have some. I have been looking after my little brothers since I was four years old. And I don't resent that. I love them. I would make every sacrifice one hundred times over for them."

"So, you chose their happiness over your own?"

He shakes his head. "No. I chose my brothers over the possibility of falling in love with someone again."

"Oh, I see," I nod. I understand him so much more than I did half an hour ago. I wrap my arms around his waist and rest my head on his hard chest. "Thank you for sharing that with me."

He runs his hands down my arms and rests his chin on top of my head. "You know, my mother always used to tell me tales of curses and witchcraft back in Ireland. But I thought she was crazy. I never believed her. Now I'm not so sure."

"You think I'm a witch?" I look up and grin at him.

"You've certainly got me under some kind of spell."

I swallow as I look into his eyes. The moonlight highlighting the darkness in them.

I have never felt more loved in my whole life than I do by him and his brothers.

"It's no spell, Shane. I love you. It's that simple. And that complicated."

He stares at me and I can't help but feel like I have just crossed a line that he didn't want me to cross.

He leans forward and seals his lips over mine, kissing me so fiercely that I almost lose my breath. Despite the cool air, my whole body is flooded with heat and desire. I have wanted him inside me since he sent me out of his office two nights earlier. He steps forward, walking me backwards until my back is pressed flat against a tree.

"Shane," I pant as I wrench my lips away from his.

He groans out loud, mistaking my desperation for hesitation. "I need you, Jessie. And there's no-one out here but us."

"I don't care who sees us," I breathe as I reach for his zipper. "I want you. Right now."

"Hacker," he growls as he reaches for the edge of my dress and pulls it up around my waist before he tugs my panties to one side. "You're going to get me. Every fucking inch of me, because you make me so hard I could come just from touching you. There is nothing I love more in this world than burying my cock in your hot cunt."

"You have a filthy mouth," I gasp as I pull his hard length free from his pants. He buries his head in my neck and growls against me as his hands drop to my ass before he lifts me until I can wrap my legs around his waist. There is no warning from him before he pushes his full length inside me.

"Shane," I shout into the darkness as a rush of my cream coats him.

"Always ready for me, my little hacker," he whispers against my ear. "Soaking wet and ready for my cock. Every. Fucking. Time," he thrusts with each word until I am coming apart around him. There is something about being out here in the open with him that makes my heart beat faster and the blood pound through my veins. Every sense is heightened.

I rake my nails down his muscular back as I take everything he has to give me.

"You want it harder?" he groans.

"Yes," I groan, and he rails into me with all his strength. The tree bark at my back bites against my skin through the thin fabric of my dress, but the pain only makes the pleasure of him driving into me over and over again all that sweeter. Soon my legs are trembling with my impending release and because he knows my body so well, he increases his pace until my walls are clenching around him and I am shuddering against him.

"Shane," I groan as the waves of pleasure crash over me.

"I fucking love the way you squeeze my cock when you come, Hacker," he growls in my ear and a few thrusts later, he climaxes with a roar.

SHANE IS quiet on the drive back to the city and I wonder if telling him that I love him has completely spooked him. Especially after he'd just spoken about never wanting to fall in love again. When we get back home, he walks me to my room. "Goodnight, Hacker," he says softly.

"Goodnight," I whisper. I stare at him, wondering whether to ask him to stay the night with me. I want to wake up with his warm, hard body pressed against mine. But I swallow the words. I know he asked me for honesty, but I have laid myself bare to him and if that isn't enough for him, then I don't know what else to do. I suppose I have to accept that this is his way, and this is the pattern we will always follow. He might never tell me that he loves me, but I feel it sometimes anyway, and maybe that is enough?

I LIE in bed staring into the darkness and listening to nothing but the sound of my heartbeat in my ears. My back stings slightly from the tree bark digging into it earlier, but it makes me smile – a reminder of the place Shane shared with me. The soft click of my door opening and footsteps padding across the floor makes me hold my breath. I know it isn't the twins because they couldn't be that quiet if they tried, and there is definitely only one set of footsteps. The scent of fresh air and his distinctive cologne fills the room as he approaches.

"Shane?" I whisper, sure that it can't be him and my senses are deceiving me, because he has never slept in my room before.

He doesn't answer me as he reaches the bed and lifts the covers. The mattress dips beside me as he slips beneath the duvet and presses his body against mine. When his rough hand skims over my hip, I know for sure that it's him and I smile to myself.

"Hey," I say as he wraps his arm around my waist and pulls me close to his chest.

"Hey, Hacker," he breathes.

"What are you doing in here?"

He swallows. "I shouldn't have let you come to bed alone."

"So, why did you?" I ask as I shift my body so I'm facing him. His hand slips onto my ass and I run my fingertips across his cheek.

"Because you make me feel things I don't like feeling, Jessie. You have my heart in a vice."

The tears spring to my eyes. I love this man so much. He and his brothers are everything I have ever wanted in life. Each of them makes me feel whole and cherished and protected, in their own unique ways. Living without them now would be like living without air. But I know that he's struggling with his emotions and I want to be what he needs too. "Well, that's better than your balls," I giggle, and he slaps me lightly on the ass before pulling me tighter to him again.

"Ow," I giggle. "My ass is still tender, you know?"

"Go to sleep," he whispers in my ear. "Or I'll put you over my knee this time."

I press my face against his chest and inhale his intoxicating scent. "I love you, Shane. I am never going to leave. I promise."

He presses his lips against my forehead. "I know, Hacker," he breathes. "Now go to sleep."

CHAPTER 46

SHANE

*M*y phone vibrates on my desk, and I look down at the screen as Erin's name appears on it.

"Hi," I answer. "Did you find out anything on the Ivanovs for me?"

"Oh, hi. And I'm fine, thank you," she snaps.

I suck in a breath. She's so fucking difficult, but I have to remind myself that she's a talented lawyer, and she knows far too many of my family's secrets. "Sorry. But did you?"

"No, nothing. Sorry."

"Nothing at all?"

"Nope," she replies breezily, and I know that she's lying. She's an accomplished liar, what lawyer isn't, and she no doubt hates that this information would help Jessie. Since we visited her office a couple of weeks back, Erin has barely contacted me.

"Oh, and next time you visit my place of work, please don't take your girlfriend into my restroom for a quick fuck," she hisses, and I have to bite the inside of my cheek to stop myself from laughing. "I had to have the whole place sanitized. I didn't realize you were so crass, Shay."

I seem to remember her dragging me into a restroom stall

more than once, but I don't remind her of that fact. Because I'm a gentleman, after all. "Well, what can I say, Erin. I just can't keep my hands off her. Thanks for the call," I say and then I press the end call button and throw my phone onto the desk.

A few seconds later, I look up as Conor walks into my office. "Did you want me earlier?" he asks.

"Yeah. Close the door."

He frowns at me, but he closes it behind him. "What's going on?"

"You remember that guy from Balthazar's place? The one whose throat Liam cut?"

Conor nods. "The one who was about to attack Jessie?"

I run a hand over my jaw. "That's the guy. My sources tell me he's still alive."

"What? Fuck! I mean, I didn't see what happened, but Liam said he sliced the guy's throat from ear to ear."

"I have no doubt he thinks he did. But, maybe be missed an artery or something?" I shrug. "Maybe the guy is a fucking superhero? Whatever happened, he's still breathing."

"You're worried he'll identify us?" Conor asks as he leans back in his chair.

"No, it's not that. Besides, he only saw Jessie, didn't he?"

"Yeah. So? Why are you looking so concerned and why have I closed the door?"

I sigh. I should have told him about this when it cropped up, but it didn't seem that important. "When that guy walked into the room, Jessie said he seemed to believe he recognized her from somewhere."

That makes Conor sit up in his seat. "What? Where?"

"That's just it. She doesn't have a clue. But, the guy called her Nataliya."

"Nataliya?"

"Yeah. But Jessie says she doesn't know anyone by that name. I thought the guy was dead and there could be any number of possible explanations, and so I dismissed it. But now that I know he's still alive," I lean back in my chair and sigh. "I don't know. It's bothering me."

"You think maybe she looks like this Nataliya? A sister she doesn't know about?"

I shake my head. "She's adamant that couldn't be possible. But," I shrug again.

"What are you thinking?" Conor narrows his eyes at me.

"Maybe her mom?"

"Wasn't her mom's name Veronica?"

"When she was in the states, yes. But what if she changed it? What if the hit on the Romanov family was really about her and not Jessie's father?"

Conor sucks in a breath and sits back as though he's deep in thought. "It's a possibility. Have you told Jessie about the guy from the bar still being alive?"

I shake my head. "Not yet. I want to find out a bit more about him first, and if he can even speak before I worry her."

Conor arches an eyebrow at me.

"What?"

"She won't thank you for lying to her," he says with a shake of his head.

"I'm not lying. I'm delaying telling her the truth because I don't want to freak her out."

"You don't want her to run?" He smirks.

"Just do some digging around on this guy. Okay? And then we can tell her if and when we find out something. There could be nothing at all to it. A simple case of mistaken identity."

"Okay. Are you telling the twins?"

I shake my head. "Not yet. I don't want Liam to know. He'll only beat himself up about it and it's not fair to ask Mikey to keep it from him."

Conor nods his agreement, and I'm glad he's on the same page. I'm not in the habit of keeping things from my brothers, but I can't shake the feeling that there was much more to the murder of Jessie's family than meets the eye. And if she's in any danger, then I'll do everything I can to protect her.

I'M SITTING on the sofa with Jessie, my arm draped around her shoulder and she's snuggled against my chest. It's not often that I spend any time with her like this, but the twins are out working, and Conor is in the club. I walked past the den and she was sitting there alone watching TV and I couldn't resist joining her.

We've been here for a while when Conor walks into the room and sits beside us.

"Hey, you," Jessie says with a yawn. "Where have you been all day?"

"Hey, Angel," he replies, rubbing his hand over her ass and onto her thigh. "Just some business to deal with."

She turns her head, and he leans forward and kisses her. I watch his tongue sliding into her mouth and I listen to her soft groans and it's such a fucking turn on. I never thought I'd be willing to share a woman with my brothers, but this feels so natural. It doesn't even feel like sharing. She belongs to each of us in different ways.

Once he's given her a good tonguing, Conor pulls away and Jessie leans back into my chest with a soft sigh. He looks over her head at me and shoots me a look that tells me he has something to tell me.

I take Jessie's chin in my hand and tilt her face to mine. "You tired, Hacker?"

"A little," she says, stifling another yawn.

"Why don't you go to bed and I'll join you shortly," I say before pressing my lips against hers. She pulls me to her, turning my fairly chaste goodnight kiss into something much more.

I pull back from her, even though it hurts me to do it

because she tastes as sweet as honey and as wicked as sin. "Bed," I growl.

She rolls her eyes, but then she stands up and I take the opportunity to smack her perfect ass. She blows us each a kiss and then she walks out of the room. "My bed, Hacker," I shout after her. "And don't fall asleep."

"I wouldn't dare," she snaps back and then she laughs, and I watch her sexy body disappear out of view.

"Did you find out something?" I say to Conor as soon as Jessie is out of earshot.

"Yes, and it's good news. The guy from Balthazar's did make it, well for a few days at least. But he's dead now."

"How?"

"Heart attack while he was in hospital recovering from having his throat cut."

"Wow! That's some bad luck." I can't help but smile though because it means that if he did recognize Jessie as a Romanov then she's in less danger if he's dead.

"He couldn't speak, but he did communicate with the nurses. He wrote a few words on a notepad when he needed a drink or something, but mostly he was in and out of consciousness."

"Did he have any visitors?"

"Yeah. Just one. A guy. But he didn't leave a name."

"But he could have mentioned he saw Jessie - or Nataliya?"

"In theory. So, do we tell her?"

"What is there to tell? The guy's dead. She didn't recognize him. She doesn't know who Nataliya is. It may have been nothing at all." I stand up. "If there's nothing else, I'm going to bed."

Conor glances at his watch. "You're stopping work before ten p.m.?" he says as he stands too.

"When there's a horny redhead waiting for me in my bed, I am, yeah."

"I never thought I'd see the day," Conor laughs.

241

"I've been thinking about what you said, too. I'm going to ask Jessie if she wants to get more involved in the business. I could use some help with the tech side of things."

Conor places a hand on the back of my neck. "So, she's really one of us now, then?"

I stare at him as he looks at me hopefully. "I suppose so," I nod.

"About fucking time, bro," he smiles at me.

I smile back. I suppose it is about time. Time to make Jessie Romanov a Ryan.

CHAPTER 47

JESSIE

*a*s I sit at the large table in the dining room that we rarely use, I look around at Liam, Mikey and Conor as we all wait for Shane.

"Any idea why he's called this meeting?" Liam asks me.

"Me? None at all." I shake my head. "I thought one of you might?" Shane spent the night with me, but he got up early this morning, although he at least kissed me this time before he snuck out of bed.

"Not a clue," Conor frowns.

The sound of the door opening makes us all look up. Shane strides into the room with a serious expression on his face. I share a quick side glance with his brothers and wonder which one of us is in trouble now.

"What's going on, bro?" Mikey asks as Shane sits down at the table.

He rubs a hand over his jaw and frowns, and then he looks at me. "Jessie here has decided that she'd like to stay. Isn't that right?"

"Yes," I swallow as I glance around the room nervously.

"Oh, I didn't realize we were doing *this* now?" Liam says as he grins at me and Conor and Mikey mumble as though they know what *this* is too.

"Doing what?" I look between all four of them.

Shane reaches into his jacket pocket and pulls out a slip of paper before passing it to me. It has an eight-digit number on it. "That's the passcode to access the alarm system so that you can add your fingerprint. You can come and go as you please, just like you asked."

I reach out and take the paper, closing my hand over it and holding it tightly. "Thank you. This means a lot to me."

Shane nods as his eyes meet mine. My heart flutters in my chest as he makes no attempt to look away.

"You do know Jessie can override that system anyway," Liam says with a flash of his eyebrows.

"Yes. But now she won't have to," Shane snaps and I smile at him.

"Is that why you called us here?" I ask.

"Partly," Shane pushes his chair back and stands up. "But also, because if we're going to make this a permanent arrangement, I think we need some ground rules, don't you, Jessie?" He holds out his hand to me and I take it.

I swallow hard as he pulls me up from my chair. "I guess so."

"Any that you'd like to start us off with?" he asks in that low gravelly growl that makes my insides turn to warm liquid.

"Mikey has to stop stealing my panties and putting them in his nightstand," I say with a smile.

Shane nods and his brothers laugh while Mikey protests at the unjustness of that particular rule.

"Anything else, Hacker?" Shane asks.

"Nothing I can think of right now, anyway."

"Okay," he smiles. "The boys and I have had a chat, and here are ours." He sits on the chair he's just pulled me up from and tugs me to sit on his lap.

"We all want you, Hacker. I'd have you in my bed every night if I could. But I know that my brothers love you just as much as I do."

I blink at him in shock. Did he just admit that he loved me?

He gives me a look that suggests he does not want to be interrupted, and I press my lips together and let him continue.

"It will always be your choice who you want to share a bed with, but it's also your responsibility to ensure that all of our needs are taken care of. This is not an open relationship and I won't have anyone feeling like they have to search elsewhere. That puts all of our health at risk. Do you understand that?"

"Yes." I breathe out and then I bite my lip. I am the one woman who gets to satisfy these four incredibly fine and passionate men. I am one lucky gal!

"We thought that a good starting point would be two nights a week each, because the twins like to share you anyway, and that would still give you one night to yourself if you wanted it. Does that seem reasonable?"

"Yes. More than reasonable."

He smiles at me and brushes my hair from my face before he continues. "There might be times when more than one of us need you. I know you enjoy being with the twins together. I assume that goes for any of us if we're willing to share, and you're feeling up for it?"

"Yes." I nod, as I feel a rush of wet heat between my thighs. Sharing is good.

"If you're one of us, then you make decisions based on what is best for us as a family unit, just like we will do for you?"

I nod my agreement.

"We do not hide what or who we are from anyone, because it's no-one's business but ours what we are to each other. And when we leave this apartment, I want to hold your hand, grab your ass, kiss you, or touch you in any way without you worrying what people might think, and I know that my brothers feel the same."

"Yes," they all nod their agreement.

"Okay," I say. I've never cared much for what other people thought of me anyway.

Shane slides his hand up the inside of my thigh as he continues talking. "Anything else you guys want to add?" he asks his brothers as his fingers reach the apex of my thighs. He brushes them over my panties before tugging them to one side and sliding two fingers through my slick folds.

I suck in a breath and am vaguely aware of Conor, Liam and Mikey mumbling that they have nothing else to say.

"Fuck, Jessie, you're dripping wet." Shane grunts as he slides one finger deep inside me, making me moan out loud. "Is it any wonder it takes all four of us to keep you satisfied?"

I bury my face in his neck as he adds another finger and presses against that perfect spot deep inside me.

"You going to make her come for us, Shane?" Conor growls.

"Please. I love to watch her lose control," Liam adds.

Shane chuckles and then he slides his finger out of me, and holds it up for his brothers to show them it dripping with my arousal before sucking it clean. "I've got a much better idea," he grins wickedly, and my stomach does a full one eighty flip. "I think we need to mark this occasion. Really welcome Jessie into the family. What do you say?"

I blink at him, wondering exactly what's lying behind those deviant eyes.

"Like a blood oath?" Mikey asks.

"Not exactly," Shane growls.

"More like a cum oath?" I arch one eyebrow at him.

That's met with laughter from all of them, and Shane presses his lips to mine and kisses me. "Exactly that," he grins when he lets me up for air. Brushing my hair back, he presses his mouth against my ear, whispering so his brothers don't hear. "You sure you can handle all four of us at once, sweetheart?"

Damn. Did he just call me sweetheart? And can I handle all

four? I've been desperate to since I first laid eyes on them. My panties might melt if they don't get them off me soon. "Yes," I pant.

"Good girl," he growls and then he stands, lifting me in his arms and placing me down on the huge table.

"I'm going to watch all of my brothers make you come, Hacker." He arches one eyebrow at me. "I'm going to sit here and watch them fuck you one by one, and when they're done, I'm going to bend you over this table and show them how hard you scream when you come for me."

Heat flashes through my entire body as his words roll over me. This should feel so wrong on so many levels, but it just feels right. The idea of having these men worship my body makes the wet heat between my thighs increase tenfold.

"Conor,'" Shane says, and it's understood between the five of us what he means. Shane sits in the nearby chair while Conor walks over to me.

"Lift your arms, Angel," Conor whispers and I do as he tells me, allowing him to slip the t-shirt over my head. He runs his hand up my arms and then onto my back, where he unclips my bra and pulls it off, letting my breasts fall free. My nipples are already hard, and he bends low and sucks one into his mouth while he pinches the other one between his finger and thumb and the heat rushes between my thighs.

I rake my hands through his hair. "Conor," I groan as I close my eyes. I know that his three brothers watch us intently, and it makes everything even hotter.

"Lie back, Angel," he whispers, and I do as he asks. I shiver as my warm skin hits the cold wood, but I hardly have time to focus on that sensation as Conor is peeling my panties down my legs as he sits down at the chair directly in front of me.

"I'm not sure I've ever eaten anything quite this sweet at this dining table before," he chuckles as he wraps his hands behind the back of my thighs and pulls me closer to his face. Then he eats my pussy like it's his last meal, savoring every single part of me. My back arches in pleasure as he coaxes an almighty orgasm from my body. He stands, and I shudder as he starts to unbuckle his belt. I watch as Shane walks up behind him, placing his hand on his younger brother's shoulder and whispering something in his ear. Whatever he says makes Conor grin wickedly and heat floods my body. He leans forward and plants a single kiss on my inner thigh, but then he steps back.

"Mikey. You're up," he says with a grin.

"Benched." Mikey laughs as he approaches while Conor and Shane take a seat and whisper to each other, like the coaches of a sports team, switching players and talking tactics – and I should hate it, but I don't.

I barely have time to think anyway because Mikey is standing between my thighs, placing his hands on my hips and leaning over to kiss me. "You look fucking beautiful, Red," he growls as his hands slide between my thighs. "It would be criminal not to eat this pussy now that Conor hasn't blown his load in it."

His words send a shiver through my entire body and despite what Conor just did, my pussy throbs in anticipation.

CHAPTER 48

MIKEY

I slip two fingers into Jessie's tight as fuck pussy and groan at the feeling of her squeezing my fingers. Her back arches off the table and she groans in pleasure as I slip deeper, rubbing the pads of my fingertips over her G-spot.

"Fuck, Red! Conor got you real wet for me."

"Sure fucking did," my older brother grunts his agreement, chest swelling with pride as I glance sideways at him. Then my eyes are firmly back on my girl as she writhes on the dining table.

"Mikey, please?" she pleads with me as I go on teasing her with my fingers.

Liam stands beside me, gripping his hard cock in his fist. "You know we love to hear you beg, baby," he growls appreciatively.

Dropping to my knees, I bring my face close to her pussy, inhaling her sweet intoxicating scent. "You smell so fucking good, Red," I say with a grunt as I slip my fingers out of her. Her cum drips out of her pussy making my cock throb with the anticipation of burying myself inside her very soon. I have a pretty good idea of what Shane and Conor have in mind shortly, and I will take full advantage of being able to eat this pussy without any of their cum tainting it. Because Jessie Ryan's cum is the sweetest damn thing I ever tasted.

I lick the length of her wet folds, enjoying the deep satisfied moan that vibrates through her entire body. "Your pussy is addictive, Red," I mumble against her slick flesh, causing her to writhe against my face.

Liam leans over her, sucking one of her beautiful tits into his mouth while he squeezes the other one in a bruising grip.

"Holy fuck," Jessie breathes out the words as a rush of her arousal drips from her hot channel.

I lap it up with my tongue, savoring the taste of her sweet juices as the coat my tongue, making my balls sear with heat and need. Reaching into my sweatpants, I wrap my hand around the base of my shaft and squeeze hard, groaning at the immediate relief, I swear I could come in my pants like a teenage boy just from eating this woman's pussy. And now she's truly ours, and I will get to eat and fuck her every damn day of my life.

I graze my teeth over her sensitive clit and she gasps.

"You okay there, baby?" Liam asks with a soft chuckle.

"Y-yes," she moans, threading her fingers through my hair.

"Mikey eating your pussy real good, huh?"

"Yes."

My twin catches my eye and winks at me. "Good because we're going to need you nice and wet so we can fuck you real hard, okay?"

"Of, fuck, yes," she pants out the words as she grinds her beautiful pussy on my face.

"That's it, ride my face until you come, Red," I urge her on, swirling my tongue over her sensitive flesh as I suck and lick her, devouring her cunt and savoring her sweetness like it's the last time I'll ever taste her.

"M-Mikey," she moans loudly before Liam crashes his lips

against hers, swallowing all of her moans and whimpers so that they vibrate through her body instead.

Then his hand slips south and he presses a finger against her clit as I move lower, sliding my tongue inside her pussy. Fuck she tastes so good. Her walls squeeze and her thighs tremble as I hold them open and tongue fuck her. Precum weeps from the crown of my cock as rewards me with more wet heat.

Her orgasm tears through her body like an explosion, and I catch every single delicious drop of it on my tongue. With a final swirl of my tongue over her wet center, I push myself up and wipe my face with my hand. Liam stands straight too, with a wicked grin on his face as she looks up at us both, her eyes dark and hooded. Her tits shudder as she sucks in shaky breaths. I grab her hips, fingertips digging in to her soft creamy skin while I line my cock up at her soaking wet entrance.

"You ready to be fucked now, Red?" I ask.

She doesn't even get a chance to get the word out before I slam into her, sinking balls deep into her tight, hot channel. She cries out, the sound echoing around the dining room and it makes pride swell in my chest that it's me currently ripping those guttural noises from her body and not my brothers. I love sharing her with them, but when I'm buried deep inside her this way, it's like I get her all to myself for a little while. As though he can read my mind, which I'm pretty sure he fucking can, Liam takes a few steps back and gives me room to fuck her.

She sinks her perfect white teeth into her plump bottom lip as her blue eyes fix on mine, dark with heat and desire. It spurs me on and I drive into her, tightening my grip on her hips so she doesn't slide up the table. My cock pulses inside her as she milks my cock with hungry little squeezes, desperate for more of me. I grin at her, aware that I'm the only man in her head right now and fucking loving that. I'm fucking feral with need for her and it burns through my veins. This cum oath—the marking her as officially ours—is long overdue in my opinion.

Shane should have gotten his head out of his ass a long time ago and made her one of us, but it's happening now. She's fucking ours and I'll never let her go.

"Your cunt loves my fucking cock, Jessie," I say with a grunt as I drive into her so hard, her eyes roll back in her head. "You belong to us now, yeah?"

"Yeah," she pants, her pink lips falling open as her back bows. "Damn, you feel so good."

Yeah, I do. I lean over her, lips trailing over her neck before I sink my teeth into her soft skin and suck hard. She loops her arms around my neck, pulling me closer as she rocks her hips, grinding herself onto my cock.

I close my eyes, trying to stave off the climax that's only a few breaths away, because I want her to fall right over that edge with me. But she's clinging to me, arms and legs wrapped around me now, panting in my ear, skin burning with heat as soft moans vibrate through her body. I nail her to the table and it's taking every ounce of willpower I have to hold on.

"Mikey," she shouts my name, thighs tightening around my waist, pussy squeezing me like a vise and tremors rippling through her entire body as she comes so fucking hard for me. The sweet fucking sounds she makes, and the way her pussy ripples around my cock, tips me right over the edge with her. My own eyes roll back as I empty myself inside her, pumping out every drop of cum I can give her as ecstasy and relief flood through my limbs.

"Holy fuck, Red," I growl in her ear as she goes on clinging to me, her chest heaving as she sucks in deep, shaky breaths.

I push myself up, my eyes raking over her trembling body as I admire my handiwork. When I pull out of her, a rush of our combined cum gushes out along with me, landing on the wooden table with a faint splat that makes her cheeks turn an even deeper shade of pink.

"Oh, you're such a naughty fucking girl Red," I tell her with a wink.

"She sure fucking is," Liam agrees as he steps up beside me, squeezing his cock in his hand as he prepares to take his turn. Jessie's eyes flicker from mine to his, and a soft smile lights up her gorgeous face. She blows a strand of hair from her forehead. "You ready for me now, baby?"

"Yes," she says the word with a soft purr. She's as sweet as fucking sugar and as wicked as fucking sin, and I love her more than I could have ever imagined possible.

I step aside, allowing my twin to take my place between her thighs. He gives me a sideways glance and I grin at him. We have been sharing women for as long as we've been having sex, but never like this. Never when we've been in love with the girl we were fucking. Never when she's meant so much to us, to all of us, as Jessie does.

"Warmed her up real nice for you, bro," I tell him with a wink.

"Fuck you," he snaps back good naturedly.

"No," I lean down and give my girl a soft kiss on the lips, "the idea is you fuck her numb-nuts."

He grins at her, pressing the tip of his cock inside her and making her whimper. "Yeah?"

"Yeah," she agrees with a slight nod of her head.

He edges in a little deeper. "You want this?"

"Yes," she whines, all desperate and needy for him despite how hard she's just been fucked.

"If this is what you really need, baby," he says on a groan as he rolls his hips, sinking deep inside her sweet pussy and making her hiss out a breath. I watch them my eyes fixed on the space where their bodies join as he stretches her pussy with his cock, pulling out slowly before driving back inside her again every time.

I glance at Conor and Shane, who are watching too. I never

in a million years thought those two would be okay sharing a woman. They're both possessive and controlling, and while Liam and I are to a certain extent too, my older brothers are not used to sharing anything. I guess Jessie is the one in a billion kind of special person that managed to change all that, and not a single one of us would give her up for anything.

I turn back to Liam and Jessie, stroking my cock as I watch my twin fucking my girl to her next orgasm.

CHAPTER 49

JESSIE

*S*hane pulls me from the table and onto his lap, seemingly not caring that his brothers' cum is dripping out of me onto his suit pants. After Mikey fucked me on the table, Liam lined up and did the same.

I'm panting for breath and my entire body is trembling as Shane takes hold of my chin and turns my face so I'm looking directly into his eyes. "You feel how hard you've made me, Hacker?" he growls as he shifts his hips slightly, so his erection is pressing against my folds.

"Yes," I breathe.

"You remember what you were doing with the twins that night? When me and Conor caught you all fucking?"

"Yes," I swallow as I stare into his eyes.

"I want that. Right now. Me and Conor."

"Now?" my voice trembles. So, that's what he said to Conor earlier? My whole body quivers from the mind-blowing orgasms that Conor, Liam and Mikey have just given me on this table and I don't know how much more I can take.

"Yes," he says as he smooths my hair from my face. "But if you're not okay with it, I'll do what I planned and bend you over this table instead, because I am going to fuck this pretty ass today, sweetheart."

I draw in a shaky breath as the idea of Shane and Conor at the same time makes my pussy throb harder. "Yes. I want to."

Shane's eyes almost roll into the back of his head and Conor lets out a loud groan of pleasure as he walks up beside us.

"Fuck, Jessie," Shane groans, and then he stands up with me in his arms, carrying me over to the huge corner sofa.

Conor is one step ahead of us, and he undresses quickly before lying down on the sofa while Shane sets me on my feet. His hands run over the skin on my ass, and up my back, until he reaches my neck. Pulling my hair to one side, he kisses me softly in that perfect spot just below my ear. "You can stop this any time you want, Jessie," he whispers.

"I know," I breathe. But I can't imagine ever wanting to. Having these two men at the same time is mind blowing.

Conor takes my hand and pulls me toward him. "Come here, Angel," he says, and I move to straddle him. "Slide yourself onto my cock when you're ready."

I take his stiff length in my hands and guide it into my entrance. I'm so drenched that I slide onto him easily. "Fuck," he grunts as I take him all the way to the hilt. "I will never tire of the feeling of your wet pussy, Angel. Now, come here," he reaches out for me, pulling me down so I'm lying against his chest. One of his hands fists in my hair as he pulls my face to his and crashes his lips against mine, kissing me so hard, I almost lose my breath. Then his other hand is on my ass, squeezing possessively, exactly the way I like it. I roll my hips over him slightly and he groans into my mouth.

I'm aware of Shane behind me and it sounds like he's undressing, but I haven't felt him yet. It's Liam's voice I hear next as my head swims from Conor's attentions. "Here you go," he says softly just before the snapping of a plastic cap indicates he's passed Shane a bottle of lube.

I brace myself for the cold gel, but it doesn't come. I heard some being squirted out, but the next thing I feel is Shane's warm, wet fingers gently gliding over my hole.

"Is she tight here?" he asks the twins as he circles it over and over.

"Yeah. But she can take you," Liam answers, talking about me like I'm not even here, which only turns me on more. The fact that all of these men have such intimate knowledge of my body makes me feel sexy and powerful.

One of Shane's hands slides over the ass cheek Conor isn't holding onto while he slips one of his fingers inside my ass. I inch forward instinctively, and he leans over me, until I am the Jessie meat in a hot man sandwich. "I'll be gentle for our first time, sweetheart. Promise," he whispers in my ear.

Conor lets me up for air, and as he does, he brushes my hair from my face with his hand. "I love you, Angel," he breathes.

"I love you too," I whisper.

Shane's lips are on my neck now and he kisses me softly as he slowly slides one of his fingers in and out of my ass. I moan loudly at the incredible feeling of these two men filling my body and my senses. He slides a second finger in and I suck in a breath as a rush of wet heat slicks my pussy and Conor's cock.

"Fuck," Conor grunts as my walls squeeze around him. "She's ready, Shane. She's milking my cock here. So, hurry up and fuck her, or I'll blow my load before you even get started."

Shane chuckles softly, and then he leans up and pulls his fingers out of my ass. I whimper at the loss of his touch.

"Hold her still, Conor," he growls as he presses the tip of his erection at my seam. "This is going to burn, sweetheart. But it will be okay once I'm in, and then you're in complete control, okay?" he grinds out the words as he edges himself inside me.

"Okay," I breathe as I resist the urge to push back slightly against him.

Conor wraps his arms around my waist. "Stop squeezing me, Angel," he groans but he does it with a smile.

"Sorry," I mouth just as Shane pushes deeper inside. "Ow," I wince. He is bigger than his brothers and he's stretching me so wide it burns.

Shane rubs his hands over my ass and spreads my cheeks further apart. "I'm almost in, Jessie," he breathes. The burning pain soon gives way to pleasure as he pushes himself all the way inside me with a satisfying growl.

"Damn. You feel so good on my cock," Shane groans.

I take a deep breath as I try to calm my racing heart and allow my body to adjust to being so completely filled. The two men stay still too, waiting for me to be ready. Their muscles flex and vibrate with the effort as their breathing comes hard and fast. Conor grinds his jaw as he stares into my eyes while Shane's cock twitches in my ass and his fingers dig into my hips. I suddenly realize that I am completely in control here. I have these two powerful men in the palm of my hand.

I roll my hips slightly and Conor groans in frustration. "You can both move now," I whisper.

"You sure?" Shane breathes.

"Yes."

"Thank fuck," Conor grunts as he grabs hold of my hips and thrusts his cock into my pussy at the same time as Shane does the same to my ass.

"Oh fuck," I cry out as pleasure and pain courses through my entire body. Conor wraps one of his huge arms around me, pressing me to him as he sucks and nibbles on my neck while he slips the other one between our bodies and rubs my clit in slow, teasing circles. Shane grabs my hips firmly, holding my ass in place as he fucks it. Then, sliding one of his hands up my back, he caresses my skin before pulling my hair and wrapping it around his fist so that when he leans over me a second later, he can kiss the other side of my neck.

Our three bodies are pressed together, covered in a fine sheen of perspiration. I close my eyes as I try to deal with the complete sensory overload of having these two incredible men worshipping my body with their hands, their mouths, and their huge cocks.

My orgasm starts in the tip of my toes, tingling and sparking through every nerve ending of my body until I am buzzing with electricity and energy. I moan into Conor's neck as I feel the pressure building like nothing I have ever felt before.

"She's on the edge, Shane," Conor growls. "And she's going to take me with her."

My body bucks between them when my orgasm tears through me a few seconds later, like black powder searing through my veins and exploding between my thighs. Conor comes too, pumping his release into me as he bites down on my neck while he and his brother hold my trembling body still.

Shane lifts his knees onto the sofa and lies over me, so that I am pinned to Conor as he finds a way to get even deeper inside me."Jessie. You are so fucking beautiful, sweetheart. I love fucking you so much," he groans in my ear as he finds his own release and pumps every last drop into me.

When he's done, he gently pulls out of me and I lie completely spent in Conor's arms.

"Fuck. That was hot," Mikey says, and I'd forgotten he and Liam were even in the room.

"You are fucking incredible, Jessie Ryan," Conor says as he kisses the top of my head before he pushes himself up and shifts back so he's sitting up against the sofa and I'm straddling him.

"Jessie Ryan?" I whisper.

Shane sits beside us and curls some of my hair around his fingers. "Wasn't that the point of our cum oath?"

"Yeah, you're a Ryan now, Red," Mikey adds with a chuckle as he sits on the other side of Conor and me and takes hold of my hand, threading my fingers between his before lifting it to his lips and kissing each of my fingertips.

Liam walks to the back of the sofa, standing behind where Conor and I are sitting and leaning down, he places his hands either side of my face and kisses me softly. "Love you, baby," he smiles. "And yes, you're most definitely a Ryan now."

We stay like that for a few moments, silent and sated. There's no need for words after what we just shared.

Shane moves first, standing up and stretching. "Right, hand her over," he says to Conor who releases me from his embrace without hesitation, allowing Shane to scoop me up into his arms. "Come on, Hacker," he says softly.

"Where are we going?" I whisper.

"I think we need to get you cleaned up."

I snuggle my head against his shoulder as he carries me out of the room and to my bedroom. He places me on the bed and orders me not to move while he goes to my bathroom. The sound of rushing water makes me realize he's running me a tub. A short while later, I must have drifted off to sleep as I'm vaguely aware of his strong arms lifting me again as he carries me to the tub. "Come on, sweetheart," he says softly. "You can't sleep just yet."

"Sorry," I yawn. "I feel exhausted."

"Well, I can't say I'm surprised. You were incredible, Jessie," he says against my ear and my heart flutters in my chest.

When we step into the bathroom, I smell the sweet scent of my favorite vanilla scented candles and bath soak. He places me gently in the tub of hot, soapy water and I sigh contentedly. "Move up, Hacker, I'm coming in with you," he growls.

"In here?" I pop one eyebrow at him.

"You think I'm passing up an opportunity to have your soapy, naked body pressed up against me? I know you're tired, sweetheart, but I'm not dead," he winks at me and I can't help but laugh as I scoot along the large tub, allowing him to climb in behind me. Once he's seated, he pulls me back until I'm leaning against his chest before he wraps his arms and legs around me like a koala. Then he takes a soft washcloth and slips it between my thighs, gently cleaning my most intimate areas before dragging it up my body and swirling it over my stomach and breasts.

"Why are you being so nice to me, Shane?" I groan as I tilt my head back against him. He plants a soft kiss on my neck.

"I'm always nice to you, Hacker," he chuckles.

"No, you're not. You're usually an ass to me. And I like it. I don't know how to handle you when you're being sweet to me like this."

"You know exactly how to handle me, Jessie, and you're well aware of that fact. But, I'll go back to being an ass to you tomorrow if it means that much to you?"

"Yes, please," I purr. "I love asshole Shane."

"Oh, sweetheart. I'm going to make you pay for that tomorrow," he growls. "But, I love you too."

My heart almost bursts out of my chest and I close my eyes and enjoy the feeling of his arms wrapped around me and the way our bodies slide together in the hot soapy water. There was a time when I thought I would never know any kind of happiness again. But here with the Ryan brothers, I finally feel like a part of something. I feel loved and protected – and cherished. I'm finally home.

CHAPTER 50

JESSIE

*G*roaning, I roll over, off of one hot, hard body and onto another. Every part of me aches, but I can't help but smile as I recall the reason why. After my bath with Shane last night, Mikey and Liam cooked us all an incredible meal and then Conor gave me a lovely neck and shoulder massage, followed by a foot rub while we watched some TV. The twins spent the night in my bed, but they were perfect gentlemen and we actually only slept.

"Morning, Jessie," Liam growls sleepily as he wraps an arm around me and softly kisses the top of my head.

"Morning," I purr as I press my face against his chest.

Mikey rolls toward us, pressing his body against mine, and I sigh contentedly as I lie cocooned between the two of them.

Our bubble of happiness is shattered by the door bursting open and Shane's voice echoes around the room.

"Boys," he shouts. "We're leaving in fifteen minutes. Get your asses in the shower and get dressed."

Liam and Mikey groan loudly, but they both do as Shane asks, each of them kissing me on the cheek before rolling out of bed and strolling out of the room.

Shane sits on the bed beside me. He reaches out, dusting my cheek with his knuckles. "How are you feeling this morning, Hacker?"

"Deliciously achy," I smile up at him.

His green eyes twinkle as his mouth curls into a smile. "Your fingerprint is in the security system now, so, you can come and go as you please. We have something to take care of upstate, so we'll be out for most of the day. Will you be okay on your own?"

"I'm a big girl. I'm sure I'll be fine."

His eyes narrow slightly as though he's deep in thought. "Or you could come with us?"

"I'd rather stay in bed a little longer," I grin at him. "Besides, I have an appointment at the salon at three. I'm getting everything waxed. You wouldn't want me to miss that now, would you?"

The fire flashes in his eyes. "Everything?" he growls.

I sit up, placing one of my hands on the back of his neck and lean in close to him. "Ev-er-y-thing," I purr against his cheek.

He sucks in a breath and a low growl rumbles in his throat. "Then it's a good thing that after this job today, I have nothing to do for two whole days. Nothing to do but you."

"Two days? But you never take time off," I breathe as my heart flutters in my chest.

"I know. So, you get some rest today, and tonight. Because you and your freshly waxed pussy are mine, sweetheart," he growls before running his hand over my ass. "And maybe we can have another spanking session. One that ends the right way?"

"And what's the right way?" I purr.

"You coming on my cock," he whispers, and my insides contract as he presses his lips against mine and kisses me.

"I thought you were looking for the twins?" Conor says as he walks into the room and flops onto the bed beside me.

Shane's head snaps up and he turns to his brother. "I was. I found them. And now I'm kinda busy with my girl. So, get lost," he says with a wicked grin.

"Our girl," Conor winks at me before he leans down and kisses me too. Shane sits back and sighs as Conor devours my mouth.

I run my fingers through his hair and a few moments later he pulls back from me with a groan. "We gotta go, Angel. You have a good day and we'll see you tonight."

I lick my lips as I look at them both. they're so damn handsome. "I'll make something nice for dinner."

Shane gives me a last kiss on the lips before he and Conor get up and walk out of the room. I lie back against the pillow and close my eyes. I'm going to enjoy being a Ryan.

IT BEGINS to rain as I'm heading back to the apartment after my appointment at the beauty salon. I duck into the alleyway next to our building and head toward the garage entrance. I'm just about to press my finger on the external keypad when a voice behind me startles me.

"Jessica," he says in a thick Russian accent.

I spin on my heel as my heart starts to pound in my chest and I come face to face with a giant bear of a man wearing mirrored aviator sunglasses. My own reflection stares back at me. Flame red hair and my shocked face as pale as the full moon.

"You need to come with me," he says as he grabs hold of my arm.

I wrench myself from his grip. "The hell I do," I snarl. "And my name isn't Jessica. You've got the wrong girl." I glance at the keypad and then at his throat. I could punch him in the jugular and make a run for it.

He sighs deeply and lets go of my arm, taking a step back and holding out his hands in surrender. He removes his sunglasses and his face softens. "I'm not here to hurt you. But you must listen to me. You're in grave danger here. You need to come with me."

"You know nothing about me. Who the hell are you?" I frown at him.

"I know everything about you. But you need to come with me. We don't have much time." He glances up and down the alleyway.

"I'm not going anywhere with you. Do Shane and his brothers know anything about this?"

He narrows his eyes at me. "The Ryan brothers are not the saviors you think they are, *Moya kroshka*. They won't protect you. They will feed you to the Volk without a second thought."

My blood freezes in my veins at the mention of the Wolf's name. "Who are you?" I stammer again as I take a step back from him until I'm pressed against the steel door.

"Please, Jessica. Your father is waiting for you," he says softly, holding out his hand to me.

I shake my head as I look at his outstretched hand. "My father is dead."

"No. He is not," he insists.

I look up at him, glaring into his dark gray eyes. "Yes, he is. I saw him murdered myself. And nothing you can say is going to make me believe otherwise," I snarl as I stand taller, preparing for a fight. I'm not going to go quietly. I will scream down this whole neighborhood if I have to.

He lifts his hand and I steel myself for the blow, but he only reaches inside his coat and pulls out a cell phone. He dials a number and holds it to his ear. Then he speaks in Russian.

"She won't believe me. You'll need to come." He glances at me. "I know," he sighs. "Yes, but unless you want me to kidnap your daughter, I don't see that we have a choice." he's quiet for a moment before he speaks again. "Okay," he nods and then he ends the call and pockets his phone.

I watch the entire exchange with an open mouth. What the hell is this guy's deal?

"The Boss will be here shortly. But you'll need to get him inside quickly. He can't be out in public for too long and risk being seen."

I frown at him. Does he really believe that his boss is my father? "Look, I don't know what's going on here, but I'm not hanging around here to meet your boss, no matter who he is."

He glares at me and we both know I'm not going anywhere, because if there is the tiniest glimmer of hope in my heart that my father might be alive, then I will stand here and wait. A black Sedan pulls up at the end of the alleyway and the door opens. My heart feels like it might pound straight out of my chest and my eyes are so fixed on the door of the vehicle, I wonder if they might burn a hole through the metal. A man steps out. He wears a baseball cap and keeps his head bent low as he walks toward us. I strain my eyes, desperate to see his face.

My blood thunders through my veins, pounding in my ears and blurring my vision. I don't know if there are tears in my eyes, but I can't seem to focus on his face. His footsteps draw nearer as he keeps his head bent low. It feels like it takes an eternity for him to reach us. The man who looks like a bear stiffens as his boss approaches, as though he's expecting to be reprimanded.

And then he reaches us, and I still can't see his face. His hand shoots up, reaching for his cap. He removes it at the same time as he raises his head and looks me straight in the eye.

"Privet, printsesssa." *Hello, princess.*

"Papa?" I blink at him as my heart stops beating in my chest. He looks like my father, but not like my father. Ten years have passed since I last saw him. He has aged. He has scars on his face that I don't recognize. But it is him.

He nods and holds out his hands. "It's me, Jessica."

"But you? I saw you?" I stammer.

He steps closer toward, placing his hands on my face. "I survived, printsessa. But I won't survive much longer if I don't get out of this alleyway. Can we go inside?"

I shake my head, unable to process the enormity of what is happening. This can't be true. Ten years. Where has he been? "Jessica!" he snaps and breaks me from my daze.

"What? Inside? Sure," I say as I stumble toward the keypad and place my finger on the screen. The door clicks open and I walk inside, my father and the bearlike man following me.

As soon as the door closes behind us, I turn to him again. "Is it really you?" I blink the tears from eyes.

"Yes, printsessa," he smiles at me and holds out his arms and I fall into them. He smells different, yet familiar. he's different, but the same.

"Papa," I sob against his neck as he wraps his arms around me.

We stay like that for a few seconds, but then he pulls back from me. "We have to go, Jessica. There isn't much time. Let's get your things." He takes my hand and starts to walk toward the elevator.

I shake my head. "No. I can't leave. The boys..." I stammer.

His face changes in front of my eyes from one that I recognize to a face full of anger and venom. The man I remember was always full of kindness and compassion. But, I suppose witnessing what he did, and looking for me all this time, has changed him. "Those *boys* are waiting to sell you off to the highest bidder. Have you learned nothing these past years?" he snarls. "How do you think I found you after all this time? They have been reaching out far and wide, trying to find the Wolf so they can sell you back to him."

His words feel like a knife to my heart. I step back from him, shaking my head from side to side. "No. They wouldn't," I insist.

"They would, and they have, Jessica. Open your eyes. I have looked for you for ten years, and now I finally find you. That's no coincidence, *printsessa*," he says, his voice softening again. "Now, let's go and get your things and get out of here. It would be best if you leave them a note, so they don't come looking for you."

"But won't they come anyway? If they really intend to hand me over to the Wolf?"

He scowls at me. "We are running out of time. I am your father. That is all you need concern yourself with right now. I'm sure you have hundreds of questions for me, and I'll answer them all. But right now, we have to move."

I swallow as I blink at him. The thought of leaving the brothers feels like a knife twisting in my heart. But this is my father. He would never lie to me. He would never put me in danger.

TWENTY MINUTES LATER, I have my backpack containing my laptop, a change of clothes, and a few toiletries slung over my shoulder. I place the small handwritten note on the center of the kitchen table, propped up by the vase containing the flowers the twins had bought for me a few days earlier.

I stare at the note. I've kept it short and polite. My father insists I don't leave any clue as to the fact I know they were planning to hand me over to the Wolf.

HEY BOYS. Thanks for everything. It's been a blast, but it's time for me to move on. I'm better off on my own, after all. Please don't come after me.

Love Jessie x

. . .

I STARE at the note as the tears roll down my face. This feels so wrong. Only a few hours earlier, I had believed they were my new family. I had believed that they loved me.

"Come on," my father orders from the doorway and I turn to look at him. My real family. For a moment, I am torn between my old world and my new one.

"Printsessa," he calls softly, and I realize where I need to be.

"Coming," I say as I wipe the tears from my cheek and turn away from the life and the home that I stupidly thought belonged to me. He holds out his hand and I take it.

Then we walk to the elevator and I walk away from the Ryan brothers for good.

CHAPTER 51

SHANE

"Will you get that bear's ass out of my face?" Liam snaps as the four of us crowd into the elevator with a stuffed teddy bear that's almost as big as Jessie.

"Quit your whining," Conor replies with a roll of his eyes.

I can't help but smile at the three of them as they argue good-naturedly between themselves. they're eager to see our girl, and so am I.

"She ain't gonna appreciate that monstrosity, you know?" Mikey says as he holds up the bear's arm and then lets it go with a look of disgust.

"She'll love it," Conor replies confidently. "And if she doesn't, I'm sure she'll love the diamond tennis bracelet he's wearing."

She will love it, but not because it's made of the finest pink diamonds – our girl isn't really that into material shit. She will love it because he chose it for her.

We step out of the elevator and into the hallway.

"Jessie. We got you a present, Angel," Conor shouts.

There is no answer.

"Jessie."

"Maybe she's working out?" Liam suggests with a shrug as he heads off to the gym.

"Or the shower?" Mikey adds. "I'll check her room."

The twins head off to look for her while Conor and I make our way to the kitchen. I see the note as soon as we walk into the room, and my heart drops through my stomach.

She wouldn't do this to us. Not after I let her in. Not after yesterday. It could be perfectly innocent. Maybe she's gone to pick something up for dinner? Or some ice-cream for dessert. But why wouldn't she just text us? Why leave a note?

Conor has a giant teddy bear in his face and doesn't notice the piece of paper on the table. I walk over to it with my blood pumping furiously around my body and a feeling of dread in the pit of my stomach. Picking it up, I read the words, and it seems like time stops. I'm vaguely aware of Conor talking to me in the background, and then Liam and Mikey run into the room.

"Jessie's not here," they say in unison.

"What?" Conor asks as he places the stuffed bear on the floor.

"She's gone," I say, handing him the note.

I watch his face as he reads it and so many emotions flood my body I feel like I'm going to explode. He was only just getting back to being something like his normal self again, and she has broken him. She has broken us all.

"No," Conor shakes his head as Liam takes the note from his hand. "She wouldn't do this to us. Someone must have taken her," he snarls as his face turns red with rage.

"Go check the security feeds," I say to Mikey and he runs out of the kitchen, returning a minute later with a laptop.

I STAND in the kitchen staring at the small screen and watching our whole world fall apart. Jessie is there, as clear as day, walking to the elevator, hand in hand with some guy. It's hard to see who it is. He's clearly used to living in the shadows and he shields his face from view. But it doesn't really matter who she left with. What matters is that she left.

She has betrayed us. Torn out our hearts and left my brothers in pieces.

I will never forgive her.

"We have to find her," Mikey says as he looks up at me.

"Oh, we will." I place my hand on the back of his neck. "And when we do, she will wish she'd never heard the name Ryan."

* * *

READY TO FIND out what happens next?

Ryan Redemption is available now.

ALSO BY SADIE KINCAID

If you haven't read the full New York Ruthless series yet, you can find
them on Amazon and Kindle Unlimited

Ryan Redemption

Ryan Retribution

Ryan Reign

Ryan Renewed

Sadie's latest series, Chicago Ruthless is available for preorder now.
Following the lives of the notoriously ruthless Moretti siblings - this
series will take you on a rollercoaster of emotions. Packed with angst,
action and plenty of steam — preorder yours today

Dante

Joey

Lorenzo

New York Ruthless short stories can be found here

A Ryan Reckoning

A Ryan Rewind

A Ryan Restraint

A Ryan Halloween

A Ryan Christmas

A Ryan New Year

Want to know more about The Ryan Brothers' buddies, Alejandro and
Alana, and Jackson and Lucia? Find out all about them in Sadie's
internationally bestselling LA Ruthless series. Available on Amazon
and FREE in Kindle Unlimited.

Fierce King

Fierce Queen

Fierce Betrayal

Fierce Obsession

If you'd like to read about London's hottest couple. Gabriel and Samantha, then check out Sadie's London Ruthless series on Amazon. FREE in Kindle Unlimited.

Dark Angel

Fallen Angel

If you enjoy super spicy short stories, Sadie also writes the Bound series feat Mack and Jenna, Books 1, 2, 3 and 4 are available now.

Bound and Tamed

Bound and Shared

Bound and Dominated

Bound and Deceived

ABOUT THE AUTHOR

Sadie Kincaid is a dark romance author who loves to read and write about hot alpha males and strong, feisty females.

Sadie loves to connect with readers so why not get in touch via social media?

Join Sadie's reader group for the latest news, book recommendations and plenty of fun. <u>Sadie's ladies and Sizzling Alphas</u>